Eve Edwards grew up loving films like *Four Weddings and a Funeral, Mamma Mia*, and *Father of the Bride*. Thanks to her sister, who worked as a registrar of births, deaths and marriages in the English county of Suffolk, her interest in weddings was rekindled. The idea of telling someone's life story through the lens of the weddings they presided over was born and *The Summer of Wishful Thinking* was the name registered for the child.

Eve herself was married on a sunny April day some years ago and now lives with her husband and three children in Oxford. With a career as a diplomat and Oxfam policy adviser behind her, she has written many novels under three pen names.

The SUMMER of WISHFUL THINKING

Eve Edwards

OneMoreChapter

One More Chapter
an imprint of HarperCollinsPublishers
1 London Bridge Street
London SE1 9GF

www.harpercollins.co.uk

First published in Great Britain in ebook format by One More
Chapter 2020

A catalogue record for this book is
available from the British Library

ISBN: 978-0-00-835639-2

This novel is entirely a work of fiction.
The names, characters and incidents portrayed in it are
the work of the author's imagination. Any resemblance to
actual persons, living or dead, events or localities is
entirely coincidental.

Typeset in Birka by Palimpsest Book Production Ltd, Falkirk,
Stirlingshire

Printed and bound in Great Britain.

For my sister, Jane, the real registrar of Suffolk. Any resemblance to actual weddings, birth and death registrations is entirely on purpose. People of Suffolk, I love your inventiveness and I wish I could've found space for more of your stories. Enjoy your special days.

Chapter 1

'So he said' to me "Would you mind wearing a costume?"' Gemma smoothed the black skirt over her thighs, wondering if anyone would spot the ladder in her tights.

Diana's laughter lines deepened around her eyes. She turned down Beyoncé so she could concentrate on the directions now they were almost there. 'Ooo, kinky.'

'Stop it, Di. He didn't mean it like that.' Gemma refreshed her phone to check they hadn't missed the turning. In high summer, the Suffolk lanes were overflowing with grasses and lacy cow parsley, that obscured signs and even some of the narrower turnings. 'They were sweet about it. Next right – no, other right – I mean left.'

Diana signalled, used to Gemma's erratic grasp of directions. 'And did you agree, Gem?'

'I had too.'

'Uh-uh, no you did not. All we have to do is turn up, officiate, do the paperwork and go home. We do not have to agree to join in anyone's fantasies, unless we want to, of course.' She directed a suggestive eyebrow wiggle at Gemma, making her laugh.

'But they were making such an effort, Di. He's wearing a replica of the doublet and hose in Henry VIII's most famous portrait and she's made herself a version of one in a painting of Anne Boleyn.'

'Correct me if I'm wrong but they're having, not just a Tudor-themed, but a Henry-famous-for-his-six wives wedding?'

'Exactly.' Gemma held her phone up, hoping 4G would be restored as she wasn't exactly sure where they were now. 'I think the irony escapes them.'

'So, what costume did they want you to wear? Axeman?'

Gemma snorted. 'I think Anne was dispatched with a sword.'

'You're such a history buff.'

History was a passion – one she wished she had more time to indulge. 'A long skirt was all they specified, so I agreed.'

'If you like them so much, you should go all out – hire something – a bishop's robe.'

'You know we're not allowed any religious references.'

'Well then, a doublet and hose deal. You've great legs, you know like Gwyneth Paltrow in *Shakespeare in Love?* I couldn't carry it off myself.' Diana often complained she was developing the same comfortable roundness of her mother, rather than the beanpole stature of her father. Gemma, however, thought 'comfortable' looked great on her friend. Who wants their best mate to be supermodel thin?

'The female registrar in a codpiece, Di? I think that might rather detract from Jerry and Mary's special day.'

'Whereas getting married as the world's most famous wife serial killer won't?'

'Good point.' A white sign flashed past in Gemma's peripheral vision. 'There – it was back there!'

Diana slammed on the brakes, forcing them both forward in their seat belts, and threw the car into reverse. 'Damn, girl, give us more warning next time!'

'Buy a sat nav if you don't like my directions.'

'The council should provide us with one.'

'Yeah right. Let's put that on the agenda for our budget right after they discuss funding adult social care and filling potholes.'

Diana turned her car into the long drive leading to the castle. 'What do you know about this new venue?'

'Not much. Sounds like some vanity project of a Londoner, someone who thought he'd buy himself a bit of English history and pay for it by making it into an exclusive wedding destination.'

'I thought it was derelict.'

'It can't be a complete ruin. I was told yesterday that we'll be doing the ceremony in the Norman keep while the reception is held in the orangery.'

'The what?'

'You know, an old hot house? Claremont used to have a famous garden but it was left to run wild. The landowner is restoring that too. I saw some photos: it looks really pretty, a kind of lost garden, like Heligan down in Cornwall.'

'I can't manage our six square metres at home; I'd say he's got his work cut out for him.'

'That's because your boys use your plants for target practice.'

'True.' Diana's boys, aged thirteen and eleven, were the

most destructive children Gemma had ever met – but in a nice way, as she always felt she should add. Her own son, Leo, aged fourteen, had bypassed the whole kick-a-ball-through-a-neighbour's-window phase; she sometimes wished he'd had one.

The drive turned a corner and the castle appeared before them, top floor peeking out of the trees on the brow of the hill, flag flying from the roof of the keep. Gemma felt an unexpected pang of excitement.

'Oh my word, Di, it's wonderful! I used to draw castles like this when I was a kid.'

Di wrinkled her nose. 'Bet it's draughty, cold and impossible to heat.'

'Yes, but the romance!'

'Sugar, when was the last time you had any real romance in your life?' Diana pulled up in a space that had been reserved for them.

'Not that kind of romance.'

'Is there any other kind?'

'Stories, fairy tales – that kind of thing.'

'You, honey, need more of the other in the real world. When did you last go on a date with a man?'

'They're more trouble than they're worth.'

'Your evidence?'

'My ex – and Henry VIII.'

'Gem, you weren't married to the cockroach and if you're appealing to six-hundred-year-old examples, I'd say you're reaching.'

They got out and went to the boot to fetch their bags and

document case. Guests were already beginning to arrive. A minibus crunched into the car park drawing their attention. Everyone inside was wearing a quiffed black wig and rhinestone suit.

'You did not mention that this was an Elvis wedding!' hissed Gemma.

'Cute, isn't it?' Diana chuckled, pleased with her surprise. 'That's how the couple met – at a convention. Makes a change from getting married by an Elvis impersonator in Vegas. Here we're the only ones who won't look like the King of Rock and Roll.' Diana did a little hip wiggle.

Groaning, Gemma grabbed the document case. They took turns on the duties. Diana was officiating at their first ceremony so Gemma's job was to be the admin backup, filling out the registry forms and certificate. The full horror of the next hour dawned on her. 'Oh God, it's going to be vows with promising to "love me tender, love me do", isn't it?'

'I'd say that's a cert.'

'I'm pleased it's you, rather than me, having to do the "repeat after me".'

'Aw, Gem, it's going to be great. Phil and Neil are nice people. You'll love them.' Diana gave her outfit a last check. She'd come in an orange suit, which contrasted well with her dark complexion. She'd just spent a fortune having her hair straightened so it curled around her plump cheeks like a Norman helmet, making her the jolliest guard that had ever been on duty at this keep. Gemma began to think her own black trouser suit and up-do was a bit dull for this flamboyant occasion.

She dug in her bag hoping for at least a scarf to brighten up the suit but came up empty. 'I wish you'd warned me. I could've at least gone for the Dolly Parton look. I look like a funeral director.'

'Girl, you just don't have what it takes upfront for Dolly.' Diana adjusted her own generous bust. 'But I would've made a fine black one if I thought of it.'

Gemma spotted a man not in Elvis gear heading for them. 'Time to put on your game face, Di. Here comes our host – or should I say, Milord Bitten-off-more-than-he-can-chew?'

'Ooo, I like what I'm seeing. He can lock me in his dungeon any day.'

Gemma snorted. 'Cease and desist, Di. You're a respectable married woman.'

'And ain't that a shame?'

Sam Ranworth was not having a good day. His first wedding and already the caterers had messed up, not reading the detailed instructions he had sent them in advance about there being no generator yet in the orangery to run their equipment. He'd had to jury rig a line from his own cottage which would probably get him barred if Health and Safety decided to make a surprise inspection. Then Neil had had an attack of wedding nerves. Sam loved his old friend dearly but Neil was famed for his histrionic moments. Sam knew he should've anticipated that Neil would indulge in one on this, the most theatrical day of his life. He had calmed Neil down with a stiff drink and an equally stiff talking to in the guest room at the cottage but Sam had the feeling that while he was doing that the details of the event were darting away from him like air from a punctured tyre. And the last thing he wanted for the launch of this new venture – and his friends – was the day to fall flat.

At least the registrar was here on time, in fact ahead of time. He liked it when people were efficient at their job. He strode across the car park, hand outstretched to the smiling woman in orange, only then really noticing her companion, who looked a bit like orange-lady's shadow in her *Men-in-Black* outfit.

'Welcome to Claremont, ladies. I'm Sam Ranworth.'

'Lovely to meet you. I'm Diana Erikson and this is Gemma Whitehall – I think you talked to Gem briefly yesterday on the phone. She's so looking forward to exploring your facilities.'

The brunette gave her companion a pained look which Sam couldn't quite understand. Diana seemed a friendly soul. What was her colleague's problem?

'Can you show us where to set up?' asked the brunette.

'Of course. Follow me.' Over-compensating for his bad mood, Sam thought he probably sounded too hearty but he couldn't tone it down now. 'Are you OK with candles? The keep doesn't have power yet.'

'As long as we can all see each other and I marry the right guy to the right guy then we'll be fine,' said Diana.

The other one's phone rang. 'Excuse me,' she muttered.

'Do you want me to make an announcement about switching off phones at the start?' asked Sam, a not-so subtle reprimand for the registrar taking a call when she should be focused on what they were doing here.

'Oh, are you going to be part of the wedding party?' asked Diana.

'Neil's an old friend from college. He's asked me to be master of ceremonies.'

'I see. Good. I'm happy for you to do it, though I'm used to doing the stern-faced thing if you prefer to relax and enjoy yourself.'

No chance of that and Sam couldn't imagine Diana would do a warning effectively anyway. 'It's fine. I'm good at barking out orders.'

'Dammit no, Leo!' exclaimed the brunette.

'Gemma?' asked Diana, swinging round to her colleague. 'Are you OK?'

The woman waved her away and turned aside in an attempt to keep her conversation private, but Sam still couldn't help eavesdropping her end of the call. Old detective habits died hard, and if anything was threatening Neil's special day, then he had to know. 'Tell him he can't, Leo – that I'm not giving him the money. What? Really? Bastard. Sorry, darling. I shouldn't swear, I know, but . . . Look, I can't sort this out now. I've got a couple of weddings to do before I get back. Don't give him anything until I get home – and don't let him in whatever you do! You have? What did he take? Oh God. That's the last straw, Leo! I'm sick of this! Yes, it does matter. He has to stop treating us like a cash machine put on earth to solve his "temporary difficulties"!'

Sam was embarrassed to see that the woman's eyes were filling with tears, quite at odds with her furious tone. She pushed her hand through her hair, making her neat twist sag around her ears.

'Yes, yes, darling. I know he's your father. But he's not my partner any longer. He's stealing from me, you do get that, don't you?'

Sam felt ashamed of himself, even though Diana was also listening. Definitely nothing to do with Neil's wedding so he had no excuse for his curiosity.

'In here.' Sam gestured to Diana to enter over the drawbridge. Once across, they climbed the steep stone staircase, leaving Gemma outside to complete her call. 'So, er, Diana, do you have everything you need?' Sam was proud of how the guardroom looked. The bare bones of the building was a stone box with hammer beam roof. To go with the Elvis theme, it was now draped with crimson cloth to give it a Vegas show feel. Flowers and candelabra brightened up the coldness of the space. It was a shame his first wedding didn't make more use of the historical connections but he'd persuaded himself that offering versatility was a better business model.

'I think we're all set. I'll just move this table a little so we can benefit from the natural light.' Diana had pounced before he could offer to do it for her. She was right about the darkness of the corner though. The high windows were glazed with small panes of old glass which gave the place an underwater feel even in bright sunlight.

Sam looked to the door where the second registrar had failed to appear. 'Your colleague? Is she OK?'

'Sounds like the bastard ex has struck again,' said Diana with a shrug.

'Perhaps not a suitable topic when we're about to start a wedding?'

'Honey, when better? I'm just keeping it real.' She winked and set about arranging the seats to her satisfaction.

Chapter 2

Gemma found it hard to concentrate on the ceremony despite the fact that she was facing an audience that included thirty Elvis impersonators. They came in all shapes and sizes, most going for the late period glitzy look, though one woman made a surprisingly convincing young Elvis straight out of *Jailhouse Rock*.

'Repeat after me,' said Diana, managing to make the words sound special rather than silly. 'I, Neil, promise to love you tender, love you sweet, and never let you go,'

Gemma straightened the paperwork in front of her, aware that her jaundiced view of men was spoiling what was actually a lovely ceremony once you looked past their dubious taste in decorations. Red velvet? Arum lilies? It was all so clichéd and the flowers funereal. She would've themed each arrangement on Elvis' most famous films – *King Creole* in dark blooms and white, Germanic *GI Blues*, a pop of flamboyant Hawaiian style. They would've made a fun talking point as guests had to guess the references. These flowers depressed her. Most weddings tended to fall into stereotypical gestures no matter how original the couple tried to make their

11

day. It was the rare relationship that didn't veer off course even from the start.

Was Leo OK? She could not believe – no, cancel that – she could *completely* believe that Ray had done that to them. The bastard ex knew she often had to work at weekends so would choose Saturdays to drop in on the son he usually neglected. Last time he had made off with Leo's bike, saying he was going to get the brakes fixed. He'd sold it to a mate who had then flogged it on eBay. It had cost her eighty pounds to replace it with a decent secondhand one otherwise Leo wouldn't have been able to cycle to school. This time, according to Leo, Ray had taken the laptop. Her laptop, but also the one Leo used for his schoolwork. The password was of course 'password' because she was useless at remembering that kind of thing. Ray would be able to get into it, wipe it and flog it before the end of the day, all to support his drinking habit. Should she report him to the police? What would that do to Leo? It was bad enough having an alcoholic feckless father without adding a criminal charge to the picture.

And tomorrow, if she bothered to track Ray down in the vain hope he still had the machine, he would be so apologetic. To stave off prosecution, he'd probably weep and tell her how sorry he was, how he knew he'd messed up, promise it wouldn't happen again – until the next time he'd run out of money and the thirst was upon him. He always claimed he wouldn't have been like this if he'd made it as a musician. The early promise as front man in a local band had fizzled out as the flutter of interest around their music subsided. He was the only one to have put all his eggs in the one basket and ended up scrambled.

Band mates had gone on to be teachers and taxi drivers; only he had clung on expecting the call, the contract, that would change everything. Thankfully, they'd already split up as a couple by then – in fact, the bastard had left her when the band looked as though it might actually make it. A teenage girlfriend expecting a baby had been too much for him to cope with, he'd claimed. She cramped his style.

Gemma swallowed bile. After starting with heady infatuation for what she thought the coolest guy in her sixth form, she probably reached hatred of him now. How sad was that?

Diana cleared her throat and Gemma became aware that there was a long pause in the service. What had she missed? The happy couple were standing right in front of her. Dammit, it was time for the signing of the registry already. She had to do her bit, telling the couple and their witnesses about the special ink and pen. She leapt up, making the table wobble. She had a strong and ineradicable klutz streak.

'Congratulations, Neil, Phil. If you'd just like to sign here. I've listed you alphabetically, so Neil, you're up first.' She was speaking too fast, earning an odd look from what's-his-name, the owner. He was acting as one of the witnesses. She handed Neil the pen, having to work around his huge black quiff.

'Father's occupation? Are we out of the ark or what?' scoffed Neil.

Gemma had already filled out most of the form. 'Yes, I know. Seems a little archaic.' She stepped back so the photographer could take her shots.

'I see you didn't put down "homophobic prick" like I suggested,' muttered Neil.

'No, I thought "retired" might make the document more valid.'

'Work it, baby, work it,' teased Phil as Neil did the Elvis lip curl to the camera.

Neither Phil nor Neil would qualify as GQ models, both reaching that stage in life, in their late thirties, where the hair was making a discreet retreat up the forehead and the middle had begun to expand. Their friend though, Milord Castle-owner, and fourth in the chair to sign the register, made a better subject with his swept back black hair – natural, not one of the many wigs in evidence – and broad shoulders. He reminded Gemma of the models in those classy watch adverts in the Sunday supplements, steely blue gaze fixed on something far more interesting in the distance. She needed a fault to cut him down to size. Studying him, she decided that perhaps his features weren't as perfect as they should be, nose just a little too big and a faint scar on the side of his jaw. He made the pen look ridiculously small in his hands. It appeared he did a fair amount of the work around the place himself if the state of them were anything to go by.

Diana cleared her throat again. *Crap*, Gemma realised she'd been daydreaming about what his hands would feel like on her skin while he held the pen out to her to take back. Diana was right: it was far too long since a man had touched her, years since she'd been kissed.

'Yes, thank you. That's all done now.' Gemma could feel her blush creep up her neck, bane of her life was her high-coloured complexion.

Neil and Phil led the way back to the waiting guests, greeted by a burst of 'Can't Help Falling in Love' sung by all the impersonators. It was actually really moving, even cynical Gemma could see that. A lady in a silver jacket, who had to be Phil's mum from her place in the front row, was dabbing her eyes, delighted that her boy had finally tied the knot. Her husband looked a little shocked at the ranks of Elvises but had come in sympathy with the theme with his wide-lapelled suit – either that or he hadn't bought formal wear since the early 70s. Neil's mother stood forlornly on her own dressed in sober grey. Her husband, Neil's father, had decided to boycott the event, according to Diana.

Good riddance, thought Gemma, imagining what it must've been like growing up gay in that household. As bad as getting pregnant at fifteen in hers, she decided.

'I think that went off OK,' said Diana once the wedding party had exited the keep to take photographs outside.

Gemma nodded, concentrating on making sure she'd filled out all the forms correctly. She could not cock this up on an otherwise very cocked-up day.

'I take it Ray's been up to his usual tricks?'

'Oh yes.' She nodded like that dog in the advert.

'What did he take this time?'

'Computer.'

'You're going to tell the police?'

Gemma shook her head.

Diana sighed. This was an old argument. 'Then you should move – go somewhere he can't just drop round on a whim.'

Renting a street away from where Ray still bunked with his parents was probably a mistake but Gemma hadn't wanted to separate Leo from his grandparents. Besides, it was a cheap part of Bury St Edmunds, the pretty market town in Suffolk where she had always lived.

'Doesn't your lease come up for renewal soon?'

She buckled the document case closed. 'Yes.'

'Then move.'

'But what about Leo's friends – family?'

'Gemma, does Leo actually have real friends rather than virtual ones?'

'A couple from school robot club, but they live in the villages, not Bury itself.' That was one of her big worries. He spent so much time alone.

'And his grandparents, do they, or do they not, have a car?'

'They do.'

'He's hardly of an age where they're needed to babysit. You can loosen some of your ties without doing any damage.' Diana could be blasé about moving, having started in inner city Hackney and moved progressively northeast away from London during her married life, first Harlow and now rural Suffolk.

'I don't know.'

'Will Leo notice?'

'Probably not.'

'Then do it. Maybe he'll find more friends; new place, new people. Villages are usually friendlier than a town.'

Gemma was half persuaded. 'Maybe.'

'And it might be cheaper.'

That was a clincher. 'You're right. The rent is a drain and I don't need to be in Bury. I'll start looking.'

'Avoid ones on the bus route to make Ray's life more difficult.'

'Yes, yes I will.'

The next wedding was a conventional do at a local golf club for a couple of divorcees. *Hope springs eternal*, thought Gemma as she administered the vows to the sixty-somethings who had found love again. All the paperwork complete, Diana dropped Gemma at the gate to her house and drove off with a perky toot. Looking up at the peeling woodwork of the windows on the first floor and weeds in the front garden, Gemma felt the weight of all her responsibilities settle back on her shoulders, somehow worse after spending the afternoon in Diana's invigorating company. She was only just surviving financially and each time Ray came by it was like he was a woodcutter taking another hacking blow at her just-managing tree trunk. She could feel the precarious creaking as things shifted. How was she going to replace the laptop? No chance of claiming it on insurance without reporting it so she was stuffed.

'Hi, darling!' she called, dumping her bag in the hall and kicking off her pinching low-heeled shoes. Bliss. Wriggling her toes, she padded through to the kitchen-dining room. No Leo. She went upstairs to change but he wasn't in his bedroom either. He was probably out catching those digital creatures – one of the few things that got him some fresh air so she wasn't going to chase him up just yet. Other kids might've stopped with the Pokémon Go craze years ago but Leo would keep on going until he'd got every one he could, visited every PokeStop and Gym. He was always that little bit embarrassing with his choices – something she knew she shouldn't feel as his mother, but she remembered who that kid had been in her own school and she died a little to see that her son was taking that role. He minded far less than she did.

'I'm an awful parent,' she told her reflection. 'I should appreciate the fact that my child is an original.'

Feeling the need for a glass of wine to reward herself, she went down to the kitchen and opened the fridge. For heaven's sake, Ray had raided here too, taking the nearly full bottle that she rationed to last the week. Of course he had. She hung her head over the sink.

'I hate him, I hate him, I hate him.'

She could almost hear that other voice in her mind, the one that sounded a lot like Diana, saying: *don't get mad, get even*. Fine. She reached for the laptop to begin her search for a new place to rent.

Oh right.

With a sigh, she got out her phone and started scanning the local possibilities. She found a site that offered her a price range filter. Plugging in her numbers, only two came up: one a few doors down and another, a cottage back where she'd been for the Elvis wedding in the village of Claremont Magna. The notes were suspicious – in need of renovation – but she was desperate.

Just do it. She sent off an email asking for a viewing and then put her phone on charge. Cheered up considerably by positive action, she began slicing the vegetables for the stir fry she had planned as a quick dinner.

The front door banged.

'Leo?'

'Yeah?'

'Hello.'

'Hi Mum.' She could hear him beginning his journey up the stairs.

'Aren't you going to come and say hello properly? Talk about what happened?'

'No.' His bedroom door banged shut.

'Can this day get any better?' she asked the cheery face of Jamie Oliver on her recipe book. 'Sometimes I hate you, Jamie, you and your perfect family – your Jules and the kids and your mates. But dammit, man, you know how to cook.' Gemma decided it was pathetic to be talking to a celebrity chef's photo so flicked on some Ed Sheeran to fill the silence. Suffolk's most famous son, he was everything Ray had wanted to be. Both had cruised sofas and busked but only one had gone on from there to fill Wembley Stadium.

'And it wasn't you, was it, you laptop-stealing arse.' She toasted the absent Ray with a glass of water.

Chapter 3

Sam was the last to leave the orangery as the final load of Elvises headed away in their minivan. The event had gone OK, though he'd had to offer up his kitchen to the caterer when the power had failed at a crucial juncture. It meant the main course was a little tepid by the time it arrived on the tables but fortunately the guests were well oiled by drink and finding everything hilarious, even cold green beans. Sam had enjoyed seeing old friends from university, though hearing about their kids made him realise how in some ways he'd been left behind. He'd always imagined he too would have children but now it looked likely it would never happen. He wasn't sure he had regrets as he was convinced he'd make a bad father. When it came to cutting the cake, Phil had made a sweet speech about hitching up with his soulmate; Neil had gone on far too long but everyone knew to expect that and charged their glasses to the brim. Sam had spent the time usefully, chatting up the photographer who agreed that he could use a couple of her best stills for his website if he put her on the list of recommended suppliers for his future bookings.

If there were future bookings.

There had been a moment where it looked like the photographer might stay for a late-night drink but then it had passed, both tacitly realising that if they were to meet professionally again, they should avoid entanglements.

He locked the door on the neatly stacked tables and chairs and swept floor, leaving the rubbish sacks to be removed in daylight. It was a relief not to have to entertain a guest, no matter how attractive. His dating instincts had been frozen for a while now and trying to thaw them out would be painful. It was easier alone. He headed back to his cottage, walking in the dark by memory and night-sight rather than bothering with a torch. His path led from the orangery past the Norman keep in the centre, through the rockery garden that he was reviving in the ruins of the curtain wall, and out across the drawbridge to the carpark. Beyond that lay the wilder parts of the estate. Pausing for a second, Sam looked out across to his woods; he could see in his mind's eye the remnants of a once great park hidden under brambles and ivy. In his time in the Metropolitan police, he'd got used to patrolling in the small hours so this was a walk in the park by contrast. His own park. Despite the headaches of owning such a place, the thought made him smile. His own shambolic beauty just waiting for him to reveal her true loveliness, He'd seen so much ugliness, he wanted this to be his legacy.

Taking a path on the left to enter his cottage (once the humble home to the estate gardener), Sam switched on the kettle. Things had been left spotless but in the wrong place – that was going to bug him for days. He would have to light a fire under the electrician and get him to sort out the power in the main buildings as a priority because he didn't want caterers trooping through his home. It would set back the renovations on the cottages that came with the estate – another hoped for source of income – but he had to get his estate up and running as a venue so he could accept more bookings. There had been a bite just the day before from a couple planning a Tudor-themed one. They'd originally booked a marquee at home but when they heard he was opening Claremont for events they had had second thoughts. They sounded perfect and he was prepared to cut them a good deal just for the photo value alone. All the guests were going to dress up: it would look amazing if they were lucky with the weather.

Remembering they'd promised to get in touch, he checked his emails. There were two pieces of positive news. His letting agent had sent a notification that someone had requested a viewing of the gatehouse cottage and the Tudors had confirmed their interest. He did a quick run of the numbers. If both went ahead, that represented the possibility of being able to employ someone to help next month with the gardens. Sam moved to the wall planner to enter the details for the wedding.

9th September.

He hadn't registered that when he discussed with them about booking the second Saturday in that month. He normally made sure he was somewhere on his own that day, up a mountain or running a half marathon, some activity that pushed him to the limit and stopped him thinking. It was not a day for him to hold the hand of a nervous bride and groom. He couldn't be needed.

His fingers hovered over the keyboard. He almost sent an apology that the booking was no longer available.

It's been five years. Surely you can hold your shit together for twelve hours?

The kettle clicked off, a prod to make a decision.

Don't be a coward.

Dear Jerry and Mary,

I'd be delighted to host your wedding at Claremont Castle on 9th September. Please fill out the attached booking form.

Hoping he wouldn't regret it, Sam pressed 'send'.

Gemma checked her watch. The last client – a death – had just left with the certificate declaring her husband of fifty-five years was no more. She'd seemed surprisingly cheerful at the prospect and mentioned booking a holiday abroad, something her Terry wouldn't allow as he didn't like to deviate from their caravan in South Wales. The world was an odd place. Gemma tidied away the forms. The twelve-thirty appointment was running late and she was already cutting it fine trying to view the cottage during her lunch hour. She called up the list on the screen. What was it? A death or a birth? Birth.

The sound of a wailing baby heralded the arrival of the next client. She went out to the waiting room to invite them in directly.

'Sorry we're late. Nappy stop. We've not got the hang of it yet – poo everywhere,' gushed the mum. 'We couldn't believe how much such a little person can produce – and what a colour!'

You know there's such a thing as too much information, right?

thought Gemma, ushering them to a seat. New parents were very often brimming over with it as it was hard for them to believe anyone else had experienced the miracle of a newborn when it was all so fresh. Gemma recalled the bewilderment of holding Leo for the first time, though 'gushing' about how incredible he was hadn't been an option in her case.

'Nice to see you all. How old is baby?' she asked, hitting her routine mode.

'Two days. Only kicked me out of hospital yesterday,' said the mum, before launching into a blow by blow account of the delivery.

Gemma had a rule not to judge the people who came to see her – and that was everyone eventually – but she had a good feel for what kind of name was going to come from the parents just by how they dressed. This couple were following the fashion for being tattooed and pierced on every body part, the mum on the large side, Dad skinny and a little vacant in expression – though to be fair that could be just the result of the new phenomenon of sleepless nights. She thought they might've been in the year below her when she was at school. Gemma ran a little bet with herself and so far her hit rate was eighty percent correct. The name was unlikely to be a private school bound Charles or Beatrice, more likely an unusual spelling of a not quite normal name – Shanara or Flynnt – and it would be the mum's choice. Gemma's contemporaries liked challenging names; she'd been quite boring going with Leo.

'So what do we have here? A little boy or girl?' she asked, opening the certification page on her computer.

'We don't believe in imposing socially constructed ideas of gender on our little one,' said the mum, crossing her arms.

Gemma revised her assumptions of where the couple fitted in the social spectrum of East Anglia, from ordinary to politically aware. Activists of some kind, switched on to current debates about gender identity. She hadn't had the training course on this yet but knew she had to tread carefully. She was not to bat an eyelid.

'Right, I'll put "indeterminate".' She clicked on the third option on her drop-down menu. 'So what about the name?'

'Tobyn, spelt with a "y", Peace Taylor.'

'Right.' She typed it in carefully. 'Is that Peace with an "ea" rather than "ie"?'

'Of course.' The mum looked at Gemma as if she was the one who needed her head examined. 'We didn't want to go for anything too predictable, you know? Tobyn is so special – little one needs a special name.'

Welcome to the world of avoiding gendered pronouns for the rest of your life, Tobyn, thought Gemma wryly as she typed in the rest of the information required. She had no problem with the whole fluid gender thing but was always struck by just how awkward it made conversation, like walking over a wooden bridge with far too many planks missing. So easy to tumble through into unintended offence thanks to the limitations of the English language.

Mum appeared to want to chat, Dad was content playing with his child's tiny fingers. Conscious of the time, Gemma tried to hurry them along but was further delayed by a printer snarl. Keeping a strained smile on her face, she silently cursed the manufacturer as she fished out a scrunched-up document. Pressing 'print' again, it then told her it needed a new cartridge and, of course, she didn't have one to hand.

'I'm so sorry about this. I'll just send this to the printer in reception.'

She had to wait behind the receptionist who was printing out the weekend duty roster.

'Come on, come on,' she muttered under her breath. It was fifteen minutes at least down country lanes to Claremont Magna and it was five to one already. The landlord was due to meet her at one and she didn't have a number with her to say she was going to be late because in a rush that morning she'd left the details at home.

'Here you are, Ms Holder and Mr Taylor, Tobyn's birth certificate, hot off the press! Sorry to hurry you along but I've another appointment.' All but forcing them out of her office, Gemma grabbed her keys and ran for the car. Surprised by a rain shower and coatless, she was soaked by the time she slid into the front seat. She'd left the directions on the dashboard and took a quick glance at the address again. Gatehouse Cottage. From her phone, it looked as though it was in the middle of the village so all she needed to do was remember how to get to Claremont Magna.

At quarter to two, she was still circling the deserted village. It looked like everyone had fled a zombie apocalypse. Finally, she found someone to ask. She wound down the window to catch the attention of a woman walking her Labrador. The walker had a hearty Duchess of Cornwall air about her with her flicked back ash blonde hair and green waxed jacket.

'Excuse me, can you tell me where this is?' Gemma held out the bit of paper she'd scrawled the directions on. 'My phone can't seem to find it.' And if she had a bloody laptop still, she could've printed off a proper map last night.

The woman peered at the address. 'I bet you put in the postcode, didn't you? That covers practically the whole village and then some. Gatehouse Cottage? That's easy. It's at the entrance to the castle. Do you know where that is?'

'Yes, yes I do.' Her heart sank.

'There's a farm track where you can turn around just down there. Good luck!'

Gemma pulled into the drive of the cottage at the entrance to the castle at one fifty-five only to find no sign of the landlord.

Bloody time waster. Sam hammered the nails into the cold frame he was mending out the back of his own cottage. He'd waited half an hour and the person had been a no show, not even a message to say they'd had second thoughts. If there was one thing he couldn't abide – actually there were lots of things he couldn't abide – but one was definitely rudeness.

'Sorry to bother you, Mr Ranworth.'

He looked up to see the registrar from Saturday, the one with the life meltdown. She was looking a little frazzled, standing there without a coat despite the light shower. 'Hi.'

'I couldn't get a reply from your cottage so followed the hammering.'

'What can I do for you?' He got up, conscious that he was wearing the dirtiest of jeans and she was standing there in one of her pristine short-skirted suits, nipped in at the waist to reveal a decent figure and very nice legs. 'Did you leave something behind? Because if you did, I didn't find anything.'

She swallowed and looked away. The light hit her face at a new angle revealing her eyes to be an unusual green-grey colour ringed with a darker line.

'I have to apologise.'

'For what? You were a bit slow on Saturday, but you were distracted, I get that.'

She pressed the back of her hand to her forehead. 'Oh God, I was, wasn't I? Sorry for that too. No, it is about our appointment at one o'clock.'

Oh.

'I can make excuses about running late, getting lost and leaving the number for you at home like the idiot I am, but that doesn't change the fact that I left you waiting for me – so rude of me.' She glanced down at her watch. 'And now I've overshot my lunch hour and I have to dash.'

Sam did a quick bit of thinking. He didn't like the idea of someone he would meet professionally living at the end of his drive, particularly when he happened to know the gatehouse was a mess and barely worth the rent. On the other hand, she represented his best chance at getting enough income to have a serious go at clearing the gardens before winter.

'It's OK.' Not that he forgave her. He had developed an instinctive aversion to women with chaotic lives, having been so badly burned in the past. 'Why don't you come by after work?'

She bit her bottom lip. 'I have to attend a parent teacher conference with my son.'

'Then bring your son too, either before or after. He'll be living here as well, right? What time works?'

'Um, six-thirty?'

'Fine. I'll meet you down there then.'

'Right, OK. Thanks. Sorry.'

'No problem.' He picked up his hammer again, which she rightly took as the signal that she was dismissed. 'You might want to wear more sensible shoes.'

Startled, she looked down at her kitten heels. 'What's wrong with these?'

'The path to the front door – it's a bit uneven.'

'Oh, OK.' Confused, she toddled off back to her little clunker of a car.

'Didn't you read the bit about "in need of renovation", sweetheart?' he murmured to himself, whacking a nail into place.

Chapter 4

'So, Leo, how do you think it's gone this year?' asked her son's form teacher, Mr Hilton.

'Fine.' Leo was slumped in the chair like a puppet with his strings cut while Gemma sat bolt upright beside him, in vain willing him to offer a little charm or politeness in the cheerless surroundings of the school gym. It didn't seem that long ago she'd been a pupil here herself and she still felt the humiliation of leaving under a cloud whenever she came into this environment. Didn't Leo realise that these were the people who would be writing him references in a few years? Of course he didn't: he was only fourteen.

'You don't feel too isolated? The teachers have noticed that you don't seem to have a special buddy in the form.' Mr Hilton glanced at Gemma, signalling that the concern was widespread and serious.

Oh God. Gemma wanted to weep. Her son was a social pariah. Where had she gone wrong?

'Nah, I'm fine.' Leo studied his scuffed trainers through his sandy fringe. He was in need of a haircut and she would have to have the talk with him about shaving the wisps on his upper lip. His dad would never think to have the puberty talk. 'I don't mind.'

But I do, thought Gemma. 'Mr Hilton, could we perhaps consider moving Leo to another form?'

'Not so late in the year. School breaks up in a week or so.'

'Mum,' muttered Leo mutinously.

'I didn't mean now. I meant next year, when they begin their options?'

'The form won't spend much time together as they will all be following different timetables. In fact, the shake-up might be just what Leo needs, introduce him to students with similar interests. We pride ourselves on the fact that everyone eventually finds a friend at St Bartholomew's.'

'I'm fine,' Leo said again.

Gemma pleated the loose material of her skirt nervously. 'I see. I suppose it would be good for Leo to keep with you as form tutor as you understand him.'

'I'm afraid I won't be his tutor next year. I'm being promoted to Head of Year 10. We've not decided who will be taking over but I'll make sure whoever it is will be up to speed on Leo.'

'Oh, congratulations.'

'And as head of Leo's year, I'll keep an eye on him.'

'Thank you.'

'I'm sure this will all pass as Leo gets older and more confident, finding his niche.'

'I thought he had, with the robot club?'

Leo looked up at the ceiling.

Mr Hilton shuffled his papers. 'That's not been running this year since Miss Green left to have her baby.'

'Oh, I see.'

Mr Hilton's eyes drifted to the next parent in the chairs behind her. 'Keep in touch, Miss Whitehall. Email me if you have any concerns.'

Where to start? 'Thanks.'

Gemma marched stiff-backed out of the gym with Leo slinking along a few paces behind. Mr Hilton was their last appointment. Leo's academic report had been fine; the form tutor, though, had clearly been delegated by staff to speak up about the social disaster aspect of Leo's school life.

'Why didn't you tell me about robot club?' she whispered, fixing the 'everything's fine and dandy' smile on her face for the parents she knew from the primary school gate. They had been much simpler days when her oddball son was in a supportive atmosphere where they'd known him since nursery.

'Because you liked the idea that I went to it.' Leo sounded so world-weary.

'So you were, what? Managing me so I wouldn't fret?' Her voice sounded shrill. *Turn it down, Gemma, turn it down.*

'Yeah. Mum, did you have to embarrass me like that?'

'Me, embarrass you?'

'I don't need special treatment. The students in my class are horrible. Why would I want to hang out with them?'

'They can't all be like that!'

'You don't have to spend every weekday with them: how would you know?'

That was an argument she couldn't knock down. She

unlocked her car. The Fiesta was so old this was done by the key in the lock. Leo got in quickly, leaving her gazing bleakly over the school fields. She dug deep for her parenting skills, learned from a library book rather than her own judgemental mother and undemonstrative father. Try to accentuate the positive. Keep up the communication.

'I was really proud to hear how well you're doing in the sciences, and computing,' she said as she slid into the driving seat.

'No, you weren't.' He unwound the wire from his ear buds about to shut her out with a retreat into music.

'No, Leo, I really was.'

'You want me to be popular.'

'I want you to be happy.'

'I am happy. You're the one who isn't happy.'

He was right. 'Maybe this new cottage will be the answer. It's right by a castle. How cool is that?'

'Mum, don't say "cool". It's not cool.' He pulled up his hoodie and went into blocking mode.

Fifteen minutes later, they turned into the castle drive and pulled off into the little slip road that led to the gatehouse. The cottage was hidden by an out-of-control hedge of black-thorn and brambles. Gemma told herself it was mysterious and atmospheric rather than creepy. At least they wouldn't run short of blackberries come harvest. They were scattered across the bushes like little hard green jewels. The cottage itself was built in the nineteenth century as a miniature architectural echo of the castle behind it, little crenellations over the front door and tall chimneys like a turret. With some care and attention, it would be fabulous. Right now, with the boarded-up window on the first floor and the cracked stone-work, it looked barely habitable.

The front door opened as the owner heard the car draw up. 'Miss Whitehall.'

'Gemma, please. And this is my son, Leo.'

Leo hadn't taken out his earbuds. He was scanning the place like he had a Geiger counter and was checking for radiation leaks.

'Mum, it's got a gym right outside!'

'I'm afraid there's no gym here,' said Mr Ranworth. Gemma noticed he hadn't invited her to call him by his first name.

'Not real, virtual,' she explained. 'You won't have to do a hard sell to my son if it features in Pokémon Go.'

He looked bemused.

'I take it you don't have kids then? The game – catch digital creatures on your smart phone? Everyone was playing it a few years ago.'

'Do I want to know?'

'Probably not.'

'Let me show you around.' He gave her that smile that wasn't a smile but tolerance.

'Great. I changed my shoes as ordered.' She displayed her multicoloured sparkly tennis shoes, an impulse buy in a sale last January.

'If you take the cottage, you might want to get yourself some boots.' He pushed aside a ratty door curtain. That would have to go. 'Obviously, it needs a lot of work. I'm planning on renovating it entirely but for now I'm offering it at a low rent for anyone happy to put up with its current condition. I'll engage a cleaning service to give it a thorough going over from top to bottom. I think from the evidence of letters on the doormat the last occupant moved out in the 1990s.'

'The house that time forgot,' she murmured, walking through the chilly rooms. It was hard to see past the cobwebs and sagging furniture but somewhere under everything was potentially a beautiful home.

'Most of the furniture will have to be chucked out – not up to fire regulations and possibly home to several generations of mice.'

'Oh.' She lifted her hand quickly off the back of the chintz sofa.

'The wooden furniture in the dining room is fine, as is the kitchen set. The bedsteads are iron so they're in good shape but I'll order new mattresses and get the lounge kitted out with basics, that's unless you have furniture of your own?'

'No, I'm renting a furnished house. I don't own much. Can we see upstairs?'

'Of course. Mind the third stair. I'm going to have to replace the tread.'

She climbed the steep staircase gingerly. It turned sharply which didn't bode well for getting large items up here. She opened the door off the dark corridor. There was a nice light room overlooking the front drive and up to the castle – that could do for Leo. The master bedroom was a disaster zone: window boarded up and what little light did enter was filtered through obscuring ivy.

'I'll get that fixed too,' Sam said, rubbing his neck awkwardly.

'It's not really ready for renting is it?' No point beating about the bush.

'The basic house is sound – roof OK. It would only take a few weeks to turn it around.'

Her first impression of him was right: he had bitten off more than he could chew.

'Heating?'

'Not yet. I'll make sure you're sorted for winter though.'

'Is the wiring safe?'

'First thing I'll get checked.'

He was making a lot of promises. Her experience of men suggested that she should pay no heed to them.

'So you want your tenant to live here while the work gets done around them?'

'Will that be a problem?'

'Not if you drop the rent by another fifty pounds a month.' Listen to her: bargaining! Diana would be proud.

'It's already at the bottom of the price range for round here.'

'OK, I understand. Good luck finding someone else.' She headed for the door.

'All right, fine. I'll drop the rent while the work is happening, but when it's done it goes back on again. Agreed?'

She'd pay the fifty pounds extra happily if she were sitting in a toasty refurbished house. 'Agreed.'

'You'll take it?' He sounded astonished.

'Isn't that what we just discussed?'

'Yes, yes. OK. Oh, and one more thing. You know that I'm turning the castle into a wedding venue and restoring the garden? That will involve lots of building work and heavy machinery. Renting the gatehouse does not equal rambling rights over the rest of the estate. Please make sure your son understands that. I can't be held responsible.'

'Fine.' There were lots of other green spaces if Leo suddenly developed an outdoorsy streak.

'So, I'll get the agent to send you a contract?'

'You promise to have the place fit for habitation by the time we move in?'

'I said I would so I will.'

'Then send the contract.'

Driving away, Gemma wondered if she'd made the right decision. The landlord was turning out to be such an unsympathetic character, next to no human warmth, but if he came through with his part of the deal then she would be better off than she was at the moment, paying less in rent and far from Ray. The final task, though, was to convince Leo it would be a great adventure – and that was possibility her biggest challenge.

'How do you like our new home?'

'Hmm.' Leo was flicking through his music.

'Leo, are you listening? I've taken the cottage.'

'You didn't! Mum, the place is a dump! And how will I get to school? It's like miles!'

'There's a school bus – I checked. And Mr Ranworth promised he'd have it ready for us when we move in.'

'But I don't want to move there.'

'Well, we are. I can't live in Bury any longer – can't afford it.' She meant that she couldn't afford Ray's depravations but allowed Leo to interpret that how he liked. 'There's a nice bedroom for you with a view of the castle. That's, er, whatever I'm allowed to say that's not cool.'

'What about the Wi-Fi? Did you ask about that?'

No. And the chances of a house abandoned in the 1990s having it were minuscule. 'Actually, I didn't.'

'Mum!'

'But we'll sort something out. Mr Ranworth was very . . .' *cold* '. . . helpful.'

'I can't believe you did this to me.'

So much for Leo not caring where he lived.

'I'm not doing it to you – I'm doing it with you – giving us a fresh start in a lovely cottage.'

'I'm not leaving Bury.'

'I think you'll find that you are.' Trying not to lose her temper, she pulled into the cinema complex on the outskirts of town. 'Shall we celebrate with a film – or a go in the bowling alley? We've not done anything fun together for ages.'

'I just want to go home – while I still have one.' He pulled his hoodie over his eyes and crossed his arms.

'OK, we'll do that then.' She pulled back out and drove home in silence, resolving to check out that library book on parenting again.

Chapter 5

Sam stepped out of the miserable excuse that was the shower over the bath in his cottage to see he had five missed calls from his sister.

'Hey, Helen? Sorry I didn't pick up earlier. What's the matter?'

'Sam? Oh, thank God you rang me back. Dad's home has been in touch. It's finally happened. They're closing with immediate effect – simply can't afford to keep going, the manager said. London wages, rising costs and everything.'

Sam sat down heavily on a kitchen chair. 'That's bad – a total disaster. He likes it there.' But not really a surprise – the manager had been saying for a while that their future looked shaky. Sam had been hoping that the home would last long enough for his frail confused dad to live out the rest of his days in familiar surroundings.

'Michael, get down off of there! Excuse me a moment.' The phone was dumped on a table and there was the sound of a toddler protesting in the background. 'Sorry, sorry. Little tyke should be in bed because he's running a fever but won't stay put. I think it's chicken pox. It's going round his nursery.'

'You seem to have your hands full.'

'Tell me about it. Dexter doesn't know how lucky he is to be deployed right now. Peacekeeping? Someone needs to be peacekeeping right here or I'm going to go crazy. Anyway, I've drifted from the subject. Where was I?'

'You were telling me the bad news about Dad's home. I'll get searching right away for an alternative. How long have we got?'

'That's what I'm trying to tell you – we have no time at all. The home has been declared bankrupt – they can't pay the existing staff so naturally, they, poor sods, are leaving. We have to fetch him tomorrow. Social services have appealed to those with family there to do their bit as they have to give priority to those with no one.'

'So what are you going to do?'

'Me?' Helen's voice went shrill. 'Sam, I simply cannot have Dad here. I have a toddler with chicken pox, a four-year-old who demands her full share of my attention, and a husband deployed in South Sudan. In what universe is it my responsibility to pick up our father who suffers from dementia and add him to the mix here? In the it's-always-the-women-who-clear-up-shit universe?'

Sam kicked himself. He was so used to her managing or he would've registered her obvious appeal for him to step up earlier. 'Sorry, yes, you're right. But I can't have him here either. I'm living in a building site.'

'Better that than he gets shingles from Michael. You've got to do this, Sam, got to – either that or our dad is the only parent left standing on the doorstep tomorrow with his bits of things in a cardboard box.'

Sam swore under his breath. He hated it when he was manoeuvred into being needed. The only thing that kept him steady was the feeling that he was not responsible for anyone. 'Helen, I'm not good at this. I'll mess up.'

'Sam, you have to stop with the pity party. It's been years. You are a good man under your selfish git act. You'll be a hell of a lot better for Dad than some scary social services temporary care. He knows you. Park him in front of the TV with the remote for a few days while you sort it and he'll be fine.'

'I don't have a TV.' Even he could hear he sounded like he was whining.

'Then get one. I have to go. Michael is now pelting his sister with Lego. I'm sorry this is landing on your plate but, hey, don't you think it's time you got back into actually, you know, caring for someone?'

How to explain that he just wasn't ready for this? He'd cock it up. 'Helen . . .'

'Love you. Speak tomorrow OK?' She ended the call.

Sam stood dressed just in his towel, too numb to realise how cold he was on the quarry-tiled floor. Was he really the only option? He booted up his computer and did a quick search for local homes near to Helen in Hammersmith. Nothing available. He repeated the same for ones near to him, not surprised to find there weren't that many out in the sticks. Some didn't list if they had room or not so he'd have to ring them in the morning. Dad had special needs with his dementia so they had to be set up for caring for residents with that condition. What was clear was that Sam was unlikely to be able to solve this overnight.

There was one thing he could do though. Following Helen's hint, he ordered the first TV he could find online, priority delivery, and put in a call to his electrician's mobile, asking him to bump up to the top of his list sorting out a connection. It would have to be satellite or through a TV aerial as he was too far away from a high-speed broadband cable which had only just reached the village.

The electrician messaged back. *So you don't want me to start on the gatehouse or power in the orangery?*

This first, then those jobs. It's an emergency. And I am made of money, thought Sam sourly.

Not according to the bank. Sam had bought the estate with the money from the sale of his London home. He'd entered the property ladder wisely in the 2000s – a detached house which he'd purchased for a couple of hundred thousand with help from an inheritance from his grandparents and a hefty mortgage, fixed up and sold for two million and change. He'd then completely jumped off the housing ladder in a wild fit and spent it all on Claremont. His friends had told him he was insane but he had known that buying the estate was his last chance at making anything of his life. He was that close to giving up. There were three exits he could see from his predicament: death through alcohol, death through pills, or a new purpose. He chose life and jacked in his job with the police and reinvented himself as castle owner. This was not the moment to become full-time carer to his father but who else was there? His mother was living the life of a spry divorcee in Bournemouth and hadn't had anything to do with her ex-husband for twenty years. Helen was clearly near breaking point with her responsibilities.

OK, man up, Sam told himself. *Fetch Dad, look after him for a few days, find a good home for him, perhaps one near here where it would be easier to drop in and see him.* That sounded a plan.

Leo darted up to his bedroom as soon as Mum parked outside their house. He did not want to talk to her ever again, the oppressor! She was so unfair to him, always acting so disappointed and never understanding what it was he wanted to do. She thought he was antisocial but he had loads of friends. He chatted to them every day via the PlayStation, had hundreds of followers for his game footage uploaded on his YouTube channel, and he'd even earned a couple of dollars through advertising. She had no idea. To her, he was poor little Leo Whitehall, class outcast; online he was Lionz, one of the top players in the football league game. He had earned respect.

Dad understood him though. He'd stop this well out of order attempt to move him away from civilisation.

He rang his grandma because Dad didn't have a phone at the moment.

'Hey, Gran, can I speak to Dad?'

'Leo, dear, how was your school meeting?'

He could hear the rattle of pans. Gran was probably doing her usual fry up tea for Granddad. 'It went OK but I've got to talk to Dad.'

'One moment, love.'

He listened as she shouted in the hall for Ray to get his lazy bum off the sofa and come talk to his son.

'Leoster, how are you? Giving the teachers hell, I hope? Sorry I couldn't be there. That place gives me seriously bad vibes, crushes my creativity.'

Dad was so cool. Always talked like school was a prison or something. He really got that these days kids made their way outside conventional education. It was a whole new world online that his mum did not understand.

'That's fine and, yeah, I am. Mum was well pissed off about it all.' He liked his father to think that he was a bit of a rebel.

'Great. So why do you need to talk to me?'

'You've got to stop her.'

'Stop who?'

'Mum. She's trying to move us to some creepy cottage out in a field somewhere. Says she can't afford to live in Bury any longer.'

'Hey, man, that sucks.' Dad didn't sound as alarmed as Leo expected.

'So tell her she can't.'

'Leo, you know I can't tell your mother anything. She doesn't listen to me.'

'But she's lying! You told me that her parents give her two hundred a month to help with my education. She could spend that on rent. That's enough, isn't it?'

'Should be.'

'I never see any of it – she hasn't done anything about replacing the laptop and it's been like two days already.'

'Yeah well . . .'

'You said the only way to get her to buy me decent stuff is to force her hand, like we did with the bike.'

'Be fair, man, a bike's a bit cheaper than a new laptop.'

'It doesn't have to be new – a good second hand one would be fine as long as it has a reasonable graphics card. The PlayStation and screen is OK but I can't edit my videos on it. I'll lose followers if I don't upload at least a video a week.'

'We can't have that.'

'And now she's trying to move me somewhere and I don't even think it has Wi-Fi.'

'Shit, then that's a definite deal-breaker.'

He'd been formulating his pitch. 'So, Dad, I was thinking, how about I move in with you, part-time? I could do my videos on those days and spend the rest of the time out in exile with Mum.' He loved his mum – he didn't want to abandon her altogether.

'You know I live here with Gran and Granddad, right? There's no room for another person.'

'Then you could rent somewhere on your own. Why don't you take over this house? Then I wouldn't even need to move out.'

'Leo, man, I'm sorry, I can't afford to rent somewhere. I have nothing to live on but crappy benefits.'

'You could . . . you could get a job maybe? They're hiring as the new coffee bar. Mum's friend got a job there.'

'Leo, do I look like the kind of guy who would be happy making cappuccinos all day?'

'But if you needed the money for something important . . .?'

'Sorry, no can do. I've got to keep things loose, you understand? I've got a couple of auditions for bands in Ipswich coming up. Maybe something will come of that. I'll talk to your mother, tell her how you feel about the move. Got to go now. Gran's putting dinner on the table and you know how she hates us talking on the phone during a meal. Stay strong, man.'

Leo threw his phone on the bed. He hated his parents sometimes – they never understood, never helped him out like he wanted when he had a problem. They did nothing for him. He was not moving, no how, no way. He wasn't going to talk to his mother, not until she realised how wrong she was.

'Leo, supper's ready!' called Mum from downstairs. 'I've cooked your favourite – burgers.'

He contemplated staying in his bedroom, but his stomach rumbled.

'Coming.' Leo picked up his phone, slipped it in his back pocket, and jogged down the stairs.

Chapter 6

'So kind of you, dear boy, so kind.' Dad sat in the front seat of Sam's car looking heartbreakingly dapper. The staff at the home had wept to lose their 'gentleman' as they called William Ranworth and dressed him this final time as he liked with his cravat and handkerchief in his top pocket. Now, winding through the country lanes, Sam wasn't sure his father had the first idea where he was, why he was there, or even who Sam was.

'We'll find you a nice new home to live in, Dad. Maybe somewhere with a view of a garden and fields.'

'I like gardens.'

'Yes, yes, you do.' William had spent his career at Kew as one of the head gardeners and inspired his son with his love of plants and landscaping. Sam's childhood had been spent as much in the greenhouse as inside a schoolroom.

His father hummed something then made an abrupt 'hah!' sound. He made these random noises these days which was OK once you got used to them and knew not to get alarmed. Sam wondered if Dad was just testing that he was still alive. It didn't make for relaxing driving though.

'I've got a garden at my new place, Dad, but it needs a lot of work.'

'Gardens are ninety percent toil, ten percent pleasure.' He'd said that often when Sam was growing up. 'How big is it?'

'Big. Fifty acres.'

'Then you've got your work cut out for you. Boy, oh boy.'

'Yes, I have, but the structure is there – mature planting, some interesting shrubs. I've just got to strip it back to reveal the beauty.'

'That's good. You can't buy time – that's what any gardener knows.'

'True.'

'Plant a tree and your grandchildren will thank you.' That was another of Dad's favourite pearls of wisdom.

'That's right, Dad, and someone did plant them for me. We're turning in now.'

Sam glanced sideways and saw that his dad was admiring the avenue of beech trees with shining eyes. He paid no attention to the castle visible above the trees, his focus was all on the approach.

'You've hit the jackpot here, dear boy. These are wonderful specimens.'

Sam grinned. Maybe having his father here for a few days would work out fine.

The bedside clock showed that it was only six. Sam lay with the duvet pulled up to his ears, wondering what had woken him. The house was quiet, only the clicks from the boiler switching on to heat the water disturbed the silence.

Dad.

Sam leapt up and checked in the spare room. As he suspected, Dad's bed was empty.

The moat.

Shoving his feet into sandals, he ran for the castle. The moat was low at this time of year and covered in green algae. A confused old man could mistake it for grass and step into it. There was nothing there, no sign of disturbance, only a couple of mallard ducks leaving trails of brown water as they paddled their way peacefully across to the bank.

What other hazards could be death traps? There were almost too many to count. He scanned the battlements but there was no sign of anyone up there and, besides, he kept the castle locked. His dad wouldn't have had time or inclination to find the key in his son's desk, surely? The drive? Thank goodness that there was next to no traffic and the builders didn't start until eight but if he reached the country lane . . .

Sam sprinted to the gate. There was no sign of his father. He checked the gatehouse cottage, reminded that he had to do something about it as his tenants were arriving in a week. That would have to wait. Dad was now his priority.

He heard a vehicle approaching. Running out into the road, he flagged down a lorry.

'All right, mate? You OK?' asked the driver.

Sam only now realised that he was wearing nothing but boxers. 'Yes – no – I mean I'm looking for my dad. He's got dementia and goes wandering. Have you seen him on the road?'

'Ah, bad luck. There's nobody on the road between here

and the village. I'll drive slowly in the other direction and if I spot him, I'll bring him back, OK?'

'Mate, you're a life saver. Thanks.'

'No problem.' The driver pulled away, as good as his word taking the bend with extra care.

Worry that his father might be knocked over subsiding, Sam made his way back to his cottage, calling all the way, alternating between 'Dad!' and 'William!', not sure which he would recognise. Perhaps he'd over reacted? wondered Sam. Maybe his dad was somewhere about the house or back garden?

The glint of sunlight on the orangery windows caught his eye. Of course. He opened the unlocked door and found what he was seeking. Trowel in hand, Dad was standing over some pots Sam had meant to fill for his front step but never got round to. Dressed only in his Marks and Spencer pyjamas and slippers, he was contemplating his choice of annuals: a tray of pansies and another of petunias.

'Lovely flowers, simple, some say common, but they'll give you a splash of colour like no other,' he said, looking up with a smile. 'Here, dear boy, see the yellow markings on this one – looks like a little face, doesn't it?'

Sam bit back the torrent of 'how could you scare me like that?' in recognition that for William absolutely nothing had happened. 'That's right, Dad.'

'I'm not sure I like this brand of potting compost. I prefer our own well-rotted stuff from the heap.' He rolled up his pyjama sleeve.

'Of course you do. Dad, what do you think you're doing?'

'Working, of course, Sam. How do you think we pay the bills?'

Sam felt a constriction in his throat. 'I think you might've come to work without your uniform.'

'Have I? Good gracious. This won't do. And what are you doing standing there in your pants? What if your mother or your sister sees? You're not a little boy anymore, Sam.'

'No, I'm not. Let's both go in and change. We can have some breakfast, then you can get on with the pots while I do some of the grunt work, OK?'

William put down the trowel and looked around him in some confusion. 'This isn't Kew.'

'No, it's my garden. Remember: I brought you here yesterday. Fifty acres.'

'Oh yes. My boy said he'd bought himself a beast of a place but he can see the beauty. Do you know him?'

'Yes I do, Dad. Come on in. Neither of us are dressed for the garden.'

His sister rang mid-morning.

'How's it going, Sam? I've been so worried about you both, feeling guilty how I dumped it all on you.' How like Helen to be wracked with guilt. If he was honest, Sam felt he deserved a little suffering after all the years he'd left her to cope.

'It's had its moments but now I'm fine as I've worked out I can use Dad as slave labour in the greenhouse.' He kept an eye on his father who was tying up some straggling plants in the cottage border. Several lupins had taken drunken dives over the cornflowers.

She laughed.

'No, it's true. He's loving it. We can't shut him back in a home with no garden. I hadn't realised how much he missed it.'

'But London . . .'

'I know. I was thinking we'd find him somewhere out here.'

'Sam . . .'

'You said it yourself: you're over-stretched with the kids. And it's only a couple of hours by car if you want to visit at the weekend.'

'I . . . no . . . actually, you're right. I'm being a bitch: wanting you to deal with this and still trying to have it my way. I've got to train myself to *let it go*.'

'Why are you singing that?'

'*Frozen*?'

'What?'

'Ask your four-year-old niece sometime. See what you can find. Dad needs to get earth under his nails to be himself.'

'How's Michael?'

'A dot-to-dot version of a grumpy toddler.'

'So it was chicken pox?'

'Oh yes. What joy. I suppose it had to happen sometime.'

'Hang on in there, Helen.'

'And you. Love to Dad – and to you. Don't forget to keep him hydrated.'

'Helen.'

'Sorry. Love you.'

Actually, she was right. He hadn't thought about fluids. Inspiration striking, Sam dug in the back of the cupboard and found the old flask his dad had always taken to work. He filled it up with tea just how Dad liked it and took it outside with his coffee.

'Time for a break, Dad.'

William stood up. 'I'm ready for one. It's going to be a scorcher later.'

By then, Sam fully intended for his dad to be inside having a snooze in front of the TV. 'I think so too. Here – take a pew.' He brushed off bird droppings from the old set of iron garden furniture with a rag. He'd not yet had time to sit on them himself since moving in a few months ago.

'Lovely. Hah!' Echoing in the little dell where the cottage was situated, Dad's exclamation scared the rooks in the trees behind the castle. They circled and cawed a protest.

Deal with it, birds, thought Sam wryly. He wasn't a fan of rooks, finding them sinister, but he realised they gave the castle an authentic *Macbeth* vibe. It could make for a great Halloween party venue – another idea for the website he had yet to update. All he had was the most basic front door with contact details.

'So, er . . .' Dad looked at him with that slight panic that showed he'd lost contact again, like his brain functioned on an intermittent Wi-Fi signal.

'Sam, Dad.'

'So, Sam, how's that lovely girl of yours – Jennifer? I haven't seen her for a while.'

Of all the names in the lottery of what his dad forgot that was the one he remembered. 'She left.'

'Oh, shame. I liked her. Perhaps you can make it up to her,

lure her back now you have all this?' He gestured to the garden. 'What girl could resist a man with his own castle?'

'Dad, she died.'

His tired old eyes filled with tears. 'I'm so sorry. I didn't know.' He did – he'd been at the funeral five years ago. 'What happened?'

'I'm not exactly sure.' He couldn't talk about this now, not with someone who would promptly forget and then ask him all the same questions another day, reopening old wounds. 'Did you know that Michael's got chicken pox?'

'Michael?'

'Helen's youngest – your grandson.'

His father chuckled. 'Little monkey.'

'Yes, that's the one.'

'Hah! Hah-hah!'

The rooks billowed and cawed as Sam sipped his coffee and William drank his tea.

Chapter 7

Diana's house was packed with people for the end of term barbecue, a tradition that grew up during primary years when parents constituted a much more cohesive group. For the children, it was the start of wonderful freedom; for parents it was their last hurrah before tackling the impossible riddle of how to occupy their offspring while also holding down full-time jobs. Diana had squeezed the cooking into the little patch out back but guests spilled out into the downstairs rooms and some into the front garden. All the boys, except Leo, had gone to the local park to kick a ball while the food was being prepared. Gemma frowned as she spotted her son slumped on a beanbag, content now he'd got the broadband code.

'Look at him,' she whispered to Diana as they set out the salads on the kitchen bar.

'I see a normal teenager, Gem.'

'I'm so worried about him. He has no friends.'

'You can't live your kids' lives for them.'

'I know, I know.' She'd read that in a book too. 'Doesn't stop you wanting to though.'

Diana went over to her husband, a cheerful giant of a man who worked as a plasterer, and had a brief word.

'Leo, my man, all the other boys have abandoned me and I have some serious heavy-duty grilling to do. Not for sissies. You in?' asked Henry.

Gemma watched with bated breath as the internal debate played across her son's face: virtual or real world?

'OK.' He slipped his phone away. 'What do you want me to do?'

'Ever barbecued ribs? Now that's a challenge. Come on, I'll show you.'

Gemma choked up as she saw her son smile at the man who bothered to give him some serious attention. 'God, I love your Henry, Di. I need a man in my life for Leo's sake if not mine.'

'Yeah, he's good with boys.' Diana smiled. 'Are you going to enjoy yourself now?'

'Sorry, I've been such a misery these last few weeks.'

'Only the last few weeks?'

She slapped her friend lightly on the shoulder. 'It's just all piling up – getting ready to move, my parents threatening a visit, and high season for weekend work. There aren't enough hours in the day. I'm only half packed.'

'Here, have a glass of wine and get half-cut. Sounds like you need it, particularly if the parents of doom are circling. Have you been back to the cottage?'

'No time but Mr Ranworth swore it would be ready. He's not going to let me down, is he, when he knows we are often asked for recommendations for where to hold weddings?' She took a sip of the cold tangy white. Ah, that was good. She'd stopped buying wine as an economy and she was missing it. 'He must know that hell hath no fury like a registrar scorned.'

'You're right. He'd be mental to do that. And if the worst comes to the worst, you could always demand to share his little love shack until yours is sorted.'

'Di, stop it.'

'It's just that he's so . . .' She twirled her hand. 'That aside, we're still on to help move you. Henry can borrow a van from work.'

'I'll say it again. I love that man. Fight you for him?'

'Girl, you're on!' Diana chuckled. 'Handbags at dawn? But if you win, you'd have to deal with his smelly socks and embarrassing tendency to laugh too loud in public.'

'You're right. You can keep him. There's no such thing as a perfect man.' Gemma dipped a carrot in hummus and crunched down.

'Did you enjoy helping Henry?' Gemma asked Leo as they walked back to their house in the dusk.

'Yeah, it was cool. Can we do ribs at home one day? I'd like to show Dad I can do it.'

'Maybe in the new place. There's lots of space. We could probably build a barbecue without too much expense. That could be a summer project for you.'

Leo dug his hands in his pocket. 'Mum, I'm not moving.'

'Leo, we are.'

'I want to stay here.'

'I know you do but I've given up the lease on the house. It's sorted.'

'Why are you ruining my life?'

'I'm trying to make it better.'

'But I like it here. It's so unfair! You don't care about me – about what I want!'

Anger flared. 'Unfair? Do you want to know the real reason why we're moving? It's because I can't have your father raiding our house every time he's short of a quid or two.' Gemma stopped before she made an unforgivable comment about Ray's drink habit and all-round loser status. 'Sorry, I didn't mean to tell you that, but there it is. I don't feel safe knowing he can barge in whenever he wants.'

'Dad's not a threat.'

'He made off with your bike and our laptop: that's a threat in my book.'

'But you've loads of money – you've got a good job and my grandparents give you money for me. You're just being mean.'

Gemma stopped on the corner of their road, an unlovely spot smelling of dogs. 'Who told you that?'

Leo kicked a stone against a wall.

'Your father? And you believed him.' She shoved her hand through her hair. 'Why not? He's your parent after all.'

'He says you can afford to replace the stuff with better things. It's not as if the money is yours in any case; it's meant for me.'

Certain facts began lining up in new and unpleasant ways in Gemma's mind. 'You let him take that stuff, didn't you?'

'I'm going in.'

She grabbed his wrist. 'Oh no you don't, Leo Whitehall.

Did you let your dad take our laptop because you thought I'd get you a better one?'

'I don't want anything special, just one that can handle graphics. The old one sucked.'

'Oh my God, you did.' Gemma swallowed. 'I thought you were a victim but you were scheming with him. How could you, Leo? I'm not made of money, no matter what he tells you.'

Leo was quivering, part-anger part-shame, his poor complexion going all blotchy. 'Don't blame me. You're the one not spending the money given for me – *for me not you!*' He pulled his arm roughly out of her grasp. 'I hate you.' He ran past their front gate, heading towards his grandparents'.

'You all right, love?' asked the busybody from Number 5 who had watched all this drama while watering his hanging baskets.

'Fine, thanks.'

'He needs a clip round the ear, that one, talking to you like that.'

'He's just angry we're moving, Mr Nielson. He needs to vent at someone so it might as well be me.' Gemma hurried inside and let herself have the meltdown that she'd been holding off out on the street. Ray. The bastard. He'd turned their son against her. She'd been so careful to try to shield Leo from the truth about Ray that she hadn't realised he was feeding Leo such poison about her. A good job? Council wages were among the lowest for public servants. Two hundred pounds a month? Her father put that straight into a trust fund for Leo's university education and it never came anywhere near her bank account as her parents didn't want to make her 'life choices', as they put it, too easy. They wanted her back under their control before they trusted her with money in case she did 'something foolish' again. They were still disciplining her even though she was almost thirty.

And as for her life choice: she'd had unprotected sex a couple of times at fifteen, got caught out and decided to keep the baby because she didn't believe an innocent life should suffer for her mistake. How was that a bad decision? It was making the best of a no-win situation. She could've had it so much easier if she'd had an abortion or given her baby away but she'd stuck it out, raising Leo alone when Ray lived up to his feckless reputation. Both of them abandoned, she had lavished all her love on the little protesting scrap of humanity she had managed to produce. Her parents had been so embarrassed by her then, and still now it would seem. Did no one actually think she was admirable for having made the decisions she did? Apparently not. There was no one with a lower social status that a single mother, even one working all hours she could to pay the rent on a crappy house in a crappy part of town.

Gemma threw her shoes in the corner and collapsed on her bed, letting angry tears flow unchecked. Sometimes she just wished she could have someone to carry part of her burden. Even someone who could mend a tap or put the rubbish out would be welcome – she wasn't choosy. Her top fantasy was a man who would greet her when she came home from work with a cup of tea, chat about her day, and then serve the casserole he'd already put in the oven. He'd help Leo with his homework then they'd relax with a Netflix session, just the two of them, until bedtime. And at bedtime, well then, the fun would really start. It was a simple dream that so many had as their reality. She must've really messed up her previous life to be born into this one. Not that she believed in reincarnation; it sounded too cruel to be expected to go through all this again.

The phone rang. She groped for it, blowing her nose on a fraying tissue. Look – even the quality of her tissues was crap!

'Yes?'

'Gemma, it's Miriam here. Just to tell you that Leo's turned up in a bit of a state. I've calmed him down with a hot chocolate but what do you want to do?'

At least he was safe – not that she thought he wouldn't be. Leo's gestures of defiance to date had never gone too far. Underneath it all, he was sensible. 'Can you put him up on your sofa? We've had a bit of an argument and I'd appreciate the space for the night.'

'Well . . .'

'Isn't Ray there?'

'No, dear, he's off in Ipswich tonight.'

'It's just for one night.'

'Oh, all right. I'll dig out a sleeping bag for him. Do you have to move so far away? He's really upset about it.'

'Yes, I do.' Right now the cottage seemed like the best idea she'd had in a long while. 'I'll invite you and Gordon over once we're in. You'll see what I mean. It will do Leo good to be in the countryside.'

'I suppose so – trees to climb, woods to explore.' Miriam

had romantic memories of her own childhood as a farm worker's daughter in Essex. 'You're right. He spends too much time indoors. He's quite pale and his skin will never clear up if he carries on like that.'

'I think that's just his age.'

'They grow up so fast, don't they? Don't worry about him tonight. I'll send him back tomorrow after breakfast. Does that suit you?'

'Could you keep him till lunchtime? I've a morning wedding to do at the office.'

'You work so hard, love.' At least one person understood that, partly because Miriam had been the one keeping her own household afloat for years after her husband had retired early on grounds of ill health. 'He can come shopping with me.'

Gemma smiled. Ah, so her son was getting a punishment after all. His gran would take him into charity shops and ladies clothes stores on her weekend browse for bargains. He'd hate it. 'Thank you, Miriam.'

'I'll try and talk him round. He has some silly notion he can move in here.'

'I'd be grateful if you'd head that one off.'

'I will, don't you worry. Good night, dear.'

Moving day arrived and Gemma was depressed to see that her entire worldly goods only half filled the small van Henry had borrowed from work.

'Are you bringing this?' Diana held up the chipped garden gnome with a wheelbarrow Leo had bought her at a school jumble sale when he was eight.

'Do I have to?' It had been a sweet gesture then but now it reminded her of lost innocence.

'He'll be offended if you don't.'

Gemma doubted he'd notice. It had been hidden among the weeds in the front garden for years. 'OK, load it up.'

Diana passed it to Henry who was standing in the back of the van with Leo. 'You almost forgot him.'

Leo took the little figure, a childlike grin appearing on his face. 'You found Doc. Wow! I'd forgotten about him. Mum, look!'

It was the first time he'd deigned to speak to her in anything but grunts for days. 'You bought it for me as a Mother's Day present, remember?'

'Yeah. He's so bad he's sick! He's going in our front garden in the new place, right?'

Her grumpy feelings towards the gnome vanished as it had proved a bridge to her son. 'Of course. We can hardly leave without our good luck charm, could we?'

Henry jumped down to the pavement. 'Ready?'

'Can we drop the key at the letting agent?'

'No problem. Let's get the show on the road.'

By midday they were turning into the castle drive. Gemma was repeating a little prayer that the landlord had been as good as his word. Pulling up at the cottage, her heart sank. The upper-storey window was still boarded up and the ivy running wild. Leo, however, was so eager to plant Doc in his new home that he ignored all the negative signs.

'Where do you think, Mum? Hey, someone has put a pot of flowers on the step. That's nice. Let's put him in there.'

Taking the pot as encouragement, Gemma got out and fished the key from the old upside-down flowerpot, left as arranged. She opened the door. Thank God, the cleaners had been. The room looked very empty as all the old furniture had been taken away and only the barest minimum of new pieces put in their place. She forgave the landlord that because there was a row of salmon pink geraniums on the window ledge.

'I'll just look upstairs,' she told Leo. 'Check it's habitable.'

'Hey, Mum, there's a note.' Leo picked it off the draining board where it had been wedged under a mug.

Gemma opened the envelope.

Dear Ms Whitehall

I apologise that the window has not yet been mended and no start made on updating the electrics. I have met with some unavoidable delays. However, I hope you'll find it in reasonable state. Expect the builder next week to start work. I'm looking into broadband but the nearest connection is in the village and I have no record of a land line to any of the castle cottages. It might be prohibitively expense at this stage to arrange for a hook up. I'm using my mobile signal to access the internet but admittedly the reception isn't great. This might be the best solution for the moment.

I'll call by later this week to check you've got everything.
Sam Ranworth

How was she going to break the news to Leo? She didn't have a generous data package with her mobile provider and she had next to no bars on her phone in any case. Delaying that moment, she headed upstairs. At least the tread on the third stair had been replaced. Opening the doors to the bedrooms she found them spotless but spartan. They needed decorating and her room was dark thanks to the boarded pane. Still, Sam Ranworth was right: it was habitable, if you weren't fourteen and had a life that revolved around being able to go online. She had to sort that out first if she was going to make a success of this move.

'Let's unpack,' she announced cheerfully for the benefit of her companions. 'Then I'll make us a cup of tea.'

Diana and Henry left after lunch. On the driveway, Henry had assured her with his professional judgement that the cottage was sound, despite its age. The cabling was passable if not up to modern standards so she need not worry about killing herself when she plugged in the kettle. The plumbing was OK but the downstairs loo was in need of complete refurbishment to be the least inviting. He knew people if the landlord didn't.

After waving them off, Gemma sensed that showdown time with Leo was fast approaching but she pretended all was fine. The first thing she unpacked was her box of history books and novels. There was a sturdy shelf unit built in beside the fire which held them all. They looked great there, much better than on the flimsy Ikea bookcase in the old house. Gemma took that as a good sign. She tended to like modern history but maybe she should get something about medieval castles, do a little research on where she now lived? Her Open University course, one she had yet to finish as she was very slow in accumulating credits, didn't cover that.

'Mum?'

Uh-oh.

'Mum?' Leo wandered into the living room, phone held out in front of him. 'What's the broadband password?'

She cleared her throat. 'There isn't one.'

'What!'

'You'll have to use our mobile data allowance but go easy on that. The contract only allows us five hundred megabytes – a couple of YouTube videos and we'll exhaust it.'

Leo stared at her, aghast. Yes, that was the perfect word. If she hadn't realised how serious this was to him she would've laughed at his expression. It could be a meme – Modern Deprived Child.

'I can't stay here.' Leo looked panicked.

'I'll sort it out with the landlord as soon as possible, Leo. You can live offline for a few days, surely? Go and explore the village for example?'

'Is there a café with internet?' he asked hopefully.

She remembered the zombie apocalypse streets. Unlikely. But she didn't need to be the bearer of bad news. 'I don't know. Why don't you look while I send a message to the landlord about it? Oh, and remember to keep out of the castle gardens – he's renovating them so they're a building site.'

The door banged on her last words. Gemma sighed. At least he was outside.

Chapter 8

Sam wheeled the barrow of manure to the flowerbed by the car park. He was concentrating on doing quick makeovers to the parts of the garden visitors saw first and had decided on a colourful border on the path between parking and the draw-bridge. He was hoping to finish preparing the ground today as he had a mechanical hedge cutter coming on Monday, which should allow him to begin to make inroads to the overgrown parts of the formal gardens close to the keep. He was content to let the parkland gardens run wild for another year. Take back control little by little. A lesson in life if ever there was one.

Tipping the contents onto the freshly dug earth, he eased out the spade from where he had planted it and began to work in the manure. Hazel poles at the back, maybe, with a rambling rose? Herbs, rosemary, lilies, periwinkles, heartsease which could spread out into the lawn? Perhaps he should do some research, visit local gardens to get ideas for what grew well locally? He wished he had more time to do these things; he wasn't that keen on the study he knew he should do into the history of the place but he really enjoyed seeing solutions other gardeners had come up with in comparable situations.

His back was beginning to protest. Sam unbuttoned his shirt but didn't take it off: his dad had drilled it in to him that gardeners were more sensible than builders. William had been thinking of keeping up a certain standard of decency but his advice applied as well to the avoidance of sunstroke and skin cancer. Reminded of his duties, Sam checked the app he'd installed on his phone. Dad, if he'd remembered to keep his phone on him, was shown to be inside where he'd left him for his post-lunch snooze.

A message flashed up.

Can we talk about getting broadband through a landline? Mobile signal is really bad in gatehouse. Gemma

The new tenant. He'd forgotten she'd be in by now, having left a note for her yesterday when he'd delivered one of Dad's pots as a welcome present and some spare geraniums for the window ledge. He really should go down and check she had everything she needed. He felt bad about the window. The new pane was sitting in his shed and he'd meant to fit it himself but time had run away from him. And the ivy – damn, he'd forgotten to trim that back too. He couldn't be blamed for the mobile blackspot though.

Sam hung his head, feeling exhausted by the list of things he had to get done. Well, she'd just have to wait in line. He couldn't get to it right now. He had to finish here, cook supper for Dad, see that his father had a proper wash today and got to bed so Sam could have a few peaceful hours to himself to catch up with his administration. Tomorrow they had a visit to a local care home scheduled so that was out too. Monday, that was the earliest he could do anything.

I'll come by on Monday.

A reply came through immediately. *I meant today. Please. It's very important to my son.*

Sam decided not replying was a reply. He'd offered his first available slot.

She didn't get the message inferred by his silence. *I'm working Monday.*

I'll come by before you leave. 8 am? He put the phone away and wiped his forehead on the towel he'd draped on the handle of the barrow.

You chose this, he told himself. You picked this over investigating crime. Rotted manure versus rotten humanity: you'd make the same choice every time.

Something made him look up – a flicker of movement over by the keep. Dad? No, there was a boy clambering on the half-collapsed curtain wall that made up a rockery in the castle garden. Having ignored the many 'Do not climb' signs, the kid was trying to get up to the battlements.

'Hey, you! Get down!' Sam shouted, running towards the invader.

Startled, the boy gave a squawk and lost his footing. He disappeared, fortunately falling down onto the shelved slope of the rockery rather than taking the plunge into the moat. Sam cursed. He shouldn't've yelled. He knew better but, dammit, he'd been scared for the lad.

He collared the boy limping away from a patch of squashed edelweiss. It was the tenant's son. Why was he not surprised?

'Are you crazy? You could've been killed!' He was tempted to shake some sense into him but years of police training saved him from getting physical. A firm but non-bruising grip on an arm was all that was required to exert his authority.

'Let go!' growled the boy.

'No chance, mate, you're trespassing.'

'I'm not your mate.'

'No you're not – so you don't get mates' roaming rights. Leo, isn't it? Didn't your mother tell you that you were not allowed into the castle gardens?'

'She might've.' The boy's eyes skittered away, sure sign that he knew he was in the wrong.

'Does she know you're here?'

The boy shook his head.

'It's time then that we had a little chat about castle rules. Come with me.' He released his hold. Funny how he could tell what the kid was thinking. The boy obviously wondered about running but worked out it wasn't worth it. That showed he did have some brains. In a bristling silence, they walked down the drive to the cottage. Sam knocked on the door. His tenant appeared, checked shirt tucked into distracting cut-off shorts. How was he supposed to have a sensible conversation with a woman showing that much length of tanned leg?

'Oh, hey.' She smiled but then it faded when she saw who he stood beside. 'I thought you said Monday?'

'Ms Whitehall, I caught your son climbing on the castle keep.' He knew he sounded a prick but he was still suffering from shock of the near miss.

'Oh. Oh, Leo!' She glared at her son. 'I told you not to go into Mr Ranworth's garden. What were you thinking?'

Leo shuffled his feet. 'There's a rare Pokémon, Mum. A Magikarp. It's in the castle. I haven't got it in my collection.'

This nonsense seemed to make sense to his tenant because she was nodding sympathetically. 'I understand, Leo, but you have to ask Mr Ranworth permission before you try to catch Pokémon on his land.' She looked up at him expectantly. 'Would that be OK? It would really make Leo's day.'

The only explanation Sam could come up with was that she was crazy too. 'You do understand that your son almost broke his neck climbing on the ruined part of the keep?'

'He did? Wow, Leo, I didn't realise you were getting to be so . . . um . . . bold doing this Pokémon thing.' She looked almost pleased for a second before covering it with concern. 'But you have to understand that the real world has real dangers. You don't get a second life if you take a fall.'

'Of course, I understand that. I'm not an idiot, Mum.'

Sam begged to differ. 'And he damaged some plants.'

'Naturally, I'll pay for any damage. Leo, apologise to Mr Ranworth.'

The boy muttered an ungracious 'sorry'.

His pretty tenant nodded, relieved. Did she think that was enough? 'Well done, Leo. Now perhaps Mr Ranworth would let you catch the Pokémon safely?'

'You're kidding?' marvelled Sam.

She frowned. 'What's the problem?'

'The problem is I don't have time to escort the boy to catch this . . . this carp thing. I'm not a babysitting service. Tell your son to stay out of my garden. I've got work to do.' He turned on his heel and began to walk away. 'What the heck is that?'

'A gnome.'

He glanced behind and saw his tenant was watching him with narrowed eyes, arms folded. 'Ornaments aren't allowed. They lower the tone.'

'I rather thought the cracked window did that. Besides, it's my rented cottage, my gnome. You may call the shots up at the castle, but here I am king.'

Sam stamped away, feeling that this wouldn't be an argument he could win. One thing he could do, though, was make sure he left her hedge untouched on Monday and hide the whole damn mess she was making of his cottage.

It's just a little gnome, Sam, his less-grumpy self nudged him. *Where's your sense of humour?*

Give them a gnome and they'll take a g-mile, he shot back. *Next it will be illuminated toadstools and fake woodland creatures.* Boy, he was now really ready to dig manure.

'Leo, you should be more careful.' Gemma had put her son on washing up duty as punishment for his incursion into the castle grounds. 'It's not just that he might have a good point about it being dangerous, but that it is his land and he requested you don't wander there. It's trespassing.'

'But you don't get it – a Magikarp – that's like epic! None of my friends have got it – not even Aki in Kyoto.' Leo splashed the water over the sink on to the floor as he dumped their lunchtime plates into the tub.

Gemma silently cursed the logarithm writers, or whatever controlled the game, for deciding anywhere with 'castle' in the title needed some special characters. 'Strangely enough I do

74

get it. I collected My Little Ponies when I was a child and I never did get the flutter one.'

He rolled his eyes. 'Mum.'

'It was hard to get hold of in the UK and cost more than several months pocket money. People kept buying me the unicorn as they didn't get that each pony was different and I wanted the whole stable.' She'd chucked them out when she was thirteen which was a shame as they'd probably be worth something now.

Leo stacked a sud-streaked plate on the rack. Gemma resisted the urge to rinse it off. 'It's not the same.'

She thought it was exactly the same but knew better than to try to make her son see that her generation wasn't that much different from his. 'You're not to go up there again without an invitation.'

'But it's just waiting there to be caught! Mr Ranworth might decide to ban Pokémon hunts on his land.'

'Unlikely as he doesn't even know what a Pokémon is . . .' *lucky man*, '. . . so he's hardly going to go to those lengths over something he doesn't understand. I'll ask him on Monday when we talk about getting the cottage online.'

'Mum!'

'It's the best I can do, Leo. This whole situation is the best I can do. I'm sorry if it isn't good enough for you.'

'I just think he's selfish – wants to keep it all to himself.'

Gemma remembered the Oscar Wilde story of the Selfish Giant. Maybe Sam Ranworth was worried about health and safety but she rather suspected he just didn't want to be bothered by people. 'Whether he is or not is his business, not ours. He can be any way he likes as it's his castle. Just stay away, OK, until I fix this?'

'All right, OK, stop going on about it.'

'Promise?'

'Yeah.'

'Right, so while we are finally actually talking about stuff, about the laptop and the internet.' He said nothing but she could tell he was listening from the methodical way he was washing the plate. 'You need to understand about my budget.' She picked up a drying cloth, remembering that the book on raising boys suggested not sitting head to head but having a side by side activity. 'The money your grandfather and mother are putting aside for you doesn't come to me; it's going into a savings account for your university education.'

He wedged the plate in the rack. 'Really? I've got, like, a trust fund?'

'Yes. It's very generous of them. But don't get carried away: it's to help you get started when you reach eighteen. It's not for squandering – and I certainly can't touch it to help out with any difficulties we might have now. Like the fact that I have to replace our computer.'

He went back to washing up.

'Getting a connection to fast broadband is also going to be costly. There'll be a monthly payment and that's before we even find out about how much they'll charge to run a cable to here. They might not be able to do it so we'll have to look into mobile and that's expensive and might not as good with the poor signal. Contrary to what your dad said, I don't earn much – barely enough in fact. I have to watch every penny.'

Leo clearly didn't like what he was hearing. 'I told you we shouldn't have moved.'

'The rent is cheaper here but you might have to choose between a laptop and broadband: I can't afford both.'

'Broadband,' he said quickly.

That's what she thought. 'Then I suggest you find a job over the summer and earn the money to buy us a secondhand laptop. After all, you owe me one.'

'A job?' Leo sounded distressingly like his father.

'Yes.'

'But who would pay me for anything round here? There's not even a shop in the village.'

'Dog walking, gardening, odd jobs: there are loads of possibilities. You'll just have to knock on a few doors, won't you, see if anyone needs any help?'

'I can't do that. I don't know anyone. It'll be embarrassing.'

'Leo, all of us have things we don't like doing. Learning to do them anyway is part of growing up.' She might as well get all her stock of issues off her chest. 'Oh and by the way, I bought you a razor and shaving gel when I did the shop. Have a look at your top lip. I think you might need to start using it.'

'Seriously?' Leo felt his face gingerly. 'Cool.'

Gemma took another plate to dry and turned away, smiling. Thank you, book. That hadn't been so bad.

Chapter 9

'So Mr Ranworth, your father will have a lovely bedroom of his own and be able to spend as much time as he likes with the other residents in our lounge.'

Sam followed the manager down the corridor that smelled of boiled cabbage and breaded fish, vowing his father would not die in a place like this. He had had high hopes for the residential home in Braintree but it had turned out to resemble a low security prison crossed with a budget hotel. All the old people he'd seen out of their rooms had lacked any spark or interest in life. If he was told that he would end up here when he hit eighty then he would throw himself in the castle moat rather than make that a reality. He didn't blame the lady giving him the tour – she was doubtless handling the situation as best as her finances and facilities would allow – but this would be a living death for his father who was often too aware to settle for this.

Turning to see what had become of William, Sam found him checking the soil on a pot plant at the reception desk.

'Do you have a garden?' Sam asked, giving it one more try.

'Only a little one in the front. I'm afraid we can't let residents out there, particularly those with dementia in case they wander off. It's a busy road. But if you father likes plants, he's welcome to have as many as he likes in his room.'

'Thanks for your time. I'll let you know what we decide.'

The woman gave him a nod. 'Please don't leave it too long. Rooms are snapped up in a matter of days in this area. There's a severe shortage of accommodation.'

Was he squandering his one chance to get his father somewhere safe?

'Look at this, Sam,' said his father, mercifully in one of his more lucid moments. 'It's plastic. And there was I worrying it wasn't getting enough water!' He chuckled.

The manager held out her hand. 'Mr Ranworth, lovely to meet you. And, William, I hope we'll see you back here soon.' Sam also wasn't keen on the way she didn't use his father's surname. He knew it was supposed to be relaxed and friendly but it came across as disrespectful when she wasn't doing the same for him.

His dad shook her hand politely but his gaze went to his son, worried. 'Why would I come back? Do we know anyone here, Sam?'

'No, Dad, I'll explain in the car. Thanks, Mrs Andrews. I'll be in touch.'

He helped his father into the passenger seat of his Outlander, standing behind in case William lost his balance on the high step into the SUV. William sat down and stared bleakly up at the converted hotel that was now an old people's home – a dirty brick skirt with a half-timbered faux Tudor upper storey. Sam could see why it had gone bust as a place to stay. Last resort of the very desperate.

'Don't worry, Dad, you're not coming back here,' Sam said quickly as he got into the driver's seat.

'Is that why you brought me – to see if it would suit?'

'Yes, as I explained on the way.' Which to his father was probably further back in the mists of time than the things of his youth.

'I liked my old place. I had friends there. Why can't I go back there?'

'That home had to close, remember? Put your seat belt on please.'

'You're really not bringing me back here?'

'No, Dad. I think we both need to find something that suits you better than this.'

'What's wrong with your place?'

Nothing, when William was living in the present; too many things to list when he was in one of his confused patches and went wandering or did something unintentionally dangerous like putting a teaspoon in the microwave or leaving the grill on high. What Sam really needed was another pair of eyes, someone to head off these potentially serious lapses. His father wasn't stubborn when a danger was pointed out, nor resist being steered in a safer direction; he just needed the nudge. 'I don't think it will work in the long term. I haven't got a stairlift or adapted bathroom for a start.'

'Oh, you can get those fitted easily.' His dad waved those problems away as if they were no more than a bad smell to be expelled.

'No, I can't, Dad. My place isn't suitable for adaptation. You need somewhere more sociable. You don't want to be stuck in my cottage on your own day in, day out.' He turned on the playlist he'd downloaded for his father which he had filled with the hits of yesteryear. As he hoped, his dad got distracted by singing away to Chuck Berry and Elvis.

That reminded him: Neil would be back from honeymoon soon. His friend was good with family dilemmas having suffered through so many of his own. He should invite Neil and Phil up for a few days so they could see what he was dealing with and advise.

After a late lunch, Sam left his father sleeping in front of the TV repeats of *Inspector Morse*. He had not taken any time for himself for weeks now and he was desperate to go for a run. Gardening was good exercise but used different muscles and he never completely relaxed while working his way through his endless 'To Do' list. Deciding he could risk it as William usually slept for at least an hour and a half, Sam slipped into his running shoes and kit and headed out, taking the woodland path that led directly into the village rather than the drive. As much as he appreciated the sight of a pretty woman, he did not want his tenant to see him taking a break while he owed her so many repair jobs. He ran past the pub – the Castle Inn – and waved to some of the locals he recognised sitting on the picnic benches out front. That prompted another thought: he'd discussed with the landlady the idea of linking up the two businesses so wedding guests could stay at preferential rates in the pub's accommodation. He really had to come back one day next week and hammer out the details.

Muscles tensed across his shoulders as he recalled all the things he had not done that he had intended to do by now.

Relax, Sam, he told himself. *The run is for not thinking about anything.*

OK, brain, switching off now.

His feet hit the tarmac in a mind-numbing rhythm and his consciousness began to float like one of the dandelion seeds drifting from the hedgerow.

'Mum, there's an old guy poking at the pot on our doorstep.'

Gemma woke up from her Sunday afternoon doze on a rug on a patch of weeds that had once been the cottage lawn. 'What?'

Leo shrugged. 'What I said. I went inside for an ice cream and saw him.'

Gemma had suspicions about the safety of the gnome. 'Not the landlord?'

'No, much older. He looks kinda . . . lost.'

'Oh.' Deciding this was not a problem that would go away by ignoring it, Gemma stood up and slipped on her T-shirt over her bikini top. She went through the dark interior of the cottage and opened the front door. There was no one there – if you didn't count the gnome. The earth around the pot, though, looked wet. She had to hope it was just water rather than some local drunk caught short. Gross.

Leo passed her. 'I think he went that way – towards the road.'

'Leo, it's not our responsibility . . .' Too late, Leo had gone out onto the drive and she could only follow him. When had her son become more civic minded than her? She found him gently taking the elbow of an old man about to wander into the lane. A car drove by a second later, taking the corner far too fast.

'Excuse me, sir, are you lost?' Leo asked.

The man blinked at him. 'Michael?'

'No, I'm Leo. You don't know me.'

'I've got to get home, dear boy.'

'Right, OK. Have you got a car nearby, or are you with someone?'

'Car?' The man put down the watering can he was carrying and patted his pockets. 'No, no, I don't think so. I don't have the keys with me.'

Gemma reached them. 'Can I help you? Drive you somewhere?'

The old man stood up a little straighter now he was faced by a woman. 'That would be terribly kind of you, young lady.'

'You watered our pot for us, didn't you?'

'Yes, yes, they need a lot of watering at this time of year. I like your gnome. Very jolly.'

Gemma smiled, thinking this old man might be confused but he clearly had a sweet nature, so unlike the grouch up at the castle. 'So just tell me where I can take you? Are you from the village?'

'Village? No, I live in Kew.'

'Kew, London?'

'Of course.'

He was wearing slippers so he can't possibly have come that far. 'Maybe you're visiting one of your relatives here?'

'Where is here, my dear?' He dropped his voice to a conspiratorial tone. 'I'm afraid I can be a bit vague at times.'

'Claremont Castle – or Claremont Magna if your people live in the village.'

He smiled happily at her. 'I'm sorry, I've never heard of it.'

'Right.' What to do? Phone the police? That seemed a bit drastic. Take him to the pub in the village and ask if anyone recognised him? It couldn't be good for him standing out here in the heat of the day. 'Would you like a drink of water?'

'No need, my dear. I have my flask with me.' He patted his pocket. 'Oh, I must've left it behind.'

'He's got a phone, Mum,' whispered Leo, having spotted the telltale outline in the man's linen jacket.

'Can we call someone for you?'

'No, I'm fine. Just doing my job.' He sloshed the almost empty can.

She tried another tack. 'I'm Gemma, this is my son, Leo.'

'Pleased to meet you both.'

'And you are?'

He frowned, then his expression cleared. 'William, yes, I'm William.'

'William, would you mind showing me your phone?' asked Leo. 'I'll show you mine.' He held out his mobile.

The old man chuckled. 'Cheeky little monkey. Mine's nothing special.' He handed it over.

Leo expertly flipped through the menus. 'Mum, he had just two contacts – Sam and Helen.'

'That's right: my son and my daughter. They must be around your age,' he said to Leo. 'Do you go to school with them?'

'No, I don't think I do.' Leo returned the phone to him. 'Here you are.'

Gemma took his elbow. 'William, we think we know where you live – up at the castle, right?'

'Do I? I thought I lived in Kew.'

'Well, let's go and see.'

'Is it far?'

'No, not far.'

'Let me carry that for you,' said Leo, taking the watering can from the old man.

Gemma's heart swelled with pride. She often forgot just how brilliant her son could be. He'd always been good with old people having spent so much time with his grandparents in Bury while she went out to work.

'It's a scorcher today,' commented the old man, gesturing to the cloudless skies.

'Yeah.' Leo steered him towards the shade of the beech trees.

'Better make sure the palm house isn't overheating.'

'We'll get right on that,' said Leo.

Sam came back from his run and stripped off his shirt as he entered the cool of the house.

'Dad?' He mopped the back of his neck.

Silence. He checked the sitting room and then his dad's bedroom.

OK, don't panic. You've been here before. He'll be in the garden somewhere.

Pulling out his phone he tapped on the app. His father was shown practically on the road by the main gates. Oh God. There was no way he could get there in time to stop him stepping out in front of a car.

Sam sprinted down the drive, only slowing when he saw three figures making their way towards him. Relief hit him like a brick, making him feel sick and shaky. He leant over putting his head down. The last straw would be to pass out now.

'I think we found something that belongs to you,' said his tenant cheerfully. Oh, the irony.

'Thank you. Dad, are you OK?'

'He was just watering our plants,' she continued, giving him a look conveying the fact that he wasn't to alarm his father by making too much drama out of the crisis.

'Yeah, and he's worried about the palm house,' chipped in the son. 'Have you got one?'

'He means the one at Kew,' Sam said absently. 'He time travels – thinks he's back there.'

'That's kinda awesome,' said Leo.

Sam looked up in surprise at the boy, cheered by this robust way of regarding dementia. 'Yes, I suppose it is. You just have to run with it and he comes back eventually.' Though Sam feared one day William might not.

'I didn't know he lived with you,' said his tenant.

'It's recent. His old home had to close and I've not found a good place for him yet.' Sam breathed through the stages of coming down from full blown fear to 'move along, nothing to see here'.

'Hah!' his dad exclaimed, alarming his escorts.

'Don't mind that. It means nothing.'

'He's been in the sun for quite a long time,' prompted Gemma.

'Yes, sorry. Dad, time for your tea.'

'Where are your manners, Sam?' scolded his father. 'Gemma and um . . .'

'Leo, sir,' whispered the boy.

'Leo. Would you like tea with us? I think there are Jammy Dodgers.' How did his father remember that when he forgot so much else?

Leo's eyes brightened. 'Great. Mum never buys nice stuff like that.'

'Well then, we'd better put the kettle on.'

Sam let his father and Leo pass him so he could fall into step with his tenant.

'Thank you, Ms Whitehall.'

'Please, call me Gemma. I already said you could and Ms Whitehall sounds formal. I'm living at the bottom of your garden after all.'

Had she? To be honest, he didn't think he'd ever met her when he was functioning properly. He'd fallen into his police training habit of calling everyone by their surnames.

'Gemma. You live at the bottom of the garden? Like fairies – very good ones as it has proved today. Sorry about Dad.'

'No problem, but he did almost go right out into the lane.'

'Damn. I was only gone for an hour.'

'I see you've got your hands full?'

'Having Dad move in put a bit of a hitch in my step, it's true, but that's life.'

'Certainly is. And I'm glad you saw my son in a better light as a result. He's not a bad kid – just lives for different things than we do.'

Sam was only just now recalling how rude he had been in his last encounter with his nearest neighbour. Not his finest hour. He had some making up to do.

'I can relate. I was the only teenager in my neighbourhood obsessed with garden design. My mates thought it funny to call me "Chelsea" after the Chelsea Flower Show until I thumped them.' He smiled at the memory. 'Digging builds up a certain core strength they hadn't bargained on.'

Her eyes flickered flatteringly to his biceps. He was reminded he was here without his T-shirt. '"Chelsea" is not the first nickname for you that springs to mind.'

'Sorry, I was about to get in the shower after a run. I dashed out when I saw Dad was missing.'

'I don't mind. I've always admired the views around here.'

He laughed, surprised by a sudden burst of happiness. It had been too long since he had bantered with someone of the opposite sex. 'It's all part of what you're paying for in the rent.'

'Then I'm getting a bargain.'

Oh no, had she really just said that? Gemma turned away so he wouldn't see the full glory of her blush. She did not make flirtatious comments like that as a rule. It wasn't her fault he was treating her to a display that left very little to the imagination.

Had she mentioned that she liked a man who worked out? Thank God, no. At least her lapse hadn't gone that far. After Ray's tortured poet physique of skinny limbs and pallid skin, her landlord was quite a treat for the eyes. The few men she'd managed to date while raising Leo never got this far stripping off before her. No one had a more vestal existence than a single mum with strict rules on whom she invited home. The only men she'd seen with less on during the last fourteen years were Olympic divers on TV. And wasn't that a pity? Ray had this to answer for too, stealing her identity as a sexual being and leaving her the all absorbing role of parent to handle alone.

It wasn't as if she hadn't dipped her toe in the water. There had been that nice teacher she'd dated for a while – Graham something, taught Economics at the Further Education College. He'd felt safe and sane but she'd realised after a few weeks that wasn't enough on which to build a future. She'd gently let that fizzle out, rather to the relief of both sides she believed. The spark just wasn't there and what they'd done with the lights out had been very unexciting.

And then there had been that unwise fling with the wine merchant from Woodbridge. Less said about his sweaty hands and fumbling moves in his Jaguar the better. He'd turned out to be married, of course – totally bogus entry on his online profile. That had put her off risking these perilous dating waters for years. People could look great, sound ideal, and yet when you met them, you soon grasped that they were either liars or limp disappointments – or both. That route might work for others but Gemma didn't think it was suited to her. She couldn't afford another heart-breaking mistake.

They took a path she hadn't yet explored that led them through a barrier of rubbery-leaved rhododendrons to Sam's cottage. It was unexpectedly charming: a long low building made from the same old grey stone of the keep with a reddish-brown tiled roof. He'd done much more on the presentation than at hers, having made a border either side of the door that looked right out of a picture by Helen Allingham, delphiniums and foxgloves making a splendid rear guard to the forward troops of lavender which were currently under assault from bumblebees.

'Why don't you sit in the back garden while I change and make the tea?' Sam suggested.

She could hear Leo and William inside, already setting about getting a tray together with much serious discussion over the point of artificial sweeteners. Following Sam's directions, she made her way around the side of the cottage, past a neat row of gardening tools, and out into another little haven. Sunflowers vied for first prize in 'who can be the tallest' along the brick potting shed; hollyhocks poked through the perennial geraniums, brazen flowers in white, reds and pinks. She went closer. Some even had an almost black bloom.

'That's *Alcea rosea* "Nigra". I'm quite pleased with it,' Sam said modestly, putting down four mugs and the milk bottle. He was now decently clad in a fresh T-shirt. 'It seems to like the soil here.'

'A black hollyhock: who would've thought?'

'Some Frankenstein plant breeder in a mad fit of ambition. There are few things they won't attempt.'

'Did anyone mention triffids?'

He chuckled. 'I read that book when I was a teenager but it didn't put me off gardening. Came from outer space, didn't they?' He pulled out a seat for her. 'Please – the furniture is clean, mostly.' He flicked off some dirt with a gardening glove that was lying on the table.

She sat down. The cast iron had been in the shade so felt

cool against the back of her thighs. 'This is the life. So, you've always been a gardener, like your father?'

He shook his head. 'No. I was a police officer until three months ago. Gardening was strictly a hobby.'

'That's quite a transformation. You left all that for this?' She gestured to the amazing landscape before her, full of colour, movement and wildlife.

'Yes. Crazy, aren't I?'

'Probably, but a little bit of crazy is healthy or we'd never try anything new.'

He pulled a sheepishly pleased face, smoothing the semi-permanent frown and making him seem so much younger. Gemma guessed that he'd not been on the receiving end of praise for some time. 'Thanks. How about you? Have you always been a registrar?'

'For the last four years.'

'And before?'

'Before that there wasn't much outside being a mum. I was an early starter on that. There was school, then Leo, some part time work, then my first proper job.'

He rearranged the mugs and the milk. 'Sorry about earlier – the wall thing. He's a nice kid. I was just scared he was going to do himself a real injury.'

'I get it. I didn't realise at the time that you were already on duty for your dad. It takes it out of you, being on tenter-hooks the whole time – ask any parent with a child under the age of reason who has mastered locomotion.' That sounded bad. 'I didn't mean to say your dad was like a child.'

'He is and he isn't. He's vulnerable so he has that in common, but he sometimes talks more sense than most adults I know. He hasn't lost his gardening skills either – still the same green fingers.' He picked a sprig of lavender and presented it to her. 'Smell this – these old varieties have such a lovely scent.'

'Thanks.' She sniffed it and tucked it behind her ear. 'Maybe it's like music to him – the gardening. They say that songs and tunes are often the last things to be forgotten because they are so deeply ingrained in a different part of the brain.'

Leo and William emerged from the kitchen, Leo with the teapot and William with a plate from which the Jammy Dodgers were in grave danger of escaping like lemmings over a cliff edge. Gemma jumped up to take them from him.

'Your boy here told me he'd never planted a seed in his life!' said William, scandalised by the very idea.

'At nursery he did do cress on a piece of kitchen towel once, but no, maybe he hasn't now you come to mention it.'

William sat down in the seat that was half in the sun. His son reached over and put a battered straw hat on his head to protect him. 'Well, we can't have that. What do you say to sending him home with some lettuce, Sam?'

'I'd say that was a great idea, Dad.'

'Lettuce?' asked Leo; he wasn't a fan of green stuff.

'Grows fast and tastes so much better than anything you can buy,' said the old gardener with infectious enthusiasm. 'You can keep cropping it for salad for weeks if you treat it right.'

'I like the sound of that,' said Gemma.

Sam passed around the teas. 'I suppose I should've made us a jug of something cold. It might not be appropriate for what must be one of the hottest afternoons this year.'

'No, this is fine. We're English. Tea is always appropriate.'

'How's the cottage? I know I owe you a window.'

'Oh that's OK. I quite enjoy the crepuscular light.'

'Crepuscular?' Sam looked taken aback by her vocabulary. She often did that to people, coming out with words that rarely made it out of a dictionary.

'You know, like twilight?'

'I know what it means but I think you might just be the first person I've heard to use it in a sentence.'

'Mum's weird like that – reads lots of old books – drops words no one else understands into conversation like it's normal.' Leo bit off the top of the biscuit and started licking the jam. Gemma was about to reprimand him when she saw that William was doing the same.

'I don't do it all the time,' she said defensively. 'It just struck me as the perfect word this morning when I woke up.'

'Crepuscular or not, I still think my tenant should have a mended window. I'll come over now after we've finished here. That's if, Leo, you wouldn't mind staying with my dad to learn how to plant lettuce?' He gave her son a look that it was really a request to keep the old man safe for the time it would take to fit a window.

'Sure. And could you then let me catch the Magikarp?' asked her son, showing he had picked up a good life skill of knowing when to push an advantage.

'Why don't we do it first?' said Sam. 'I take it that it doesn't take long? Your mum can walk with my dad over to the orangery where we've set up a potting bench while we go on our hunt.'

'Cool.' Leo was already on his feet.

'When we've finished our tea.'

Leo sat down.

Gemma took a biscuit and bit off the top. Really, there was only one way to eat a Jammy Dodger even in company.

Chapter 10

There was something oddly illicit about being in a woman's bedroom when it was just the two of you in the house. Sam was very aware of Gemma downstairs. He could hear her humming as she scrubbed carrots at the sink just below the open window. He rested the pane of glass against the wall. It had already been cut to size so it should be a fairly simple task to clear out the old putty and slot it into place.

Detective habits never die so he couldn't help noticing the clues about Gemma as he worked, particularly the pictures on the rickety dressing table that majored in Leo and very little in anyone else. There was a group shot of Gemma and some female friends, including the registrar – Diana, wasn't it? There was a photo of Leo cuddling an older woman he took to be a grandmother, and one of a young girl on a beach with two adults standing on guard behind her, possibly Gemma as a child. There were some framed prints waiting to be hung – the front one a moody black-and-white shot of New York in the interwar period. Had she ever been? he wondered. Guessing from her brief outline of her story, she had gone straight from schoolgirl to mother. That had to have been tough. He hoped she'd had a good family around her as Leo's father sounded a first-class bastard.

'You done up there?' Gemma called. 'Because I'm tempted to crack open my "welcome to your new home" wine from Diana.'

'Almost.' He smoothed the last of the putty in place and wiped the glazing clear of any smears. Hearing soft footfalls behind him, he turned to find Gemma standing with two glasses of white wine. God, she was gorgeous, particularly in this 'crepuscular' light. She looked so young and sexy with her piled up brunette hair and shorts and suddenly she came out with words he associated with elderly librarian types.

'What?' She touched her face. 'Have I got a smudge on my nose or something?'

'No. I was thinking you looked . . .' *lovely* '. . . settled in.' He took the glass and toasted her. 'To new beginnings.'

She chinked her glass against his. 'Thank you. And you look pretty at home yourself. You know, there's something about a man with power tools that just gets to me.'

He was a little surprised by her teasing, having stopped using his own moves some years ago. 'I'll . . . er . . . get my power tools out for you anytime.' He saluted her with the battery driven screwdriver he'd used to tighten the window latch.

Flushing, she turned away. 'Sorry that was uncalled for.'

'Who doesn't like a risqué pun now and again? I know you're just joking.' Putting down the wine on the window ledge, he closed the window. 'Leave it like this while the putty hardens. I think the pane cracked because the window snapped open in the wind and hit the wall – the latch was loose. I've fixed that so it should be OK.'

'Thanks, Sam.'

It was the first time she'd said his name – and he liked it. 'My pleasure.' He had to get out of the bedroom. His thoughts kept going to what could happen on that white duvet. He needed much clearer signals before he risked that – 4G at least, rather than a couple of bars of interest from her. 'Shall we go down?'

They took the wine out into her scrubby patch of back garden.

'I must do something about this lawn,' he said, poking at the dandelions with the toe of his sandal.

'Sam, you've quite enough going on up at the castle to worry about this. Leo is around all summer. I was thinking of asking him to have a go at some basic gardening. I was going to buy some tools but would you mind very much if he borrowed some of yours?'

'How old is he?'

'Fourteen.'

'Is he OK with lawn mowers, shears and that kind of thing?'

'I don't know but he's fine in the kitchen.'

'If he's here alone without you to monitor him, I'd worry about lending him anything that could cause an accident.'

She knuckled her forehead. 'No, you're right. Bad mother. I was just hoping to get him some kind of work and thought if he started with doing odd jobs for me, he could say he had some experience.'

'I'm happy to lend you any of my equipment while you're here. And Gemma,' he reached out and tapped the back of her hand. 'You're not a bad mother. From what I can see, you're a great one.'

She smiled up at him. 'I was so wrong about you. I had you tagged as the grouch of Claremont Castle, but you can be really nice, can't you?'

'I have my days. The majority are spent in grouch mode, but the fact that you both saved my dad's life today has flipped my "be nice" switch.'

She laughed which made plenty of other switches flip too but he wasn't going to bring that up. If she crossed her tanned legs one more time, he was going to have to have a very cold shower when he got home.

'Are you serious about wanting to find him odd jobs?' Sam asked.

'Yes, very much. It's pretty urgent, actually. He's working to replace a laptop that was . . . er . . . taken a couple of weeks back.'

Delicately put. Sam hadn't forgotten overhearing her conversation on the phone that first day. He had an idea. Would she go for it? 'Look, Gemma, feel free to say no . . .'

'Uh-oh.' She took a swig of wine.

'It's nothing bad. Just I'm looking for someone to help keep an eye on Dad while I'm working. If I knew he had company even for a few hours it would mean I could concentrate on what I'm supposed to be doing.'

'Leo's only fourteen, Sam.'

'He wouldn't be responsible for Dad's safety, just be on hand to send me an alert if there's a problem – a bit like today. If Dad could potter around the orangery and garden, he'll be in seventh heaven.'

On cue, the gate rattled and Leo appeared with a tray of

baby lettuce plants. 'Hey, Mum, look what Mr Ranworth and I did together. He says we can eat them in a week or two. They'll grow like billy-o if on the right window ledge.'

Sam smiled to hear such an old-fashioned phrase come out of the boy's mouth. 'See, it could be mutual. Dad's got a lot to offer. He taught me everything I know about gardening.'

Gemma took the tray from Leo. 'Where did you leave Mr Ranworth, Leo?'

'He's inside. I got him some water. He became a bit hot on the walk down here so I left him in the kitchen. Is that OK?' Leo glanced worriedly at Sam.

'That's perfect. Thanks, Leo.' He met Gemma's gaze with a 'may I?' query in his expression. She gave a little nod. 'In fact, Leo, I was wondering if you'd like to earn some money for a few hours work next week?'

Gemma tried not to worry about Leo in his new job as she went about her work on Monday. Sam had been very clear that Leo's only role was to ring him if William wandered off or tried to do something unsafe, but it was still a lot of responsibility to put on a young person's shoulders. What if he stopped paying attention for a second and something terrible happened?

Diana bustled into her office, wearing a vibrant green skirt and yellow blouse – a blast of citrus in the grey and beige surroundings. 'How's life at the castle?' She put a coffee down on Gemma's desk, payment for a quick gossip in their break.

'It's turning out OK – better than expected. Did you know that Sam has his dad living with him?'

'*Sam* is it? I thought you said it was strictly Mr Ranworth and Ms Whitehall between you both.'

'Don't look at me like that, woman. And stop wiggling your eyebrows. It's all your fault in any case.'

'Oh? Do tell.'

'We bonded over your bottle of wine last night. He's given Leo a job keeping an eye on his dad who's got dementia. Leo should be able to afford a laptop in a few weeks if he sticks with it.'

'That's wonderful.'

'Is it? Did I do the right thing letting Leo take the job?'

Diana put her coffee down so her hands were free to gesture. 'Are you insane? Of course, it's right! Gemma, you've got to stop looking at your son as if he's still in primary school. How old were you when you were left in sole charge of a baby?'

'Fifteen.'

'And is Leo being left alone with this old guy?'

'No, Sam's around – just busy.'

'That sounds entirely appropriate to me. Anyway, I'm not here for your gossip . . .'

'Oh really?'

'Not just your gossip – though you would tell me if he made any moves on you, wouldn't you?'

'Sam's dad?'

'No, Mr King-of-the-Castle!'

'Well, I've seen his biceps and they're mighty fine.'

Diana waved that off. 'When you get to see anything more intimate, then let me know.'

'You'll be the first.' Gemma grinned. 'OK, playtime over. Why are you here?'

'I'm worried about our eleven o'clock wedding.'

Gemma checked her daily diary. 'You mean Niyazov and Motherwell?'

'It has all the signs of a fake one. I recognise some of the guests in the waiting area from the rent-a-mob crew.'

Gemma had presided over a number of these weddings where it was clear the bride and groom did not know each other and that money was exchanging hands so the foreign national could strengthen their application for a right to stay in the UK. They were tricky ones to judge. The registrars had a number for head office to ring when they were faced with a couple they did not believe were really together but that didn't help in the moment. And all that head office could do is pass on the information to Immigration and, as far as Gemma was aware, nothing was ever done.

'Great – just what I like on a Monday morning: a moral dilemma.'

'So, what do we do?'

'Have the couple made any errors in their paperwork?'

'No, they gave the twenty-eight-day notice and the authorities for marriage have come through from Colchester – everything seems in order.'

'Do they list the correct venue?'

'Yes.' Diana sighed. 'OK, we go ahead. Who knows, maybe true love will flourish between them?'

'And maybe pigs will fly.'

'I hate this part of the job sometimes.'

'We aren't border guards.'

'Thank goodness. I think it's your turn to administer the vows.'

'Di . . .'

'I did it last time – with that lady who looked like Morticia and the guy who resembled a weasel?'

'Oh yeah, you did. I think we're going to need chocolate.' Gemma pulled out her drawer for her emergency supply of Cadbury's and offered it to her friend.

'I shouldn't but . . .'

Coffee drunk, chocolate consumed, the two registrars headed out to the larger meeting room where the ceremonies were conducted. The registry office was in the elegant red brick town hall opposite the Abbey Gardens. Take away the cars and paint out the lines outside, it would be the perfect square for a costume drama, having retained all its period buildings. Inside, the public areas kept an air of gentility and small-town aspiration: chequered marble floor, pillars, white walls and crystal chandelier. The beauty of the surroundings made it popular for weddings, even bogus ones like that before her. Smiling at the fake couple, with their equally suspect family, Gemma dug deep for her professional poise. She was glad she had Diana at her back.

'Are you, Gregor Ivan Niyazov, free, lawfully, to marry Rebecca Jane Motherwell?'

Burly Gregor didn't even look at his much older bride. 'Yes, I am.'

She repeated the question to Rebecca.

'Yes, I am.' The bride had a distinctive Brummie accent, unusual for people in this part of the country.

Diana looked up abruptly on hearing the woman's accent and cleared her throat insistently. Gemma smiled blandly at the couple. 'One moment.' She walked over to Diana, trying to make it look as though this was all part of the usual procedure.

'It's her – Morticia but without the black party wig!' Diana hissed. 'I swear it.'

'You sure? But the identity documents checked out.'

Diana gave a tiny shrug. 'She can't've got a divorce through so soon. I only married her last week. This isn't legal.'

'Di, this is way above our pay grade. We'll have to get our manager. I was about to do the contracting words.'

'I'll get her. Does Morticia think we're that stupid? That's insulting!' Diana's blood was up and Gemma knew that meant there was no backing down now.

Gemma saw the woman shooting them both poisonous looks. 'Yes, I think she does think we're stupid.'

'We can't stop fake weddings but we can stop obviously bigamous ones. Stall them.' Diana grabbed the papers concerning the couple and hurried out.

Oh God, how? Some of the guests in the front row on Morticia's side did not look very patient; in fact, they looked like bouncers from a very tough nightclub who would take the message 'wait a moment' very badly indeed.

'This is a very special day, unique in the life of the couple standing before us. So, as Shakespeare says, "If music be the food of love, play on".' She beamed at the guests in a frantic fashion. 'Before Gregor and . . . Mor . . . Rebecca take the solemn binding step of pledging themselves in marriage, we are going to take a moment for reflection with the help of their choice of song.' The couple had selected a track to walk out to at the end but Gemma decided it would do nicely here. The lyrics to 'I would walk 500 miles' by the Proclaimers blared out in the meeting room while Gemma tried to maintain an expression of calm.

'What the fuck is going on?' hissed Morticia, jabbing Gemma with her bouquet. 'It doesn't happen like this!'

And she would know if she'd done this many times before. 'Problem with the ink,' improvised Gemma, stepping back and brushing off the lily pollen. Damn, that would stain her white blouse. 'My colleague's gone to fetch a new bottle.'

'Look, we're in a hurry. I've got a bloody pen in my bag.' Morticia was getting very up close and personal. Her breath smelt of alcohol. Any last doubts Gemma had about the accuracy of Diana's memory evaporated. She remembered that odour of Scotch and over-generous application of perfume from the signing last time.

'We have to use a special kind of ink to avoid fraud, Miss Motherwell. You wouldn't want any question over the validity of your union, would you?'

Gregor pulled his bride away. 'No,' he said firmly. 'All must be legal.'

Diana returned with Gillian, their manager, and the three registrars gathered for a quick conference.

'Are you absolutely sure she got married here last week?' Gillian whispered. A lady in her mid-fifties, she had the competent air of an excellent primary school teacher.

'Without a shadow of a doubt,' confirmed Diana.

'Unless she has an identical twin?'

'The odds of that?'

'I swear it's her too,' added Gemma.

Gillian frowned. They were on shaky ground here. Their job was to administer the oaths, not to do the job of law enforcement officers.

'Look,' said Gemma, 'why don't we invite a couple of community support officers to stand at the back? It's a public ceremony so they are free to come in and it might spook our suspected bigamist into abandoning the service.'

The Proclaimers cheery warble came to an end and Gemma let the music play on to the next wedding's choice, Handel's 'Arrival of the Queen of Sheba', much to the bemused looks of the guests.

'Maybe we should do nothing and just report them?' suggested Gillian.

'And be taken for fools? What if she's back next week with another groom?' said Diana. 'When are we going to say enough's enough?'

'OK, let's call them in.' Gillian left to fetch the police. Gemma and Diana looked at each other.

'How are your stalling skills?' asked Diana.

'Getting better with practice.' Gemma went back to the front of the room. 'I apologise for the delay, ladies and gentlemen, we're having a few technical difficulties.'

Morticia – Rebecca – whoever she was today – gave a harsh laugh. 'Bloody disgrace. You're spoiling my big day.'

And exactly how many of those have you had? thought Gemma cynically. 'I'm afraid questions have been raised over the paperwork. We won't be long verifying them.'

One of Morticia's rent-a-mob got up, a big guy with alarming knuckle tattoos. 'There's nothing wrong with my sister's documents.'

Interesting. Why did he think it was his sister's that were under question rather than the groom from Tajikistan? Would that be because he had forged them himself?

'Then we'll be proceeding very shortly, won't we, sir?'

The thug approached her. 'Listen, pet, some of us haven't got all day!'

'I'm not your pet. I'm a legally appointed registrar. Take a step back and resume your seat, sir, or I'll ask the town hall ushers to eject you.'

He jabbed a finger at her and growled. 'Watch it. I know where you live.'

'Extremely unlikely and I interpret that as a threat which contravenes our rules. Please leave.' Gemma was doing all this on bravado and knew she could really do with some help at this point. Diana would've contacted reception by now to get the security guards to arrive. At that moment though, rescue arrived in the shape of Gillian with two community support officers in hi-vis jackets. 'Excellent, the police are here.'

It was as though she had dropped a stink bomb in their midst. Guests fled for the exits, the thug and his sister shoving Gemma over in their haste to make for the fire escape behind her. Losing her balance, her face collided with the corner of a table. When the confusion cleared the only people left in the room were the registrars, the police and a stunned-looking bridegroom.

Gemma felt her right eye gingerly. 'Ouch.'

'What is happening?' asked the groom, probably wondering if this was all some bizarre English marriage custom.

'I'm afraid, sir, your fiancée is probably a fraud,' said Gillian, still watching her accusations carefully.

'You've been left in the lurch, sugar,' said Diana sympathetically. 'If you want your money back, you'd better get on after them.'

Gregor shrugged philosophically and patted his pocket. 'No payment until after.' He clearly did not understand that he had just admitted to intending to enter a fake marriage. 'Do you know another English lady who wants a good strong man who will work hard?'

Diana steered him to the door. 'Head out there, honey, and you'll find they are legion. Just don't offer to pay them, OK? That's not legal here.'

Chapter 11

The bump had bloomed into a black eye by the time Gemma reached home. She had made a statement to the police but, with the fraudsters scattered to the four winds, there was little they could do. They had to hope the gang wouldn't dare come back to Bury. Gregor had gone on his way with every sign he was going to take Diana's advice, starting with the receptionist on the front desk, a mature lady with a husband, so he soon moved on. Gemma liked to think of him going from woman to woman in Bury St Edmunds like a bee from flower to flower, striking up conversations about his reliability as a husband and willingness to work hard. She wished him luck in his search.

Turning into the cottage, the first thing she noticed was her parents standing on the step – oh Lord, that was all she needed. Second, and far more welcome, was the fact that the ivy had been trimmed from her windows, making a vast improvement to the appearance of the gatehouse, like a decent haircut to Leo on the rare occasions she could tempt him to the barber. She didn't need to feel ashamed about her choice of place to live before their exacting standards.

'Mum, Dad, how long have you been waiting?' Her parents had retired to Aldeburgh on the Suffolk coast, busy with a life of classical concerts and golf, and rarely came to see her. Gemma's impression of them was that their hearts were as smooth and hard as the pebbles on the wave-washed beach to which they had retired. She and Leo were expected to visit them like subject rulers paying obeisance to the emperor and empress. Her calculation as to how frequent that had to be was a computation that made Newtonian calculus look simple.

'We left you a message that we were coming,' her mother said with a hint of displeasure as Gemma gave her the obligatory kiss on the cheek. An elegant lady with dyed blonde hair to cover the grey, she always seemed a little too perfect to be real. She was never seen without make-up, never spotted lounging about in leggings and ratty T-shirt like her child did most evenings and weekends. Mother and daughter were both disappointed in the other – it wasn't all one way. 'What have you done to yourself now?' It was too much to hope that she hadn't spotted the black eye.

'Dad? How are you?' Gemma went up on tiptoes and kissed her father's scratchy cheek. He bore himself like a Roman centurion with a thatch of pepper and salt hair to add to the distinguished gent impression.

'Gemma,' he said gruffly, patting her awkwardly on the back. His jackets always smelt faintly of smoke which, as he professed to have kicked the habit in the 1960s, made her wonder.

'You said you were coming but you didn't say when,' Gemma said, addressing the first of her mother's assertions.

'Well, we were in the area, looking at antiques, so thought we'd call in. But don't think you can get away without telling me about that eye,' said her mother.

'It's nothing.'

'James?'

Prodded into action, her father tipped Gemma's head to the light. 'Have you put something on it?'

'Yes, Dad. Is it that noticeable?'

'I'm afraid so. I had one like that just before my wedding when I got a cricket ball in the eye. Your mother wasn't too pleased then either.' He showed far less alarm about it than his wife.

Gemma's mother was not satisfied by this line of questioning. 'Oh Gemma, you're not in another unsuitable relationship – not with someone abusive, are you?'

She made it sound as if this was a habit when Gemma had been living a blameless single life for years. 'No, Mum, it happened at work today. I fell against a table.'

'I imagine you were wearing high heels. I always told you when you were a teenager that they were a liability.'

'You imagine wrongly. I was wearing sensible work shoes and, for your information, I was knocked over by a serial bigamist and her criminal thug of a brother.' *Put that in your pipe and smoke it, Mother.*

Gemma's more rational self, chimed in. *Calm down, don't get irritated within thirty seconds of being in their presence.* 'Now, shall we go in and I can put on the kettle?' Her parents' visits were a trial but at least she'd learned in recent years to stand up for herself. She should welcome them as training in maintaining a spine.

'Well, I must say this is a very pretty cottage, Gemma,' said her father, trying to move the conversation on as her mother searched for some new way to make the black eye her fault. 'That hedge could do with cutting back.'

'Oh I hope not yet. I have big plans for those blackberries.'

'Not sure about the gnome though.'

'A present from Leo when he was little – and I like it.'

'Ah well.' Her father walked away with his hands clasped behind his back, giving her taste up for lost.

Her mother was inspecting the spartan living room. 'It's very dark in here.'

'Be fair, Maggie, old cottages like this often are. Now where's that grandson of ours?' Dad looked about the place as if Leo might be hiding under the furniture somewhere as he used to do when Beach Granny and Granddad arrived. He had always been a little scared of them, probably picked up from Gemma who for years found her parents intimidating. It was only recently, since she'd stopped trying to win their approval, that she'd become less cowed by them.

'He's up at the castle. He's got a job there for the summer.' Surely her parents couldn't fault that?

It seemed she was wrong.

'Oh, but we were going to ask him to stay with us. We know how bored he gets during his long holiday.' Her mother inspected the lettuce plants on the kitchen windowsill.

Gemma bit her tongue to stop herself telling her mother to leave them alone. 'I'm afraid that won't be possible now.' And it would've been nice to have been informed of this offer weeks ago so she could plan.

'But he's only fourteen. He deserves a holiday.'

'I thought you'd be pleased he had a job?'

Unexpectedly, her father came to her defence. 'That's true, Maggie. It's good for the boy. When I was his age I had a paper round.'

'What's he doing in this job of his?' asked her mother, dubious that anything Gemma had organised would pass.

'He's helping out in the gardens and keeping the owner's elderly father company,' she replied, rather misrepresenting the truth, but that was the only way to win a round with her mother.

'Humph. These need water.'

No, William had warned them that lettuce did best on fast draining sandy soil. 'That's Leo's project so please leave them. He has a schedule for watering. Earl Grey or builders?'

'Do you have any Lapsang?'

'I'm afraid not.'

'Then Earl Grey.'

Gemma had already known that would be the reply so was filling the pot. The safest way to handle conversations with her parents was to get them off the topic of her and on to them. 'So, how was your holiday in Italy?'

As her mother told her in detail about the lovely couple they met from Tunbridge while they were in Verona, Gemma wondered why bother to go all the way to Italy if all you wanted was to meet other British people? How had she come from these two almost strangers? She had speculated as a child that she was adopted, found in a basket like Moses, but no, the baby pictures suggested otherwise.

'I'm surprised you think the country life will suit you.' Her mother had jumped tracks again and was back on the subject of her failings. 'What will Leo do here all day?'

'More than he did in Bury. He'd become quite a recluse in his bedroom. As I've not sorted out the Wi-Fi, he's outside more. I think it's good for him.'

'When I was a boy, I liked nothing more than to ramble all day during the summer holidays with a Tupperware box of sandwiches and bottle of pop,' her dad piped up. 'Oh what mischief my friends and I got up to!'

Gemma was having difficulty imagining her father as a kind of *Just William* child – she'd been convinced that he was born grown up. 'You've kept that quiet, Dad.'

'Ah well. Can't tell you all my secrets, now can I?'

Wondering what had become of her son, Gemma looked out the window that had a view of the drive and saw Leo approaching, accompanied by William and Sam. They were each carrying a bunch of flowers. She waved but they didn't see her.

'Hi, Mum!' Leo burst in, full of high spirits. 'That's Granddad's car outside, isn't it? Are they here?'

'Yes – here – in the kitchen.'

Leo's face was alight with something that looked a lot like boyish joy – Gemma wanted to weep at the sweetness of it. These moments were so rare now. 'We brought you some flowers for the house, Mum. Sam said the garden had too many, but I think he just meant we should pick you some.' *Subtlety, thy name is not Leo.* 'Hi, Granny, Granddad. Would you like some flowers too, Gran? We've picked loads.'

Or maybe it was – her mother was disarmed by this gesture

in a way that Gemma had never seen before. 'Oh, Leo, that would be lovely. A few sweet peas maybe?'

Leo studied the bouquet in his hand. 'Which ones are those?'

'The pink and white ones.'

'The ones that look like butterflies? Cool.' He dumped the flowers on the drainer and selected a few stems of sweet peas. 'There you are.'

'I'll just wrap them in some damp kitchen towel for the journey home.'

Gemma recovered her wits enough to remember that she should make introductions. 'Mum, Dad, this is William Ranworth and his son, Sam. Sam owns the castle and is restoring the grounds.'

'Pleased to meet you.' Her dad held out his hand to William. 'I'm James, and this is my wife, Margaret.'

William frowned. 'Have we met before? In the war?'

Her dad looked startled. 'No, I don't think so. I wasn't born then.'

Sam held out a hand to divert attention away from William. 'James, pleased to meet you.'

'I hear you've given my grandson a job?'

'Yes, he's keeping my father company and learning how to garden. It's worked out well so far.' Sam glanced over at Gemma and his smile vanished. 'What happened to you?'

Leo caught the alarm in Sam's voice and actually looked properly at his mother. 'Mum, you've got a black eye.'

She scooped Leo up with an arm around his shoulders and kissed his cheek. 'Come here, you. Yes, I do know but thanks for pointing it out.'

'Are you OK? Ice – do we have any?'

'I'm fine, Leo. It happened a while ago at work. A wedding got a bit physical.'

Sam pulled out a chair. 'Sounds like you had a rough day. Do you have any of that wine left from last night?'

She wished he hadn't mentioned that in front of her parents. 'I'm afraid I don't.'

'I'll go back home and get you some. A black eye deserves at least a nice glass of Cabinet Sauvignon. Perhaps your parents will want a glass too? Dad, stay here for the moment with Gemma. I'm just fetching something from the house.'

His dad was looking a little confusedly around the kitchen, flowers drooping in his hand. 'Jennifer?'

'No, Dad, you remember Gemma. Leo's mother?' Sam sounded a little hoarse.

'Nice girl, Jennifer. You should've held on to that one.'

Who was Jennifer? wondered Gemma. But now was not the moment to ask.

Sam gave Gemma a brittle smile. 'Sorry, he's gone time travelling again.'

'It's fine, Sam. William, would you like me to take those flowers? Perhaps you'd inspect the lettuce – tell us if they need any more water?'

That request snapped William back to the present. He went to the window and felt the soil around the seedlings with his roughened fingertip. 'No, these are fine. Where's my apprentice? Ah, yes, Leo, give them some more water tomorrow morning but not too much. Moist but not swamped. You don't want to kill them with kindness.'

Gemma went over to her parents in the guise of refilling their cups and whispered a quick explanation. 'Mr Ranworth gets a little confused from time to time.'

'Poor chap,' murmured her father, moving to join in the discussion at the window. Gemma heard him introduce the topic of tomatoes which started William off contentedly in a new direction.

'So I see. Shouldn't he be in a home?' Her mother accepted a second cup.

'That's the plan – in the long term.'

'And what about his son? What's going on there, Gemma?'

'Nothing, Mum. He's my landlord, that's all.'

As usual her mother ignored what she said. 'He seems a good few steps up from your other boyfriends.'

'He's not my boyfriend.'

'Don't scare him off, Gemma.'

'Mum!'

'I know you: you'll ruin a relationship that promises happiness because you have a self-destructive tendency.'

'That's not true.'

'What about that nice wine merchant from Woodbridge?'

Gemma had always regretted her private life rarely, if ever, stayed private. Her mum used Leo as her unwitting spy in the camp, wheedling information out of him with a skill that the Stasi would've admired. When Gemma objected to her son being manipulated that way, her mother had laid down what she thought her trump card: *but I'm your mother!* 'He was married and a creep.'

'And that school teacher? Why did you let him go?'

'There was no spark. Why are we even talking about this? I'm renting this cottage from Sam, that's all.'

'We'll see.'

'Mum, please.'

'Gemma, you're almost thirty and single. I worry about you.' And wouldn't she love to be able to say 'my daughter, married to the castle owner'? That was enough to quash any romantic notions Gemma might've entertained about Sam.

'I'd be more worried about me if I was still hooked up with a man like Ray.'

'Well, I did warn you.'

'I was fifteen, Mum. Anyone in skinny jeans with puffy hair who plays rock guitar looks good to a fifteen-year-old girl.'

'We didn't bring you up to be a groupie.'

This was why she hated her parents' visits. None of them had moved on from the events of fourteen years ago. They rehashed the same old grievances and she was so tired of it, Groundhog Day without the happy ending. 'I think we should agree not to mention this again. It hurts me and probably hurts you too. Yes, I'm about to turn thirty and I'm single, but I have a decent job and a wonderful son. Are you ashamed of that?'

'No, no, of course not.'

'Then can we leave in the past the bad decisions I made when I was a child?' She waited a beat. 'Please.'

Her mother sniffed. It was difficult for her to let go because it was really about power, wasn't it? As long as she felt in the right, Gemma was always going to be in the wrong and therefore inferior. They had never met as equals on any ground even though Gemma had spent her twenties trying to find a space for that to happen.

'OK, you might not be able to forgive me . . .'

'Forgive you? I don't blame you . . .'

'Don't you?' She absolutely did.

'I just want you to learn from your mistakes. You seem bent on repeating them.'

'Oh yes? How many illegitimate children do I have running round the house? How many feckless partners are lounging on my sofa, living off me while they try to make it big in their music career? I think I learned my lesson long ago.'

'But you're not happy!'

'And telling me I'm not good enough and always wrong is a parenting method to help me achieve my happiness?' Her pulse was racing as her temper flared. She had to get out before she did something where she really did put herself in the wrong. 'I'm just going out to . . . to put these on the compost.' She grabbed a fading bunch of wildflowers she'd had in a jam jar on the kitchen table. 'Won't be long.'

Gemma marched outside and threw the flowers in the hedge.

Breathe. Your mother doesn't run your life or make your choices.

She kept walking until she was out of sight of the cottage window then collapsed against a fence, head in her arms.

'Trouble?' Sam had arrived with the wine.

'Can I swig that straight from the bottle?'

Studying the vintage, he gave a rueful smile. 'I'm afraid not. Perversely I picked one with a cork.'

'Don't you have some handy Swiss army knife that can sort out all life's problems?'

'Sorry no – just secateurs.' He leaned against the fence next to her. 'Is it your parents?'

'How did you guess?'

'That face is not caused by a black eye. That face reads utter frustration and desire to strangle someone.'

She laughed and scrubbed her hands over the face in question. 'Yeah, you're right.'

'Want to talk about it?'

'It's simple really. Mum and I are like two north poles on a magnet – push us together and we push each other away. She's never forgiven me for being an idiot at fifteen and getting pregnant. And with Dad, well, it's somehow worse – he's a blank, doesn't engage, just echoes Mum when she prompts him to say something.'

He said nothing just waited for her to continue. Gemma found that soothing. Her mum was always peppering her with questions and asking for justifications.

'I think it was mainly because I embarrassed them. I was all set to be university material – a lawyer or a doctor even, and instead I became a teenage single mum – quite the fall from grace. It wasn't the moral failing they worried about most, though that came up, but the stupidity of it.'

'You think you were stupid to have Leo?'

'Of course I don't. He's the best thing that ever happened to me. But they do. If I had been less naive, I might've avoided having him when I was only a child myself. I did a lot of growing up very quickly.'

'You know, Gemma . . . no, I won't say.' He looked away to the trees in the distance.

'Go on – please, I'm interested.'

'It's not my place to get involved.'

'Giving your opinion isn't getting involved. This was all over long ago – or should've been.'

'That's what I was thinking. If you can't be naive at fifteen, when can you be? In some ways, your mum is acting like the spoiled child, needing her pain, her embarrassment tended to when it should be about what's best for Leo and for you.'

He had summed it up nicely – not that she'd ever put it to herself in quite those terms. 'You think Mum's having the equivalent of a childish tantrum?'

'She's certainly grandstanding if she always turns it into a drama about how you failed her. You should've cancelled that particular family show in its first season. And as for your dad, I have to admit I think I understand him a little better. A lot of men in his generation were trained to hide their emotions. It might be more than embarrassment he feels.'

'He never says – never shows anything.'

Sam tapped his fingers on the bottle. 'What did they say about your eye?'

'Oh right: Mum accused me of being in an abusive relationship and Dad told me he got one just like it from a cricket ball – that sums them up right there.'

'OK, don't bite my head off, but maybe in some twisted way, that is how they show their love for you?'

'You think?'

'Running it through my Google translate for emotions and

I get from your mum overwhelming anxiety about you, and your dad was trying to cheer you up with tales from his own experience.'

Sam was right. When had she started to look for the negative in every little thing they said? It was like she was primed to explode at merest hint. They must find saying anything to her like crossing a field of landmines.

'But you have every right to set out the grounds for how you are going to relate from now on – particularly here,' Sam continued. 'Your rented house, your rules – as you told me a couple of days ago.

She chuckled at the reminder. 'The gnome is awful but he was a present.'

'There you are – you have your reasons and what other people think really doesn't matter.'

Chapter 12

Sam regretted sticking his neck out and giving Gemma his view on her parent situation. It was none of his business. He should've learned that lesson long ago. But she had seemed so despairing when he'd found her slumped on the paddock fence, he couldn't help himself. He'd once stepped up to help people without a moment's thought; it was what had led him to become a policeman, after all. He'd had some optimistic idea that he could make things a little better if he did his job well. Not that he had been blind to life's cruelty, but that hadn't stopped him trying to put his weight on the other side of the scales. And he'd been damned good at his job until . . .

Lingering in the kitchen, Sam opened the bottle and poured a little into a glass to test. He could hear everyone else talking out on Gemma's wretched patch of lawn, Margaret's voice rising above the others. He couldn't make out the words but what she was saying was in a tone of complaint. Gemma was right: her mother truly was a piece of work, sniffing with disdain at her daughter's attempts to make them comfortable on kitchen chairs. His own mum would be making a joke and helping fetch them, despite being a decade older than

Margaret. He had been perhaps too generous when he suggested Margaret's criticisms were a twisted method of showing she cared. Gemma's father though, he was the kind of man Sam could relate to having met many of them in his career in the police, particularly among those senior to him. He would diagnose an upbringing of nannies and boarding schools, cutting off normal instincts like an espaliered apple tree trained against a wall. He was more optimistic about Gemma's chances of bettering her relationship there, as those kinds of trees could bear a lot of fruit if you understood how to look after them.

She's not your problem, mate, his brain reminded him. *Don't make the same mistake of getting too involved.*

There had once been another vulnerable woman in his life. Jennifer had been estranged from her parents when he had met her through his job in CID at Scotland Yard. He had assumed it was their fault of course as Jennifer had told him over the months they were together the story of her many fallings out with them. He now wondered if it hadn't just been exhaustion on their part. There were only so many dramas and crises that a sane person could manage.

Insane ones seemed to have an endless appetite for them.

He took a slug of wine. *Head in the game, Sam. You're serving wine, not revisiting the ghosts of the past.* Picking up the tray of mismatched glasses, he carried it outside.

'I took a taste. It's not a bad red. Margaret, can I serve you some?'

* * *

126

His tenant's parents left after an hour, wanting to get home before it got dark.

'My eyes aren't what they used to be,' James said gruffly, kissing his daughter on the cheek. 'I don't like driving at night.'

Yes, thought Sam, there was affection under James' manner, just he always misdirected attention to some trivial comment rather than come out with it. He was really saying he didn't want to leave so soon.

Sam had heard them arranging with Gemma to have Leo to stay the following weekend which reminded him that he needed to get something more permanent sorted out for his dad. It was a shame that every day couldn't be like this one with the three of them pottering happily around the castle grounds. He'd got a hell of a lot more done than he had for weeks, whacking great chunks off the overgrown hedges with the big tractor hedge cutter. Some of them had had thorns as long as the hedge in the *Sleeping Beauty* story. He wouldn't've been surprised to find a dragon hibernating – a stone one as he knew there were many garden features buried under the rampant greenery. He had to be particularly careful he didn't hit anything with the cutter. He could do with finding some old plans or drawings of the garden to give him a clue where they might be. For the moment he had to be content with the unscientific method of probing the under-growth with a bamboo cane.

Gemma collected the dirty glasses and brought them into the kitchen while Sam was putting the cork back in the wine.

'Where do you want me to put this?' He held it up to the light. 'Only a glass left.'

'I'll save it for another crappy day then.' She put it in a cupboard on a low shelf. 'Bound to be another this week.'

'Sorry to hear that. I had a really good one, thanks to your son.'

'The arrangement with Leo's working?'

'Oh yes. He and my dad have hit it off. I don't know how long it will last – the novelty will wear off quickly I expect for Leo – but they enjoyed each other immensely as far as I can tell.'

'I'd say it will last at least a laptop's worth.'

'Then I hope he wants a very expensive one.'

Gemma smiled and started washing up the glasses. 'Oh I meant to say, thanks for cutting back the ivy.'

'Don't thank me: Leo did it with a hedge-trimmer at lunchtime.'

She put the washing up brush down. 'My son was up a ladder with one of those machines?'

'Only after training session on the ground and me standing on the bottom to steady him. It works on a battery – no electric cord.'

'Sam . . .'

'At his age I was splitting logs with an axe – believe me that's much more dangerous. He was a natural.'

Leo, of course, chose this moment to enter. 'It was sick, Mum. The blades just slice through like a samurai sword.'

Seeing Gemma's expression, Sam wondered if he should've asked the mother's permission before letting Leo have a go.

Following on from their conversation about Leo borrowing tools, he'd thought he'd done the right thing and made sure Leo did an easy bit. The fiddly stuff he'd handled himself.

'That's . . . great, Leo.' Sam could tell she was swallowing down her objections with difficulty so as not to spoil her son's achievement. 'Just I'd prefer it if you didn't do anything dangerous again.'

'It wasn't dangerous. Not like if he'd let me try the big tractor hedge cutter he hired.'

'I should think not! You can't even drive!'

'But it's private land. I can here.' He'd used that argument on Sam too.

'Gemma, don't worry: I won't let him on any of the big machines.'

She put her fist to her forehead in what was becoming a familiar gesture of frustration. 'I'd be happier if you said the same about the smaller ones too.'

'Mum, I'm not five!'

'Leo, your mum's right. I should've asked her first.'

'But you told her I would be gardening – and that's gardening. You said if I didn't learn to handle heights responsibly then I'd prat about like I did on the wall the other day.'

'Yeah, I did, but I think I overstepped. It was your mum's call, not mine.'

Leo rolled his eyes. 'Mum, tell Sam that it's fine – that you're not cross.'

'No, I'm not cross – just a bit shocked. And thanks, Sam, for the apology. I appreciate that you did it with good intentions. Just check with me first next time, OK?'

At least there might be a next time. She couldn't be too angry if she was being reasonable about it.

'But Sam didn't tell you the best news, Mum,' Leo said.

'There's more?' She smiled weakly.

'He found the old landline. It's still there but was buried under masses of ivy.'

'Someone cut it off at the wall outside at some point but yes, it's there,' Sam confirmed. 'The pole was buried under climbers in that wild patch of hedge bordering the road but it should be a simple job to clear it. I've already cut the ivy around the base so it should start dying off. If you tell BT, they should be able to reconnect the cottage. I doubt with the distance from the village it will be super-fast broadband but it will be better than nothing.'

Gemma hugged her son. 'That's wonderful.' She looked over to Sam. 'Really wonderful.'

Gemma enjoyed Friday weddings. The choice usually meant the couple were economising so they weren't splashing out on the bride's little girl fantasy wedding that would end in divorce courts a few years later. From her wide experience, she completely endorsed the research reported in the newspapers a week back saying that the more spent on the wedding, the higher the likelihood of breakdown. Secondhand or home-made dress, flowers and catering done by friends and family, laughter over mistakes – that was her idea of the perfect day rather than the strictly choreographed kind sold by bridal magazines where a hair out of place was considered a disaster.

'Sean, please repeat after me. Fiona, I promise to love and respect you.'

Sean, a sandy-haired stocky guy, was blushing fiercely but he held his bride's gaze as if she were the only one in the room. He repeated the words in a steady voice. Fiona, a petite redhead, swayed slightly on her crutches. Victim of a car accident in which she had been cut from the wreckage by the very same firefighter she was now marrying, Fiona had come a long way to be able to stand there. They'd been featured in the local paper and Gemma knew from the reports that Fiona had been determined to walk for her big day. The press were outside waiting to snap more photos; she could hear the excited murmuring on the town square as a little crowd of well-wishers gathered. Everyone loved a tragic story that turned to a happy ending.

Gemma spoke the second part of the promise for Sean to repeat. 'Helping our love grow, always being there to listen, comfort and support you, whatever our lives may bring.' A simple formula for happiness; just a shame Gemma had given up expecting it for herself.

After Fiona had said the same words, they moved on to the exchanging of the rings. Family and friends giggled when the little nephew charged with carrying the rings on a satin pillow refused to budge from his parents' side. Eventually his dad carried him to the bridal couple.

'Looks like Jake won't be dragged to the altar so easily, Sean.' He winked at his new sister-in-law.

Once the rings were wrestled from the three-year-old, Gemma continued. 'Sean, please repeat after me: I give you this ring as a sign of our marriage, and as a symbol of our love. I promise to care for you, to respect and cherish you, throughout our lives together.' The evident love with which Sean said the words gave Gemma hope that this was one couple who wouldn't end up splitting. It was hard to know but she had a good feeling about them.

When the exchange was complete, the audience broke into a spontaneous round of applause. Someone must have tipped off Sean's colleagues outside as there was a sudden burst of fire-engine siren, prompting yet more cheers and laughter. Curious to see how the couple would leave, Gemma followed the bridal party out to the steps. When they reached the stairs, Fiona passed her ribbon decorated crutches to her bridesmaid, Sean swept her off her feet, and they proceeded down the steps in a flurry of confetti. He then lifted her into the front cab of the fire engine and they were driven off to the reception to a hooting of horns and sirens.

Diana appeared at Gemma's side, wiping a tear from her eye with a tissue. 'No matter how many of these I do, there are still a few that make me sentimental. That was one fine exit.'

Gemma didn't say anything but hugged her friend.

Diana squeezed her back. 'Oh well, back to reality. Two o'clock and I have a death. You?'

'Birth.'

'*In the circle, the circle of life!*' sang Diana, as she usually did when they had this little conversation. This time Gemma joined in as they went back to their offices.

Making a cup of tea to carry to her desk, Gemma read

the notices on the staff board. A new one had just gone up, plum in the middle: an invitation to apply for voluntary redundancy.

Gillian entered carrying a little box of salad and a fork. 'That was some departure your wedding made. I hope we don't get complaints from the hotel. Half their guests were outside thinking it was a fire drill.'

'Oh, I think they'd've caught on pretty quickly. Gillian, what's this about?'

The manager frowned. 'Oh yes, I was going to raise it at the staff meeting later. Austerity cuts are hitting the service and they want us to reduce numbers to a smaller team.'

'But we're already fully stretched. I don't suppose they are talking about reducing the workload, are they?'

'They're pinning their hopes on the new software. They think a lot of what we do can be done online, increase our productivity.'

'They've said that for years but never found a way of making it work. New systems always make more work, not less.'

'I know, Gemma.'

Gemma's anger was building, sweeping away all the pleasant feelings left from the wedding. It wasn't Gillian's fault but she had to speak up or burst with the unfairness of the situation. 'They'll spend hundreds of thousands on a new programme, find it doesn't do what they want, and we'll be left with fewer staff and a bad system.'

'Succinctly put but it still doesn't mean they aren't going to try. The politicians running the council are like goldfish: they forget they've swum round this bowl before.'

Gemma splashed too much milk into her tea. 'So couples are going to be able to rock up to the front desk like to a cash machine, plug in their details, press "enter" for the vows, and hey presto they're married?'

'Not quite but I sometimes wonder if that isn't what the councillors would prefer. Registrars cost them, you see – wages, pensions, maternity and sickness benefits. We are awfully inconvenient being human.'

'I'd thought I was in a profession that wouldn't be hit by automation but it seems I was wrong.'

'No one is safe, Gemma. No one. I'm hoping to solve the budget demand by finding volunteers for redundancy but if that doesn't happen then some of us will lose our jobs.'

Gemma suddenly realised Gillian was warning her she might be affected. 'Oh. I hadn't realised it was that serious.'

'It is. Very.'

'How will you decide?' Mouthing off to her manager now seemed a foolish move.

'God knows. I'm hoping I won't have to.' Grey-faced, Gillian put her salad away uneaten. 'I'd better go. I have a phone call with head office at two.'

It was only on the drive home that the news started to sink in for Gemma. If she lost her job, it would be a complete and utter disaster. She lived with no backup, no resources to draw on for a rainy day; even a few months of job-seeking could send her into serious debt.

'Don't panic: it might not be you,' she whispered, turning into her driveway.

But then a great finger seemed to come down from the

clouds over the castle, pointing right at the roof of her car in parody of the National Lottery advert: *it could be you, Gemma Whitehall. It probably will be you.*

Chapter 13

Sam was clearing out the box room in anticipation of Neil and Phil's visit. He would surrender his double bed to the newlyweds, making do with a blow-up mattress in the little room he'd planned would eventually become his office. For the moment it had become the destination for all the stuff in his move from London that he had not needed immediately – and there was a lot of it. Moving from a four-storey Victorian house in Wandsworth to a cottage in Suffolk was like a middle-aged Elvis trying to squeeze into his teenage jeans.

'Do I really need all this?' he mused aloud. Opening the nearest box, he was suddenly transported back to his childhood. At the top was a well-thumbed children's book on gardening, pages smeared with earthy fingerprints and splashes from a watering can. He had propped this up on the potting bench in the greenhouse at home, working next to his dad. William believed in reading up on his subject and encouraged his son to do his own research in books with colourful cartoon characters like Peter Pea and Sally Strawberry. Lifting that out, Sam came across a box of Lego and a wooden train set. His sister's kids would enjoy those when she brought them for a visit. No, he couldn't throw them out. Getting a marker, he scrawled across the lid: *Toys – attic.*

Next he opened the box underneath. The problem in the move had been that at the end he had run out of time and just thrown things into the packing cases without sorting them. Kitchen stuff had got jumbled with DVDs – it was carnage. He hummed happily when he found his favourite chopping board below his dusty James Bond film collection, a Christmas present that he had never got round to watching. Having the satisfaction of being able to empty the cardboard box, he collapsed it and put it by the bins for recycling.

The third box proved a much less welcome surprise. Lifting the flaps he was first hit by a familiar scent. Jennifer had always worn Elizabeth Arden 5th Avenue perfume. It had been his standard present at Christmas and birthdays. Walking past a counter in a department store and catching a whiff of it was enough to catapult him back in time; he completely understood how his father could find himself tossing about on the seas of memory at the merest nudge from the past. Sam thought he'd got rid of all of her personal belongings but there was a scarf that still bore strong traces of the scent. She must have spritzed it heavily for the smell to last so long. It was too late to send it to her parents as he had her other things – he didn't want to reopen old wounds for them if they'd managed to find some peace by now.

'Put through the wash and charity shop,' he told himself firmly, creating a new pile. Over. Dealt with.

Fearful now of what else he might find, he excavated further. An unfamiliar blue shoe box was next. He took it out and realised it was too heavy to contain shoes. He lifted the lid. Christ, how had this slipped through the net of his clear-out? It was full of photos, all stuffed in randomly. This had to be Jennifer's own collection as he didn't recognise half the people from the time in her life before he knew her. He leafed through and was given an ugly jolt when he came across a photo from the night they met. It had been at a bar coming up for eight years ago. A group from the Yard had gone to Victoria to celebrate closing a case and ended up in a pub near the station. There she was: wide-eyed and smiling, resting her blonde head on his shoulder. He was grinning like he'd won the jackpot.

An overwhelming sense of pity for the two young people in the picture swept through him. His younger self, just moving from uniform to plain clothes detective, hadn't known that Jennifer was prey to so many demons. A management consultant who was part of a team advising the division on efficiencies, she projected such a positive image, full of the joys of life, pretty and funny – but she had been trained to do that, hadn't she? Just as he had been schooled always to be calm in a crisis because no one wants the police officer panicking. It was only at two in the morning six months into living together, and often after they both had had too much to drink, that her unbalanced side had really showed. She didn't trust anyone totally, especially not herself, but still wanted others to solve her problems. She had jumped into a relationship with Sam like a shipwreck victim swimming for a lifebelt. She'd damn nearly dragged them both under. He shuffled through the rest of the photos, seeing variations of the same pose over and over again: her leaning on him.

'You couldn't win, you poor fool,' Sam told the young man in the picture.

He dumped the photos back inside and sealed the box. He had learned from the garden that there was only so many emotional thorns he could cut back in one year.

Neil and Phil arrived in their camper van in time for supper. Sam was still weeding the castle rockery but heard the merry toot as they pulled up in the car park. Stacking his tools in the wheelbarrow, he headed to meet them. They were impossible to miss as their van was covered with decals of the king of rock and roll.

'Sam, you gorgeous man, come here!' Dressed in a white shirt and trousers, Neil was looking tanned and happy, Phil quietly pleased: the fortnight they'd spent in Memphis clearly had agreed with them.

Sam held up his hands. 'Careful: I'm not clean.'

'But still delicious.' Neil hugged him anyway.

'Steady on: you're a married man now.'

Neil smiled. 'I know – and isn't it wonderful? Phil is fully aware we can both just look and admire you like you would a Greek statue or something. No need for jealousy.'

Sam offered his hand to Phil. 'I prefer not to be thought of a statue, thanks.'

'The place is looking even better than it did at our wedding,' said Phil, thankfully moving the discussion along. Neil enjoyed flirting with Sam more than Sam enjoyed the attention, and Phil understood that. He gave Sam a wink when Neil spun round to check out the improvements.

'Someone's been a busy bee,' said Neil.

'You wouldn't believe how hard I've worked,' agreed Sam.

'And all this with your dad in tow. How is he?'

'Oh, he's OK. Still haven't found him a place at a residential home – not one that he'd like.'

'I think what you're doing for him is amazing.'

'It's just the deal – payback time for all those years of devoted parenting.'

'You know what I'd do if my dad gets to the stage when he's ga-ga?' Neil made the middle finger gesture. 'Payback.'

Sam didn't want to enter into that discussion because Neil wouldn't like what he had to say. Neil, at heart, was a softie. If his mother appealed to him for help, Sam would bet that Neil wouldn't be as tough as he suggested, not even for a moment. But hopefully Neil would never have to find out and his father would live to a good age before keeling over on the golf course still in possession of all his mental faculties. No one should be forced to watch a parent become fragments of their old self. 'Come on, let's go and find Dad. He should be in the cottage and I need to let Leo go home – he's going away for the weekend.'

'That's the boy you've got minding your father?' asked Neil.

'That's right: he lives in the gatehouse cottage.'

'With the woman who married us?'

Sam laughed. 'Glad to see you're keeping up, but you make it sound like a *menage à trois*. She was the one who did the signing part – the brunette.'

'Was she now? Oh, she was rather pretty, wasn't she, Phil?'

'No idea, Neil, I only had eyes for you.' Phil grinned at Neil.

'Good one. See, he's coming along nicely as a husband, wouldn't you say, Sam?'

'You'd know. And yes, that's the one. I wasn't sure of the wisdom of letting the cottage to someone I'll come across professionally, but she turns out to be a great tenant and her son a complete lifesaver as far as helping me with Dad goes. We all get along very well.'

'High praise indeed from Mr Buttoned-Up. So have you gone on a date yet?'

Sam looked to Phil for help. 'How have we gone from me saying she's a good tenant and praising her son to dating?'

'No idea. Neil's reasoning processes are an academic study all of their own.' Phil was a Philosophy lecturer; his Elvis impersonation a strictly leisure time activity. 'I'll let you know when I figure them out.'

Neil flung his hands out. 'Come on, guys, it's simple: Sam is a man with a need for female companionship. He's moved out here to the wilds where there are only old dears who listen to *The Archers*, but luckily a pretty single lady moves into his gatehouse cottage. It's written in the stars. Surely he has to at least take her for a spin?'

Sam groaned. 'Take her for a spin? Did you really just say something so crass? She's not a car to test drive.'

'How else should I put it?'

'Don't – because you'll put your foot in it,' said Phil.

'Yeah, you'd better shut up right now, Neil, as I'm about to introduce you to her son.'

Neil mimed zipping his lips closed. 'But you know I'm right,' he said in a low voice, showing that his resolve didn't last long.

Fortunately, for the sake of Neil's tact, Leo only stayed for a brief 'hello' then scooted off down the drive to pack for his weekend with his grandparents. William blinked at the two newcomers like a nocturnal creature dragged into the light. He was not in one of his good patches having already surprised them with several abrupt 'hah's.

'Dad, you remember Neil, from university?' Sam began.

'No, no, I can't say I do. Were you in my college?'

'No, William, I went to university with your son, Sam. We went to Bristol together.'

'You did? Oh, very good. Well done you. And who's this?'

Sam stepped forward. 'Dad, Neil and Phil are married.'

'They are? Where are their wives then?' He looked outside as if he expected two women to enter from the garden.

Sam knew something like this might happen. His dad was often stuck in the nineteen fifties in his memories so the idea of same sex relationships was not in his active memory.

'We're married to each other,' explained Phil patiently.

'Hah!' William was clearly on edge. It was a confusing world at the best of times and some changes too fast for him to absorb.

'The law changed a few years ago,' Neil carried on.

'I don't know what I think about that.' His dad fretted with his cuff.

'Dad, please,' said Sam. 'Neil and Phil are my guests for the weekend. Let's leave it at that, shall we?'

'Who?'

'Neil and Phil.'

'I was at college with you, wasn't I?' William circled back to the beginning of the conversation.

Phil glanced at Sam who just shrugged. 'I tend to just roll with it,' he said in a low voice.

'Maybe we were,' said Phil to William. 'I understand you like gardening? Tell me about that.'

The strange thing was that an hour later when they were touring the gardens in the last long shafts of sunlight, his father seemed to have clicked back into a much more with-it frame of mind, taking Neil's references to his husband in his stride. This dad who lived in the twenty-first century was completely fine with same sex marriage.

'Sorry about Dad, earlier,' Sam said to Phil.

'No problem. He wasn't rude – just scared. Lost in time.'

'You're right. I hadn't thought of it like that.'

'It's like a coma patient waking up in a different world from the one he went to sleep in.'

'It's hard to take though at times. He forgets that someone died and I have to tell him all over again and he suffers all over again. Sometimes I chicken out and lie that they're alive to spare him the pain.'

'I don't blame you. So, are you going to keep him with you? He seems very settled here.' They paused to watch William show Neil a newly discovered stone urn on a lion pedestal that Sam had wrestled out of a thick patch of nettles.

'I know: he's taken to the garden like a duck to water. But I'm worried when I turn my back something will happen to him. He's not safe to be left alone. I'm hoping to find him a residential home nearby but it's proving extremely difficult. The ones with vacancies all seem too much like battery farms for old folk.'

Phil pulled a face. 'I can imagine. We went through the same nightmare with my grandmother. In the end pneumonia got her before she was forced to move in. We all thought it a mercy.' He paused, seeing his husband coming their way. 'Look out. I know that expression: Neil has had an idea.'

'Sam, I've just been talking to your dad and discovered that he'd never missed an episode of *Gardener's World*. He seemed quite shocked I'd never seen the programme – neither has Phil,' announced Neil.

'Yes, I have.'

'No, Phil, you haven't,' Neil said firmly.

'OK I haven't.'

'I'm sure Sam has seen his fair share so I've suggested that we sit down with William this evening for our introduction to the only decent programme on television while Sam has a night out.'

'Neil . . .' Sam thought he could guess where this was going.

'No, Sam, it's all decided. But gosh, who can you go out with?' Neil put a finger coyly to his cheek. 'It would be so lame to be on your own. Happily, I think there might be a lady in the gatehouse cottage who is home alone as her son has gone away. Am I right? Isn't it your neighbourly duty to see that she is OK, ask her if she's lonesome tonight?'

Sam's lips twitched. You couldn't stay serious around his friend for long. 'My duty?'

'Yes, she might need a man to, I don't know, remove a spider or something?'

'I'll send you along then.'

Phil snorted. Neil was a famous arachnophobe.

145

'That's not happening. Would you please get with the programme, Sam? Even if it isn't anything more than a night away from here with a pretty companion, I'm trying to give you a break.'

And why not, thought Sam? He'd been making cocoa and shepherding his father to bed for weeks now. He did need a change of scene and to remember he was more than the son of an elderly dependent. Just as long as he didn't raise any expectations in Gemma's mind, surely it would be harmless? A bit of flirting, a little chat, like when he mended the window; nothing that would suggest anything serious.

'Thanks, Neil. You're right: I do need a break.'

'Go get changed first. Your gardening jeans might do for us but . . .' Neil twirled his hand at the scruffiness of Sam's appearance.

'Dress to impress?'

'No, in your case, you undress to do that. Just put on something that makes you look vaguely presentable.'

So that was how Sam found himself walking down the drive at eight wondering if he was about to make a first-class fool of himself. Leo had already told him that he was being picked up at seven by his grandparents so unless Gemma had made her own plans she should be in. There were lights on downstairs. Feeling like he was seventeen again and about to ask out a girl for his first date, he almost turned around. Only the thought of Neil's scathing comments kept him going. He approached the cottage and knocked.

Chapter 14

Gemma had big plans for her night in alone – well, big plans for her. It was so rare to have the place completely to herself that a rom-com DVD with a glass of wine was the ultimate luxury. She could lounge in leggings and a particularly baggy T-shirt, wear no make-up and ditch the bra. She'd given herself eight o'clock as her start time for movie night so was therefore appalled when someone knocked on the door – then alarmed as she really was here on her own in the cottage for the first time. It suddenly struck her that, like in the horror flicks, no one would hear her scream.

Going to the front door, she kept the chain on as she opened it a crack.

'Who is it?'

'It's me: Sam.'

'Oh, Sam.' She took off the chain. 'Is it your dad? Has he gone wandering again?'

'No, no, nothing like that. I . . . er . . . are you feeling OK?' He was looking at her attire.

Gemma decided to brazen it out. 'Fine. Just chilling.'

'Right. I was wondering if you'd like to come out for a

drink? I've got some friends watching my dad so I've got a night off.'

'Oh.'

His face fell and he was already turning away. 'Doesn't matter. Another time maybe.'

She realised she'd sent out completely the wrong signals. 'Stop, Sam. I'm sorry. What I should've said was "Yes, I'd love to go for a drink". It was just that I was thinking I totally look like crap. Just give me a minute. Come in.'

She left him in the sitting room knowing he'd soon work out just how pathetic her little life was with her glass of white and DVD bought from a charity shop. Running upstairs, she tried to think what she should wear. He was in worn jeans and a blue shirt – so something casual. Hang on, was this a date? Or was it just that she was the only one he could think of who would have no plans on a Friday night? Whatever the reason, she was about to have a real grown-up night out so she wasn't going to spoil it by agonising about motives – at least not much.

She started throwing clothes around her room in a haphazard search for the right look. Her wardrobe didn't run to that many outfits: all her work ones were too formal, the slobbing-about-the-house ones too ratty. Diving into the pile, she went for light blue cropped trousers and a lacy blouse. About to pull that on, she remembered she'd ditched her bra earlier. Time for one of her nicer underwear sets, by which she meant one that hadn't gone grey in the wash yet. Her home-making skills were hit and miss at the best and she was the kind of person who couldn't be bothered to separate out the wash into colours and whites. She wriggled into a fairly new cream satin bra and matching briefs – not that she expected anyone else to see them but they would give her confidence, as well as her bust, a boost. And Sam was the most attractive man she'd seen in years so she could hope, couldn't she?

How long had she kept him waiting? Did she have time for make-up and hair? She inspected herself in the mirror. He might not like it but she certainly needed a serious repair job on her morning make-up. In fact, she needed to start again.

'Are you OK up there?' he called.

'Yes, fine. Just getting ready.' *Don't get too excited – don't read too much into this*, she told herself.

'You looked fine as you were.'

Yeah, right, when he'd thought she might be ill. 'Won't be a moment.' In fact she'd be at least five minutes. Green shadow brought out the colour in her grey-green eyes. Finally, with a vigorous brush of her hair so that it fell loosely in a smooth brown cape around her shoulders, she deemed herself fit for the public of Claremont Magna. After all, this would be something of her debut in local society.

When she came downstairs, she found Sam sitting in an armchair. He sprung to his feet on seeing her.

'Sorry to keep you, but if you don't give a girl notice, you can't expect miracles . . .'

'You look perfect.'

It was so lovely to be flattered; she drank it up like a sunflower does sunshine. 'Thank you. Better than the sad sack who opened the door?'

'Gemma, you'd never look a sad sack even in a sack. Where

do you want to go? I was thinking the pub in the village so we don't have to drive. Are you OK with that?'

'Sounds great. I've not been in yet.'

'Good.' He held out a hand to usher her to the door. 'Shall we?'

There was something very lovely about walking side-by-side down a lane in the twilight, last blush of the sunset fading over the fields. Bats flitted overhead and an occasional owl hooted from the castle woods. It was very romantic, even though this wasn't what this was about, was it?

'I think I could grow to love it here,' Gemma confessed.

'There's something magical about it, isn't there? You don't have to go very far from a town to find sanity returns.'

'A kind of sanity at least – a slowing down of the pace.'

'Nature can be very soothing – when it isn't being a bitch and sending up brambles behind your back and scratching you to bits with thorns.'

She laughed. 'Yes, total bitch who has had decades to do her worst in your poor garden. So, why are you taking her on up there? Did you fall out of love with London?'

'I'm not sure I ever was in love with it. And doing the job I did; you get to see the very worst side of the city.'

'Why did you go into policing?'

'Same way many people do: got hooked on the idea at a graduate recruitment fair. I wanted to make a difference and went into it with noble intentions.' He said this with a sour twist to his mouth, a little mocking of the young man he'd been. 'Don't get me wrong, it's a rewarding career most of the time. I think I was reasonably good at my job.'

'You liked solving crime?' She meant it as a teasing comment but he took it more seriously.

'It's not like that in reality. A lot of it is messy and there's no justice in the end – and that can get to you. But I'm logical and like to put things in order so I suppose I had the skills that worked well in an investigation where you need to be all that.'

'And you made a difference?'

'I suppose so – often too late for the victim of the crime but maybe we stopped there being more? I hope so.'

'I'm sure you did. So why give up?'

'Oh, that was complicated, but I suppose the short answer is that I'd had enough.'

'And the long answer?'

They were at the pub door. He gave her a smile that wasn't quite a smile. 'Maybe I'll save that for another evening. I think I'd need to be a hell of a lot drunker before I go into all that. Speaking of drinking, what'll you have?'

OK, avoid the subject of the past. She got the message. His hand rested briefly in the small of her back as he ushered her to go first. Had he noticed? It felt a little possessive, like this might be a date? Gemma slipped into a spare table by the window while Sam went to the bar to order. The Castle Inn was everything she would have anticipated: old world charm of oak furniture and prints of local landmarks on the walls, with a clientele of regulars and some weekend visitors who had the fresh faces of people who have spent the day outdoors.

'Ah, if it isn't the lord of the castle himself!' bellowed the barkeeper. 'What'll you have, Sam?'

'A glass of Sauvignon blanc and a pint of St Edmunds, Tim.'

'Not seen you in here much recently.'

'I've got someone moved in with me at the cottage. I've been staying in.'

Tim's eyes went to Gemma. 'Lucky man.'

Gemma could feel her cheeks flush. Fabulous: start her social life in the village under a misapprehension.

'No, Tim, my father,' Sam said in a tone meant to quell speculation. 'He's living with me while I try and find him a good residential home. Gemma here has just moved into the gatehouse cottage with her son – as I thought the gossip network would've worked out by now. You're slacking. I'll introduce you but only if you promise to behave.'

'You can't keep all the attractive ones to yourself, mate.' The barman waved at her with an empty beer glass. 'Hello, Gemma. Welcome to the village. We're all as mad as hatters and fond of scandal so consider yourself warned.'

Gemma came to the bar to introduce herself properly. 'Thanks. I knew there was something wrong with the village when I first came here. I'd assumed a zombie apocalypse had hit.'

'You're not far wrong. They filmed *Shaun of the Dead* here.'

'Really?'

'Nope. Just kidding.' He pulled on the beer tap, sending a mischievous grin her way.

'He does that a lot, does Tim,' said Sam.

'Life and soul of the village, that's what they call me.'

'But if it's a zombie village, that's not saying much, is it?' she replied.

Tim bellowed with laughter. He put the full glass on the bar, foam running over the side. 'I like your lady, Sam. You can bring her here again.'

'Maybe it's me bringing him.'

'Ah, then that'll be eight pounds ten.'

Sam slipped the money over before she could reach for her purse.

'The next round's mine,' she said quickly before Tim could make something of it.

Sam picked up the drinks. 'Let's take these away from this crazy man.'

'Quietest table is the one over the back there. I can't see what's going on in that corner.' Tim gave them a wink.

'You're impossible, Tim.' Sam took the glasses to the one Gemma had originally picked in full view of the bar.

'And that's why everyone loves me,' he called after them.

Sam put the drinks carefully on the tabletop. 'Sorry – I should've warned you. He can be a bit much when you first meet him but I find the impression fades after a while. Cheers.'

They clinked glasses.

Gemma glanced over at the landlord to see he was now teasing another customer. 'I didn't mind. He's got used to being a character and has probably forgotten how to switch off the act. I imagine to keep going a local pub needs someone like that.'

'His wife, Gaynor, does the business side and he does the entertainment, or that's how she explained their arrangement. I think I'll bring Neil and Phil here tomorrow and introduce them to Tim. That will be a match worth watching. Neil and

Tim will either get on like a house on fire or I'll have to arrest one or both of them.'

Gemma knew she shouldn't be surprised but this policeman-turned-landowner seemed an unlikely best mate to the Elvis impersonators. 'Where did you meet your friends?'

Sam launched into an explanation of the day he had met Neil at university and how they both fitted into the extended group of mates he had made at that time. He paused at the end of the account and gave her a rueful smile. 'I don't seem to make friends so easily now – or not ones I keep.'

Gemma sensed he was saying more than he let on. His expression held a sadness that she couldn't match to his words and there were stress lines on his face that seemed wrong for someone still in their late thirties. What had caused them? 'I never went to college but I imagine you are more open to new people at that age, more willing to take a chance with them. Plus, you are mixed up with so many different types, people outside your own circle back home, it must be refreshing. It's a good opportunity to take a risk on making friends.' Her own risk had, of course, ended in disaster. The last thing Ray had been was her friend. 'We don't have so much time to spend with people now, do we?'

He spun an unused beermat absent-mindedly between thumb and forefinger. 'I would've thought you were surrounded by people all the time.'

'Not people who are friends material, not at work. I mean, Diana is a friend, obviously. I was lucky to come across her in a small office. We click. But I can't say that for anyone else – they're strictly colleagues. I have a book group I go to when

I can carve out the time to read the novel – Diana's in that too. But my social circle is quite small. I lost a lot of friends when I had Leo. I suppose you can't expect to meet best mates everywhere you go.'

'What about male friends? I can't imagine you'd go long without a boyfriend.'

Fishing, was he? That was encouraging. 'Then you imagine wrongly. Being a single mother puts a severe cramp on my style.'

'But Leo's old enough to be left home alone now. You're free to date again, aren't you?'

'Technically, there's just this little thing called money that gets in the way of an active social life.'

'Really? Is that the reason?'

He was probably right to doubt that explanation. It was easier to hide. 'Actually, I'm not sure. I got badly burned once with a not very nice man so I play it safe.' She shrugged and sipped her drink. This was embarrassing: she was telling him too much. 'How about you?'

'I definitely play it safe. There's been nobody special for some time. I did live with a girlfriend for a while, but she died, five years ago.'

'Oh, I'm sorry.' From his body language, that conversational path clearly had a 'No Trespassers' sign planted in it and was the probable answer for the stress lines.

'I learned then that I'm not good looking after people . . .'

'You're looking after your dad.'

'I mean a partner, so I prefer to keep things light, dating but not headed for commitment, so no one is disappointed.'

Gemma's hopes faded. She had no room for another man in her life who had a problem with commitment. Still, she had better not let him suspect she'd even daydreamed. 'I can understand that. With Leo, I've always avoided bringing someone else into our lives, someone he might think of as a rival. I like to keep things light too.' *Gemma, what are you saying?* her more honest side chimed in. Her fantasy man would be her equal in the relationship, involved, loving and a good friend to Leo as well as her.

But that was fantasy, she was sitting in a pub in reality, she reminded herself. If she wanted to go out with Sam, she needed to suppress that side.

'Sounds a good choice – at least for a few more years before Leo leaves home,' Sam said approvingly. 'You could be like me: date from time to time but not get too serious?'

She shouldn't let him think she was only interested in one-night stands. She owed him some honesty, some warning. 'But I'm not sure that'll always be enough for me. I get lonely. I want someone to stick – eventually.'

'I think everyone does. But that's not on the horizon for me at the moment – too much other stuff to sort first. It helps me to be with someone who understands that, someone like you. A new friend.'

'Thanks.' Gemma swallowed her disappointment.

'Another drink?'

'Yes, why not? My round. Tell me about your plans for the castle gardens.'

They walked back together in the dark using their phone lights to warn drivers they were on the road edge, but there was no traffic. Their easy conversation about the garden had subsided and there was tension in the air, an expectation about how the night might end. Was what they had been talking about in the pub been a kind of negotiation of expectations? Gemma wondered. Looking at it baldly, had they just admitted that they were both lonely adults with a need for intimacy? Had they been more or less agreeing to find it with the other, or the opposite? It hadn't been at all clear to her. When he'd said she was a new friend, had he meant 'date'? The problem was that, though she'd said she kept things loose, she did not want to be just a booty call at the bottom of the castle drive. If they went down that path, what was between them – and there was definitely something – would that ever have the chance to develop into anything else? She was attracted to him, but she also was growing to like him. She might have to choose between the two.

They arrived at her front door. She'd left the light on and moths flickered hopelessly against it.

'That was lovely. Thanks for luring me out of my den,' she said.

'It was good to sit down and have a real conversation with you.' He moved closer.

'Thanks. I don't get much chance to talk about anything that matters with people.'

'You're an interesting woman, Gemma Whitehall. Has anyone told you that?' Sam leant in for a kiss.

Her heart raced. So they were going there, were they? They were actually going to touch? 'Thank you – and no, I don't get told that.'

He bent down and kissed her gently on the cheek, leaving her uncertain if that had been a friendly goodbye or a prelude to romance. 'Then they should. Goodnight, Gemma.' Letting his touch linger, he moved back and started walking slowly away.

Yes, that was the way to end it tonight – careful of each other. 'Goodnight, Sam.'

Closing the door behind her, she leaned against it.

'Please, sir, can I have some more?' she whispered. One little kiss, one little scoop of affection, just wasn't enough.

Chapter 15

'Now, let's see what you can tell me?' Gemma heaved the old volume of gardening journals onto the foam book rest. She had just enough time before her afternoon wedding. The wretched book wasn't indexed so she had to start at the beginning and leaf through, speed-reading while flicking through to pick out any reference to Claremont. The spiced-dust smell of old paper rose as she turned the pages, provoking a couple of sneezes. She loved it here in the quiet reference section of Bury St Edmunds Library. She had caught Sam's enthusiasm for the subject during the discussion at the pub and thought she could surprise him by carrying out a little of the research he admitted he didn't have time to do. It was also, she realised, a kind of present and proof that there was more to her than her eight GCSEs and two A levels suggested, scraped together at the college of further education when Leo was a baby. She had worked towards an eighth of an Open University degree too but that had stalled some months ago. Her self-image wasn't a flattering one but Sam had said she was interesting – she wanted to live up to that.

She checked the details she'd jotted down in her notebook.

According to Sam, the grounds had been developed in the early twentieth century at the height of the enthusiasm for the medieval nostalgia of the Arts and Craft Movement. A description of the work done on what had once just been pasture land would be good; a plan of the grounds would be ideal. She had already unearthed a set of accounts for the estate, held in Ipswich, but it was the reference to newspaper article on a coronation party held at the castle that had caught her eye. She turned a page – and there it was: a full description of the celebration held in the knot garden and knight's grotto. The gardens apparently combined the best features of the famous ones at Hampton Court, and Gertrude Jekyll's garden philosophy of painterly designs. She hoped Sam would understand what that meant because she was very hazy on what that might entail. Weren't Jekyll's borders something to do with clouds of harmonious colour? She took a picture of the report on her phone, pleased with what she had managed to find out in an hour.

Conscious she was cutting it fine for the wedding, she returned the book to the librarian and jogged downstairs. She barely had time to grab a sandwich as the next couple were due at three and she was supposed to meet Gillian in fifteen minutes to prepare the room at the town hall. Making a quick dash into the supermarket, she popped the first tub of salad that she saw into her basket and queued up at the express till.

'Gemmy, how's the new house working out?'

Her heart sank. Ray. He moved in behind her, leaving her no escape unless she abandoned her basket. As usual he looked lean and short of sleep, hair limp, beard straggly. The odour of last night's drink hung on his breath. 'Fine thanks.'

'Leo said I should come and visit.'

'He's away at the moment.'

'Not today – I'm busy – but sometime soon. Can you give me a lift after work next week? Wednesday?'

Gemma glanced at those in the queue nearby. She really didn't want to have this out in front of the six other locals waiting to pay for their meal deals. 'It's better if he came to see you.' A till opened up and she scanned her items as quickly as possible. The infuriating machine, however, conspired with Ray, intent on delaying her, telling her an unexpected item had appeared in the bagging area. She looked down. Ray's BLT had mysteriously ended up among her shopping. She picked it up and handed it back to him.

'Oh come on. It's just a sandwich!'

'It's just a sandwich – it's just a bike – it's just a laptop!' She waved her card over the contactless payment, gathered her purchases and hurried out.

Ray dumped the sandwich and pursued. 'That was mean.'

'Says the man who never pays his way. I'm not your cash cow, Ray.' He was still following her. She paused on the pavement, refusing to drag him back to her work like some albatross strapped around her neck. 'I've made my position crystal clear.'

'He's my son.'

'See him on your own turf, not mine.'

'He wants me involved in his new life in the country.'

'So where's my laptop, Ray?'

'Not still going on about that, are you?' He dug out a flimsy hand-rolled cigarette from a flat tin.

'It's not unreasonable seeing how you stole it from me. Next time I'll call the police.'

'It was as much Leo's as yours – and he's my son.'

'So that makes it all right to take it? Is that how you really see him – like he's your property?'

'We share him, Gemma, remember? He's as much mine as yours.'

They were worlds apart on this and were speaking different languages. He regarded his son as a bridge through her defences –. Had she really condemned Leo to a life of fighting off his father's demands? It had to stop. If she didn't draw a line, how could Leo learn to do so?

'Ray, let me be absolutely clear as you seem to have a problem hearing me: you don't come near the cottage, you don't take anything I have bought for Leo even if he offers it to you. Next time I will report it as theft and think it justice if you get a criminal record. Your choice: cross me on this and I won't shield you from the consequences.'

'He's my son too, Gemma.'

'So start acting like a father.' She felt like the roof was lifting off her head. If she didn't get away from him, she was going to lose it totally right there in the middle of Bury St Edmund's High Street.

'You're a fucking pathetic excuse of a mother, Gemma. You're teaching him to distrust his own dad.'

'I've done nothing but tell him the truth – and not all of it. Don't push me or maybe it'll all come out.'

His eyes narrowed, little shards of flint in his pale face. 'Yeah, like how you couldn't keep your knickers on when you were fifteen – how you threw yourself at me? Real saint you were. Does he know what an easy lay his mother was?'

His crudeness made Gemma feel sick. The only effective response was to turn and fast walk back to the town hall. He didn't chase, thank God. She stumbled up the stairs to her office and locked the door. Furious tears fell. Ray wasn't an albatross: he was a rotting corpse to which she was chained.

There came a gentle tap on the door. Wiping her eyes, she opened it to find Gillian in the corridor.

'Are you OK, Gemma? You realise the wedding is waiting for us?'

'Sorry – bad hay fever. Be there in a moment.' They both knew she was lying but it was easier to go with that explanation. 'I'll just freshen up my make-up and I'll be right with you.'

'Do you want me to take the ceremony while you do the registry?'

Yes, but what message would that send the woman who had to decide on cuts? That Gemma wasn't up to the job? 'Really, I'll be fine. Give me two minutes.'

An emergency splash of water on face and quick repair job on the mascara and Gemma found herself standing in front of the glowing faces of the latest couple to condemn themselves to a lifetime together. She felt like a figure of glass and ice. One tap and she'd go to pieces.

Don't do it, she wanted to scream.

'A warm welcome to the friends and family of Casey and Janice,' was what she said.

An hour later, Gemma filed the last of the paperwork and emerged from her office.

'Is it OK if I shoot off now, Gillian?' she asked her boss.

'Yes, I'm all done here too. I think that went off well, didn't it?'

Despite the fact that the registrar marrying them moved like an automaton. 'Yes, they seemed pleased enough.'

'I'll see you Monday then. Enjoy the rest of your weekend.'

'And you. Any plans?'

'Might have.' With a mysterious smile that was quite unlike her, Gillian headed out the front while Gemma took the rear exit to the staff car park. What was Gillian up to? A secret lover? That was a stretch to imagine but why not? Gemma scanned the car park for her Fiesta. Where had she left it? Hers was the only vehicle left in the spaces as Gillian lived close enough to walk to work. Rounding the wheelie bin, Gemma caught the first hint that something was wrong. The car seemed to be sitting very low to the ground. Getting closer she realised that was because she had a set of four punctured tyres. Hunkering down by the rear wheel she immediately saw that they had all been slashed.

She swore. Ray. Had to be him, didn't it? Why would a vandal want to target her vehicle so vindictively? This felt personal. Having been warned off by her, Ray was sending his own signal. But she hadn't been joking about reporting him if she had the evidence. He might be Leo's father but he had used up his free passes from her.

Hurrying round to the front of the building, she tapped on the window to rouse the security guard.

'Excuse me, but my car's been vandalised – the tyres slashed.'

He opened the door to her. 'What? Those bastards.'

'Is there any CCTV on that part?'

'Let's have a look.' He led her to the monitors which he had been watching not very assiduously. 'Where's your car?'

'Past the wheelie bins.'

'Ah, no, sorry. It's directed at the back entrance. You'll need to report it to the police, I suppose?' He tapped in a few digits and handed her the phone. 'I've dialled the number for you. They won't come out but it should be enough to satisfy your insurance company. Oh and don't forget to take photos.'

'You sound like you've dealt with this before?'

'The deputy mayor's car was keyed a few weeks ago. Bury used to be such a nice place.'

He was right about the level of interest her report met. The details were taken down but the police showed no inclination in coming out just to view the damage considering the vandals were long since gone. Her next call was to Jason, an old friend from school and not one of Ray's crowd, who ran a garage. Closed for the weekend and already back home, he promised to bring the truck and tow it on Monday.

'Is it OK where it is?' he asked.

'Well, it's not going anywhere, is it?' She could just imagine what the mayor and councillors would make of it when they parked up on Monday morning. Her car had just gone from shabby to derelict.

'Fine. I'll fetch it then and try and return it to you by the end of the day.'

'Thanks – you're a star. How much will four tyres set me back?'

'I'll see if I can do you a special price, Gemma. Bloody vandals.'

That was the best she could do for now. Gemma went back to the car, took photos, and then looked up how to get home. Her options were limited. There was an hourly bus for Saturday shoppers that toured the villages but missed out hers. Her best bet was to take it to Lavenham and walk. She looked down at her shoes, wedding smart rather than walking comfy. This was not going to be fun.

'You just left her on the doorstep?' Neil was incredulous.

Sam sat back in the second row of the camper van. It was nice to have someone drive him for a change, even if it was Phil in their ridiculous mystery machine. His dad appeared to be enjoying the ride too, mesmerised by the little Hawaiian dancer in a grass skirt suspended from the driver's mirror. 'Yes, I walked her home then said goodnight.'

'Neil, not everyone likes to rush things like you do,' said Phil calmly, signalling that they were leaving the main road. 'Thanks for the suggestion of Sutton Hoo, Sam. Anglo-Saxon burial site plus tearoom: what more could you want?'

Neil was not to be so easily deterred from his matchmaking. 'Don't change the subject, Phil. My friend here is in dire danger of never progressing beyond a handshake with any woman ever again. He's practically turned into a monk!'

As ever, Neil's concerns were well meant but poorly aimed. 'Neil, really, I don't need your help with my love life.'

'Oh, but you do. You are so . . . so clam-like since, well, you know.'

'Let's not spoil a lovely day, please.' Naturally, Sam had wanted to sweep Gemma off her feet and tumble onto that white duvet of hers. The empty house behind her had beckoned, the fact that he found her funny and attractive lured him in, so walking away up the drive had been a struggle. Only the knowledge that he had to be certain that she didn't expect too much saved him from going with impulse. Showing that he could walk away had also been part of proving it to himself. They'd talked about maybe dating without commitment, hadn't they? They were on the same page.

The roads narrowed so that the grass brushed the sides of the vehicle. Phil slowed.

'There's someone walking on the lane.'

'Isn't that . . .?' Neil nudged Sam.

'Yes, it's my tenant.'

Phil wound down the window. 'Need a lift?'

Gemma, dressed in one of her smart office outfits with matching shoes, turned around and obviously just registered a strange van full of men and grew understandably alarmed. 'I'm fine. I'll just scramble up the bank here – let you pass.'

'Really, we're going the same way. You probably don't recognise me with my normal clothes on. I'm Phil. You married me and Neil. The Elvis impersonators?' Neil leant forward and waved. 'Sam and his dad are in here too.'

Her suspicion turned to relief. 'Of course I remember you! Thank you. I'd love a lift. My feet are killing me.'

'Hop in the back then. Plenty of room.'

Sam got up to open the rear door for her. 'Car trouble?'

'You could say.' She passed him, and he caught the scent of perfume and something that was purely Gemma.

Neil waggled his eyebrows. Damn, he'd been caught sniffing and wouldn't hear the end of it.

She buckled up in his seat so he took the one beside her. 'So, how's your day been?' she asked brightly.

'Wonderful,' said Phil, and proceeded to give her perhaps a little too much information about the exhibition they'd just visited.

'What have you been doing, Gemma?' asked Neil.

'Marrying people.' She grimaced.

'Why the long face? You don't think they have the stuff to last?'

'How would I know? Sorry, they were a perfectly lovely couple. I'm just having a bad day.'

'Is your car in the garage?' asked Sam.

'It'll be towed on Monday.'

'Engine trouble? I'm pretty good with most minor fixes.'

'Do you happen to have four spare tyres in your shed?'

'*Four?*'

'Vandals in the town hall car park.'

'I thought I'd left that kind of crime behind in London.'

'Yes, well, just because we have sheep and fields, doesn't mean we don't have morons too.'

'That totally stinks. Sounds like you need cheering up,' said Neil briskly. 'Sam, why don't you take the lady somewhere nice this evening so she can forget about it for a bit?'

'Oh, but . . .' Gemma shot Sam a flustered look.

'Your son comes home tomorrow, right?' pressed Neil. 'Not much time to have some fun.'

Sam wasn't sure if he wanted to curse or bless his meddling friend. 'How about it, Gemma? There's a gastropub in Lavenham that sounds worth a try.'

'Oh, I'm not sure . . .' She clutched her handbag on her lap and Sam remembered she was probably also worried about the cost of two nights out in a row.

'My treat. You provided me with the perfect solution to keeping Dad company so I'm in your debt.'

'Don't turn him down, love,' said Neil brightly. 'He doesn't get out much and we're off back home tomorrow. It's his last chance. Take pity on the guy.'

'Well, in that case . . .' She smiled at him and Sam suddenly realised that he really didn't care so much about managing her expectations as he thought. He wanted her.

'He'll pick you up at seven,' declared Neil, thoroughly pleased with himself.

'Hah!' said his dad, making them all jump. 'Philip, why have you got that hula woman hanging from your mirror if you're homosexual?'

Sam groaned. Recently his dad's brain lacked a filter, but at least he'd changed the subject.

'You know, William, that's a very good question,' said Phil with a grin. 'Neil?'

For once, Neil was struck dumb.

The pub had proved well worth the visit but now Gemma could feel the tension rising between her and Sam on the drive home. She couldn't tear her eyes from his forearms as he negotiated the country lanes – strong and tanned, just how she liked them. Their relationship was at a crossroads. Should she invite him in tonight and take this a stage further or should she just say goodbye and let it settle back to the friendly tenant and landlord relationship of before?

But would it ever return there?

No, she was fooling herself. The chemistry between them stretched across the periodic table. They were both adults, harming no one. They could keep this in perspective. She wasn't sure she could do the light dating with no commitment like they had discussed, but she could give it a go.

'I hope you didn't mind my dad earlier?' asked Sam.

What? Oh, he must be referring to the hula woman comment as they'd just driven past the same spot. It was a little lowering to find while she had been contemplating getting busy under the sheets, he had been thinking about his aged parent. 'No one was offended, Sam.'

'I wish you'd known him before he got like this. He was the best.'

'It's still there. Look how good he is with Leo.'

'And Leo is really good with him. He's a great boy.'

'Thank you. Is your mum . . . er . . . still with us?'

'Oh yes. In Bournemouth. Retired. She had a late career as a school librarian after she finished raising my sister and me.'

'When did they separate?'

'When I was about fourteen and my sister twelve. They sold up and bought houses close to each other in Kew so we were able to keep up with both. You couldn't do that now, could you, not on normal wages? Anyway, I gravitated towards Dad because of the gardening and I suppose my sister was closer to Mum.'

'Why did they end the marriage?'

'Why does anyone do anything? I think she just thought life would be more exciting elsewhere.'

'And is it? More exciting?'

'God knows. If you meet her, you should ask her. Your parents seem pretty solid?'

'Oh yes, stuck together like superglue. Can you imagine my mum letting my dad get away from her?'

'No. She'd hunt him down and drag him back to the family cave.'

'See, you understand them already. The good thing is that I think Dad actually likes being managed. He's happy – they both are.'

'And you – what makes you happy?'

Gemma paused. Could she risk it? Oh, why the hell not! The first part of the day had been terrible; why not end it how she really wanted? 'Right now, it would make me happy if you didn't drive away when you drop me at the gatehouse cottage.'

His Adam's apple bounced as he took a big swallow. 'OK. I won't.'

Gemma looked out the window on her side, looking at her reflection rather than the shadowy fields. Who was this stranger in the glass? Had she really just done that? Propositioned Sam? Neil and Diana would be high-fiving her but this wasn't her default mode. A streak of shyness ran deep in her.

Still in silence, Sam swung the car into her drive and parked up by the door. She got out quickly.

'Can I make you a drink?' Stupid, stupid, she had nothing to offer him but tea and coffee. She fumbled with her keys and switched on the lights inside.

'I'm fine.' He moved in behind her and put his keys and phone on the kitchen table. His hands brushed her waist and she could feel the heat of his body at her back. 'Nothing needs to happen tonight, Gemma. We can take this slow. Going out on a date doesn't mean we have to – you know . . .'

She cut him off by reaching up to kiss him. 'Sam?'

'Yes, Gemma?'

'I think slowness is sometimes over-rated.'

'Thank God!' He turned her around and boosted her up so her legs were wrapped around his waist. 'Upstairs?'

'Yes, please.'

Chapter 16

Sam woke up and realised he was still at Gemma's. He'd intended to leave after they had made love but had instead fallen asleep, more deeply relaxed than he had been for years. He had a hazy recollection of a sleepy encounter in the small hours too. There was something about her that gave him that little extra. He already wanted her again. She was lying facing away from him, her hair curling down her back in messy tendrils, tucked in waist and swell of her hips. He had no desire to be a gentleman and spoil the view by pulling the duvet further up the bed from where they had kicked it. She might be his perfect woman: offering him the warmth of human touch he craved but without emotional tangles. He inched his hand closer, wanting to stroke her skin, but worried that it would be too revealing of how he was feeling. There was definitely something very warm in the vicinity of his frozen heart.

A little scared, he rubbed his chest. The morning after: how to handle? Not by being sentimental. Tender but not too inviting. The sex had been the best he had ever had. Gemma was fun and matched his enthusiasm, laughing when a smooth move went a little wrong, being vocal in her approval when it went very right.

God, she was amazing and he didn't want this to end. And that worried him. He couldn't start needing anyone.

Perhaps she felt his scrutiny because she stirred and turned over.

'Good morning.' She wrinkled her nose in a smile.

'Good morning.' He brushed the hair off her cheek.

'I must look a mess.'

'You look rumpled and delicious. No man could possibly complain waking up next to this.'

She surprised him by leaning forward and kissing him. 'You say the loveliest things, Sam.'

'I give you the truth, the whole truth, and nothing but the truth.'

'Breakfast in bed?'

'Oh yes.' He rolled so his leg trapped hers beneath him.

'I meant toast or cereal.'

He nuzzled her neck and made her giggle. 'Hmm, I'll have to think while I tackle my first course.'

Sometime later they sat at the sunny kitchen table. Sam had decided to risk Leo's choice of breakfast cereal and was regretting the decision.

'How does he actually eat this stuff?' he asked plaintively.

'Another mystery of the teenage boy.' She took it away from him and offered a plate of toast.

'How's he doing?'

'Having a good time with his grandparents apparently. Dad took him to a pitch and put golf course.'

Sam smiled as he attacked the butter that Gemma had got out of the fridge, trying to get it to spread on the bread. 'I remember doing that with my dad.'

'It's good that my father thinks to do that kind of thing. Sorry about the butter – I'm afraid of attracting mice if I leave it out and I don't have a butter dish.'

'No problem. It'll melt eventually. Is that because Leo's own father forgets?'

'Ray is a continual disappointment in that department.'

'Which department?'

'The parenting one.'

'Maybe his relationship with his son is just different from a traditional one?'

'Hmm.'

'You're not convinced?'

She fiddled with the lid of the teapot, making it sit straight. 'I can't talk to you about this, Sam. You didn't sign up to getting involved.'

She was right but he was interested. He'd grown to care about Leo over the last week. This was about the boy, not about their fledgling relationship. 'Feel free to vent, Gemma. I'm listening.'

She searched his face for confirmation he was serious. 'Oh God: where to start? It's like Ray is the child – co-child with Leo. He encourages rebellion and irresponsibility. He persuaded Leo to hand over our belongings so he could flog them and Leo was tasked to manoeuvre me to get a more expensive replacement. That's the history behind the missing laptop.'

'He sounds a real winner.'

'Oh yes, he wins the "how much worse can I get?" prize every time. The latest is that he was possibly behind my tyres being slashed. I've no evidence but I'd just had an argument with him yesterday lunchtime. I bumped into him in the supermarket.'

That painted things in darker colours. 'And he struck back? Have you talked to the police?'

'And say what? I suspect him on the basis of a gut feeling? That's not going to fly.'

'True.' When he was on the beat, responding to domestic disputes had always been regarded as a poisoned chalice by officers having to attend the scene. The truth was always skewed. 'OK. Look, if he comes here and bothers you, give me a call and I'll get rid of him for you.'

'Thanks, but it's tricky. He is Leo's dad and my son does love his father. I have to handle this carefully.'

'The offer stands. Call me if you need back up.'

She reached out and squeezed his hand. 'Thanks, Sam. That makes me feel a lot safer even if I never take you up on it.'

Walking into his own kitchen an hour later, Sam felt the amused gaze of Neil and Phil like a heat ray. God, he hoped he wasn't blushing. He was very conscious that he was wearing yesterday's clothes.

'Slept well?' asked Neil archly.

'Fine thanks. Where's Dad?'

'Dead-heading roses out the back. So?'

'So what?'

'Coffee?' asked Phil, kicking his spouse under the table.

'Thanks. What plans do we have for the day?'

'I thought a pub lunch and then we'll head back,' said Phil.

'Do you want to invite anyone, Sam?' Neil wasn't giving up.

'No, just the four of us will be fine.' He couldn't expose Gemma to Neil's cross examination on the day after; it wouldn't be fair to her. 'I've been meaning to introduce you to the local pub landlord. You'll either love or hate him.'

'And who said village life was boring?' Neil smiled, giving the innocent phrase an air of innuendo.

Sam's phone pinged with a message from an unrecognised number. Using it as an excuse to avoid Neil's gaze, Sam ducked out to the back garden. His father was happily wielding his secateurs, appropriately dressed in cotton shirt and his gardening trousers, and someone had remembered to make sure he wore gloves.

'Morning, Dad!'

'Hello, Sam. Got green fly.' William gestured to a fine pink rose, an old-fashioned variety with a beautiful scent.

'I'll get the spray out later.' Opening his texts, he thumbed through to what turned out to be a long message. His mood swallow dived. It was from Jennifer's sister, Camille. He'd not heard from, or even thought about her, for years.

Hey Sam. I hope you don't mind me contacting you but I'd really like to talk to you. You will probably remember that I was only 18 when my sister died and it's taken me a while to realise that I have issues I need to work through. My counsellor suggested I reach out and ask to talk to you so I can get a clearer picture of what happened to her. She says that just not knowing – not

understanding – is a big part of why I can't move on.
Let me know if you're happy to see me and I'll come to
you. I've just finished college so have plenty of free time.

Little Camille out of university – that brought home how many years had passed since the darkest time of his life. He remembered her as a fresh-faced teenager making radical and not very flattering fashion choices in her Goth phase. To be honest, he did not want to see her. He had little wisdom to share because he never really understood her sister and was still as confused by what had happened as Camille. It would be unbearably painful to go over all that again.

His thumb hovered over the first letter in the 'thanks but no thanks' option.

She'd gone to counselling. That was one up on him. He'd thought he would muddle through on his own and here he was, still pretty much in emotional deep freeze, everyone told him so. How long was he going to stay there? All his life? That seemed pathetic. Maybe he could help Camille even if it was to say that he had nothing much to say. He had the photos in the blue box – she might appreciate those and it would get them off his hands. Putting it another way, if he refused, he'd have yet more guilt to shoulder.

Hi Camille. Good to hear from you. Of course you are welcome to visit. Sam

He included his address and pressed the paper plane button to send it off before he could regret his decision.

* * *

Gemma flitted about the cottage in a buoyant mood, getting ready for Leo's return. She changed the sheets on all the beds, did a wash, and rigged up a second line in the back garden to take advantage of the sunshine, all the while humming along to her favourite songs played through her crappy little speakers. She didn't even have to worry about neighbours overhearing.

Oh my God, I'm actually happy, she realised, catching a glimpse of herself in a mottled mirror on the turn of the stair as she carried a pile of clean and folded laundry to her room. She imagined her life as a pictogram set of weighing scales: on one side all the worries – trashed car, problems with Ray, shaky job situation – and on the other, like a feather floating down to rest on the pan, a night with a man for whom she was coming to care. Seemingly insubstantial, that feather sent the things on the other side shooting up to irrelevance.

'Don't get carried away,' she told herself, but somehow that advice didn't sink in as she began daydreaming about her own Summer of Love.

Leo came home mid-afternoon, dropped by his granddad who 'had to get back' for a golf dinner. Gemma didn't even mind that her father only stayed for a cup of tea. Thanks to Sam, she'd learned to translate his embarrassed little excuses as clumsy messages of love for her.

'Mum, did you remember to water the lettuce?' Leo asked, rushing back into the kitchen after having waved goodbye to Granddad.

'I did.'

Head bent over the project, he brushed them with a competent fingertip. 'Wow, they've grown so much. We'll be able to start cropping them soon.'

Gemma thought his estimation of the frail little leaves on the windowsill was optimistic but she could work with that. 'I look forward to our first salad.'

'Anything happen while I was away?'

'I missed you, of course, but I went out to dinner with Sam last night as his friends were around to dad-sit.'

On a mission to raid the fridge, Leo paused, hand on the milk bottle. 'You and Sam went on a date?'

'Yes. Do you mind?'

He pulled out the four pinter and splashed a generous amount on his cereal. 'I don't know. It's weird.'

'Why weird?'

He shrugged. 'I know him. I see him all the time.'

Gemma realised that he had a point. The few people she'd dated had rarely crossed paths with Leo. She'd made sure he was staying over with his grandparents if she had anyone back.

'We're just friends.' With spectacular benefits.

He chomped on a huge spoonful of Cheerios. 'Just don't mess it up for me, OK? I'll soon be halfway to getting my laptop.'

Coming up behind him, she squeezed his shoulders, bony little shoulder blades under the black T-shirt reminding her how vulnerable he was for all his extra inches on her. 'OK, I'll try not to.'

'I like Sam.'

That was his final word on the subject and Gemma took it as his way of saying he was OK with it. 'So do I.'

On Monday, Gemma entered the office to find it buzzing with gossip about her. Eyes in the staffroom all shot to her with slightly guilty expressions. For a confused moment, she wondered if someone had been spying on her love life, but then realised it was the more prosaic disaster-in-the-car-park that occupied them.

'It's outrageous, Gemma,' said Gillian. 'You should be able to park on council property without fearing that vandals will get to your vehicle. I'm having words with my superiors to see if we can get the CCTV coverage made more comprehensive.'

'The deputy mayor had her car keyed,' Gemma replied, hanging up her light raincoat. 'She'd probably support the idea.'

'You OK, honey?' asked Diana, moving in and giving her a hug.

'It's a real bummer but I'm trying to be positive.' Gemma collected her share of files from the pigeonholes.

Diana flicked through hers. 'So how did you get into work?'

'Leo's bike. Cycled to Lavenham and then caught the bus. There's one an hour.'

'It's going to set you back a bit, four tyres, and all the expense of setting up in the new house.'

'Tell me about it.'

'If you need a hand, you know you can ask. Don't go to any of those payday loans people. My little brother got into deep financial trouble taking that route so I feel my mission in life is to go around like a little lighthouse, warning others of the risk.'

'I know – and thanks. How was your weekend?'

'Not good actually. Henry's done his back in again. He's had to cancel his jobs this week.'

'Oh no.' Gemma resolved she definitely wouldn't be tapping her friend for a loan. 'Can I do anything?'

'Aw, sugar, that's so sweet of you. No, he's fine. He's done it before. He just has to lie flat for a few days then take it easy. We'll muddle through.' They were alone now in the staffroom. Diana glanced towards the door. 'For someone who has just had their car wrecked, you look mighty pleased with yourself.'

Gemma checked her watch. Her first appointment would be waiting. 'Di, you know what I said about biceps the other day?'

'Uh-huh.'

'I saw a lot more than that and I have to say it was definitely not a disappointment.'

'Oh my word, you haven't – you didn't!' Diana did a little boogie around the coffee table. 'Gemma got laid. You go, girl!'

Gemma tried to shush her. Diana was not known for her ability to keep a secret. 'Look, it's just a casual thing. Please don't say anything to anyone.'

'But this is huge: you get to bed Mr I'm-Too-Sexy-For-My-Castle!'

'Di!'

'OK. It's a secret.' Her eyes glistened with mischief. 'But at least let me tell Henry. He'll be so pleased for you.'

'You may tell him in a dignified manner with no details

that I am dating someone. Otherwise I'll be too embarrassed when I see him again.'

'What else can I say? You haven't given me any juicy deets just a merest hint. Oh God, I'm getting all hot thinking of your lord of the manor getting busy under the sheets with the lowly peasant at the gate.'

'Di, you read far too many lurid romances.'

'And learned a thing or two from them, I can tell you. Thank goodness Henry is into role play.'

'TMI, Di.'

Diana goosed her in the ribs. 'You can't torture me like this. Feed me something.'

Gemma pretended to think hard. 'Well, there was some torture involved, I have to admit, and it was entirely consensual – and mutual.'

'Gemma!' Diana fanned herself, grinning broadly.

'But that's all I'm going to say.'

'Cruel woman. I'll just have to get you drunk one night.' A wail in stereo broke out in the waiting room. 'That sounds like my twins. Duty calls. I'd better hurry.'

Gemma checked her first appointment and schooled her expression into more sober lines fitting the registration of death. She walked out into the waiting room to where a confused elderly man sat with his son.

'Mr Vernon? Follow me, please.'

Grimly contemplating the bus and cycle trip home in the drizzly weather, Gemma cleared her paperwork from the day of appointments. As ever, all human life had processed before her and she was still processing the diet of joy and grief. Her rather melancholy mood was interrupted by Diana, who darted into her office already speaking.

'Guess who's sitting in reception?' She looked pleased so Gemma knew it was a nice surprise.

'No idea.'

'Your man. He's been waiting out there for fifteen minutes. You'd better rescue him or a prospective bride might throw over her current choice and snag him for herself.'

Ignoring this teasing, Gemma felt the little lurch of worry that any parent feels when a person she thought would be with her son was actually outside. 'Is Leo OK, did he say?'

Diana rolled her eyes. 'I imagine he's fine as Sam didn't mention him. He said he'd come to run you back home – he had an errand so thought he'd save you the trip. Isn't that sweet? It's almost as if there's, you know, *something* going on – but my lips are sealed.'

Shoving the last papers in the file, Gemma grabbed her handbag and hurried into reception. Sam was standing in front of the notice board, arms folded, giving her a fine view of his back. Diana sighed and regretfully walked on to her own office.

'Sam, is Leo alone with your dad?' Gemma asked in a rush.

He turned round and gave her a puzzled smile. 'They're in the car outside. I told you I wouldn't leave Leo alone in charge.'

Gemma realised her comment sounded like she doubted his honesty. He wasn't Ray; his word could be trusted. She was going to mess this up before it even really got started if she carried on like this. 'Sorry, yes, you did. That wasn't how

I meant to say hello but it just came out. Shall I go out and come back in again?'

'If you like.' His lips quirked in one of his sexy half smiles.

With an exaggerated air of calm, she went out and came back into the waiting room. 'Sam, lovely to see you.'

He kissed her cheek. 'Gemma, would you like a lift home?'

'Can you take me to Lavenham? I left Leo's bike there.'

'That's fine: we can chuck it in the back of the Outlander. There's plenty of room in the boot. Are you ready to leave?'

'Yes. All done for the day.' Saying goodbye to a very impressed receptionist, Gemma felt her pride swell as she walked out at Sam's side. She was used to thinking of herself as a failure but anyone who saw her now would think she must have something going for her to have a man like this with her.

'It's so kind of you to come and fetch me.'

'We had to pick out some fencing at a garden centre so I thought I'd save you the hassle of the bus. Did you get your car towed?'

'Yes, an old school friend owns a garage so he's sorting it for me.'

They were approaching Sam's car. 'Any sign of your ex?' he asked in a low tone so Leo wouldn't overhear.

'No – but then I wasn't expecting him to do anything else, not now he's made me suffer. He doesn't stick at anything, even revenge.'

Sam opened the rear door for her. 'Right, so Lavenham first, then home. How about you and Leo come to ours for supper? I've had a supermarket delivery so I'm well stocked.'

'That sounds perfect. Hi, William.' She leant over and kissed her son which he accepted stoically. 'Good day?'

'Yeah. Hey, Mum, the telephone people came and put in a line!'

'That was quick. I'd better contact them and see if we've been reconnected.'

'Sam talked to them already. Looks like it won't be until Thursday.'

'Then we rejoin the internet superhighway?'

'Might be more of a B road with a few potholes but, yes, you'll be back in business,' said Sam, meeting her eyes in his mirror and smiling.

'We'll settle for that, won't we, Leo? Anything else to tell me?'

Leo chatted on about a second stone lion that Sam had found in a shrub. That reminded Gemma that she hadn't mentioned the research she'd done on Saturday, other things having driven it from her mind. Would he mind?

'Sam, I hope you don't think I'm overstepping but I did a little investigating in the reference section of the library. I found some material about the castle garden.'

Approaching lights, Sam braked rather more suddenly than usual. 'Mind? No, that's great! I couldn't see when I was going to get around to it. What did you find?'

'I'll show you when we get home – I photographed the article on my phone. And there's more but I'd have to call it up from Ipswich, accounts and stuff. I thought that might tell you want plants they were buying.'

'Good thought. Please, if you've time, I'd love everything you can find out.'

'You really don't mind?'

'Gemma, do I look like a guy who wants to spend his time in a library?'

She met his gaze again in the mirror. 'You're grateful?'

'Oh yeah.' His smile was only in his eyes but she knew he meant that he would show her later just how grateful he was.

Chapter 17

Once she had Sam's permission to visit, Camille didn't wait long to invite herself over. That was why Sam found himself meeting the train from London a mere two days later, his dad and Leo waiting in the car in the short stay parking space as he stood in the ticket hall. This situation with Dad, having to tow him around everywhere he went, was a foolish arrangement. He really needed to give more time to finding a solution, perhaps fork out for a carer to come in for a few hours each day so he didn't have to rely solely on a fourteen-year-old boy.

The train drew into the station. Watching the people come through the ticket barrier, Sam wondered if he would recognise Jennifer's little sister. Just as well he hadn't changed much, otherwise they were in danger of walking straight past each other.

'Sam!'

He was right: he would never have been able to pick her out of the crowd. The sullen Goth he last remembered had turned into a tall smiley platinum blonde. 'Hello! I know it's a cliché, Camille, but you've grown!'

Camille leaned in to kiss him continental fashion, once on each cheek. He was disconcerted by this confident adult. 'It's been five years, Sam. I hate the pictures of me as a teen. What was I thinking?'

He took her sizeable bag, suddenly worried that she was planning on staying the night. Neither had mentioned in their texts the duration of the stay. 'You were thinking that life sucked, you were hard done by, and everything was unfair.'

She laughed. 'That's about right.'

He held the door for her. 'Camille, I think I should warn you that I've got some people in the car.'

'Oh? Who? You've not got a family now? I hadn't heard that.'

'No, I'm not married. It's my dad and my tenant's boy.' That was a rubbish explanation. 'My dad's not well – he's got dementia – and Leo – that's the boy – helps me keep tabs on him.'

'I see.' She didn't really.

'Dad's home closed suddenly so he's with me for a few weeks. The thing is, I can't predict what Dad will say. He's confused most of the time. He often thinks Jennifer's still alive. Would you mind very much if I don't mention your connection? It will just start him off asking questions – painful questions – and I have to break the news that she's dead to him as if it is the first time he's heard it.'

'I completely understand. I don't want to put him through that. So, who am I then?'

'How about just a friend from London?'

'Fine.'

'We'll tell him you like gardens and have come to see the work I've done on the castle.'

She beamed. 'I do like gardens, Sam. It was you who made me see how lovely they can be, don't you remember?'

'I remember taking you and Jennifer to Kew once. I thought you were bored.'

'That was just an act. I loved it, despite all the dirty looks through the eyeliner and long fringe. I was bowled over by the glasshouses. Thanks to that, I decided to study garden design at college.'

'You did not!' She had managed to surprise him. That was the last career he could imagine her taking up at eighteen.

'Yep. You put me on this path.'

'Well, now that is quite something to learn after all these years!' Sam was cheered up immensely by the idea that the time he had spent with Jennifer hadn't been a total blight on everyone's life. 'You are going to love Claremont, Cammy. My tenant found some fascinating news articles about it last week. You might be able to make more of them than I can if you'd like to have a look?'

'I'd love that.'

They reached the car and Sam popped the boot to stow her bag. 'Dad, Leo, this is Camille, a friend from London.'

'Hi, guys. Call me Cammy.' Camille got into the front seat and turned round to shake hands. 'Lovely to meet you both.'

Sam was amused to see that Leo looked quite stunned by the pretty twenty-something visitor. He managed a blushing 'hello'. Dad, however, was frowning.

'Do I know you, young lady?' he asked.

'No, Mr Ranworth, I don't believe we've met before.'

'You remind me of someone but I can't remember their name. You know who I mean, Sam?'

Sam did: Camille's expressions reminded him of her sister. The arch of the brow and the shape of the eyes: nothing too obvious but the hints of Jennifer kept coming through. It was painful for him to see. She was now only a few years short of the age Jennifer had been when they met which probably heightened the resemblance. 'Don't worry, Dad, I expect it'll come back to you. Let's go home for lunch.'

After the midday meal, William normally had a sleep in front of the TV. Sam gave Leo his laptop and left him dad-sitting while he showed Camille around the grounds. She'd asked to talk so he thought it better they did this out of earshot of his father and Leo.

'This is amazing!' Camille exclaimed as she admired the planting in the keep. 'I hope you are recording the project? You'll want to look back and see how far you've come – and you can use it as part of the garden narrative for visitors.' She plucked a leaf from a scented geranium and sniffed.

'You're right. I've not done that – or only intermittently.'

'You should ask that kid, Leo. I imagine he could take photos and videos for you. From what he said over lunch, he seems pretty knowledgeable about YouTubing and that stuff. If you don't have time, you should ask if he could do your website and manage your social media. Kids always want extra pocket money. I know I did at his age.'

Sam took a seat on a bench in the shade of the north wall.

'Cammy, you've been here less than an hour and already you've come up with more ideas than I've had in months.'

'I'm sure that's not true, Sam.' She sat beside him and drew up her legs cross-legged. 'I can see what you've been doing here. It takes a lot of hard work to restore a garden of this size. I'm not surprised you don't have time to think about the extras.'

'But I need to if I'm going to make a success of this as a business. I've had my first wedding but that was for friends. Real clients start in September and I have to be ready. I've been busting a gut for the grounds to be in a fit shape to host them.'

They sat in silence for a while, listening to the rustle of the leaves and the caws from the rookery.

'I like it here. It feels peaceful, despite the hard work,' she said. 'It's like you've built your own little haven. Can I ask you something, Sam?'

'Isn't that why you are here?'

'Has it helped you come to terms with Jennifer's death?'

Had it? Sam didn't like opening the door on that rat's nest of feelings. 'To be honest, Cammy, I don't know. I've not been as brave as you: I've not gone for counselling. I'm far from sorted.'

She twirled the geranium leaf in her slim fingers. 'I didn't say I was sorted but the counselling has helped. Would you mind telling me what you remember about my sister? I just want to understand why. We hadn't seen much of each other in that last year.'

'I know. Jennifer was pulling back from some people.' And clinging on harder to others.

'Why did she do it, do you think?'

Sam swallowed. He'd agreed to this talk but it felt like his chest was being clamped open and his heart probed by an incompetent surgeon. 'Your sister was a complicated lady.'

'I'm aware of that. I lived with her too, remember, when we were growing up? Despite the age difference, I got enough clues to know she was unbalanced at times.'

He nodded. 'I think what she did was a cry for help. She needed me to be more than I could ever be. I think she wanted me to hold her together. Needless to say, I failed miserably. A career as a policeman does not make for a regular home life and when she hit her crisis, I wasn't there for her.'

He often wondered if Jennifer had intended to do it at the end. Had the overdose been meant to fail? He suspected she had been in a state where she hadn't cared either way: left it in the lap of the gods like some crazy gamble with her life. The inquest had been inconclusive and the verdict of accidental death kinder than he had anticipated. He comforted himself with the thought that it might be right. He had been expected back earlier, messaged that he was on his way, and then caught a last-minute case in Pimlico. He had texted and thought nothing of the fact that she had not replied – that was stupid of him in retrospect. She'd been wild and edgy for a few weeks. He'd been in no hurry to return because work had felt like a sanctuary where he could relax away from her demands – and that was perverse considering he was investigating serious crimes. That should've tipped him off to how bad their relationship had become.

'It wasn't the only time she attempted suicide,' Camille

said quietly. 'She tried for the first time when she was fifteen, Mum said.'.

'Really? I didn't know she'd gone so far before.' He tried to process this new piece of information, trying to distance it as he would evidence of a disturbing crime. It hadn't come up at the inquest. It could've saved him from some of the self-reproach. 'She did tell me she often had suicidal thoughts. That was part of the problem. I was used to her being moody, saying dramatic things. I didn't know that she had moved from just having the thoughts to acting on them. There were signs but I blew them off.'

'We don't blame you, Sam.'

'Thanks.' But he blamed himself. The guilt was ever-present. He'd been looking for a way out of their relationship for months but been put off by Jennifer threatening to kill herself if he so much as mentioned her moving into her own place. Their relationship had become a prison. It wasn't until he arrived home that night intending to catch a couple of hours sleep before returning to the murder enquiry that he found her dead on the sofa. There hadn't been a note, unless you took the 'You failed me' one sent by the corpse. That was in the end why the coroner had ruled accidental overdose.

If he'd understood her better . . .

If he'd known about the earlier attempt . . .

If he hadn't been late . . .

If he'd noticed she hadn't replied to his text . . .

But the very worst thing of all was that he had felt relief as well as guilt and sadness – he couldn't forgive himself for that.

'So, there was nothing specific that set her off that night?' asked Camille.

'Not that I'm aware. We'd had a few arguments as couples do but nothing recent. She'd been quieter than usual for a few days and always wanted to know where I was. That was pretty tricky as I was caught up in an investigation. There had been a spate of stabbings. I don't think she liked the fact that I was so absorbed by it.'

Camille sighed. 'No, she didn't like it when she wasn't the main focus.'

'If it is any help, I don't believe she wanted to die; I think she wanted me to save her.'

'Thank you. That does help.'

He let a few moments of silence pass. 'How are your parents?'

'They're OK. They worry about me, want me to have a stable relationship and give them grandchildren, but other than that they're managing. I think they just want to look ahead now, keep the happy memories going and forget about the bad.'

'I have some photographs that belonged to Jennifer. Some of them are really nice – from the good times. I came across them in the move. Would you like them?'

'Thanks. I'll take a look.'

He rose and offered her a hand up. 'I'm glad you came, Cammy.'

She squeezed his fingers. 'So am I. Now, why don't you show me these photos and I'll also look at the articles about the garden?'

Gillian put up a list on the staff noticeboard with times for each of them to see her individually. Diana nudged Gemma.

'Do you think this is it? The big heave-ho?'

'I sincerely hope not. I'm hoping it's more of a performance review.'

'She'll probably just ask us if we want to take voluntary redundancy. If I knew I could walk into another job, the lump sum would be attractive.'

'But what would you do round here, Di? There's not much on offer outside hospitality and care worker, neither of which pay enough to cover my bills.'

'I know, honey. I was just daydreaming about a new kitchen.' She brushed Gemma's arm. 'Don't worry. Gillian knows your situation. I'd better run. I've got a death coming in.'

Gemma couldn't concentrate on her appointments that morning, not even raising an eyebrow when a couple wanted to call their twins after two of the most blood-thirsty characters in *Game of Thrones*.

'So is Aerys the little boy or the girl?' she asked wearily.

'The boy, of course!' said the dad. 'Cersei is the girl.'

'Or do you think we should call her Lannister?' queried the mum. Gemma almost gave her opinion but then realised she wasn't being addressed.

'I thought we talked about this,' muttered the dad.

This sometimes happened: parents arriving still uncertain of the name. She needed to move them along if she was going to be on time for her appointment with Gillian.

'You could flip a coin,' she suggested.

'What!' spluttered the dad.

'Seriously, it's not as stupid as it sounds. Your instinctive reaction would tell you how you really feel: you'll either be pleased or hate the outcome and then you'll know which name you want.'

'Ooo, let's do it!' said the mum. She took a coin from her purse. 'Graham, Cersei: heads or tails?'

'Heads,' he said grudgingly.

The mum peeked at the result. 'Oh, it's tails.'

Gemma uncapped her pen. 'So how do you feel?'

The mum and dad exchanged a look. 'Disappointed?' ventured the mum.

Dad nodded.

'OK. Cersei it is then.'

Gillian was pouring tea from a pot she kept for private use in her office as Gemma entered.

'Gemma, dear, would you like a cup?'

'Thank you, yes.'

'Everything going well with your appointments?'

'Fine. That's the third *Game of Thrones* dispute I've had to resolve this month. I've never seen the series but I've had to bone up on the characters just so I know how to spell them.'

'Ah yes. Fashions in names are continually fascinating. I remember when it was all Kylie and Jason.'

'Oh?'

'You make me feel old. *Neighbours*, in the eighties. Everyone wanted to be Australian.' She handed Gemma a cup and then offered her a biscuit from her tin.

This was going to be bad, though Gemma.

'So, not to beat around the bush, I have some difficult decisions to make, as you know. I'm trying to find a solution that is fair to all my staff.' Gillian took her place behind her desk. 'I'm asking everyone the same question. Would you consider going part-time?'

'Oh. That wasn't what I expected. I thought you might ask if I wanted redundancy?'

Gillian's eyes lit up. 'And do you? You're young. I'm sure you'll have no problem finding yourself another job – retrain even.'

She had to cut off that train of thought. 'No, Gillian, I don't. I can't afford to take time out for study.'

'Ah. Then how about part-time?'

'I'm sorry. I can barely survive on my wage as it is. With Leo, I don't have the capacity to hold down multiple jobs. I've just moved to a village where there are next to no employment opportunities.'

'I rather thought you might say that.' Gillian shuffled the roster sheets. 'Everyone has been giving me pretty much the same story. It looks as though I can't do this the way I'd prefer.'

That sounded ominous. 'Sorry?'

'I am trying to find a fair way to decide who to let go. Unless something changes it will probably be on the last in first out basis.'

Gemma knew what that meant. She was the most recent employee and, with the retirement age going up every few years, even the older members of staff still had years to go before they would be expected to leave. 'You mean me?'

Gillian wasn't meeting her eyes. 'Take the next few weeks to look around, Gemma. I'm telling everyone the same as we're all at risk. At least, at your age you have a lot to offer an employer. I'll still arrange for the redundancy package even if you are leaving for another job.'

'You're giving me the sack?'

'No, I'm telling you that we are restructuring and your role might well go in the process. I'll have no choice. Here are the terms of the redundancy. Have a look and let me know if you want to take it before the deadline at the end of August.'

'But you are basically saying I have no choice?'

'Of course, another member of staff might change their mind – and you have priority for applying to another role in the council.'

But the council were cutting roles in all departments. 'Gillian, I can't . . .'

'Take the rest of the afternoon off to think about it. I'll do your wedding with Diana.'

Taking the piece of paper, Gemma walked out in a daze.

'Gem, what's wrong?' asked Diana, catching her in the corridor.

Gemma cleared her throat. 'Looks like I'm the sacrificial lamb, Di.'

'Oh God, no!' Diana hugged her. 'Look, I'll talk to Gillian.'

Gemma closed her eyes, resting her forehead on Diana's shoulder. 'It's not her fault, Di. What's she to do? She can't magically increase our budget.'

'I'm so sorry.'

'I've got to go. Have to pick up my car.' And how was she going to pay for that now she knew she was reaching a cliff-edge for finances?

'Of course. Get some fresh air.' Diana's eyes were glistening. 'We'll sort this out somehow. Don't panic.'

'Right.' Gemma grabbed her handbag from her desk. 'Like everything else in my life goes so well.'

Jason the mechanic was as good as his word and charged her cost price for the tyres. He'd always had a soft spot for her at school and she wondered how her life would have gone if she had ended up married to a garage owner. She could've happily worked two or three days a week and had more time for her children.

But there would've been no Leo. She couldn't regret her choices when she had him.

'Thank you, Jason,' she said, handing over a cheque, praying it didn't bounce.

'No problem, Gemma. Alice says hi.'

'I say hi back.' Jason had married a girl in the year below, a lovely red-head who worked at the local dental surgery. They were the backbone of their local community, unlike the spineless wonder she had picked.

'You and Leo must come over some time.'

'Thanks.' She knew Alice was unlikely to ask them. She didn't like Gemma much – perhaps because Jason liked her too much – and certainly didn't understand Leo. Their son, Bradley, was everything a boy was expected to be: keen on football, loud and adventurous. She suspected that he was one of the boys in Leo's school that her son did not want to be around.

Gemma stopped off on the journey home to fill the tank. Her spirits began to lift a little as she left town behind and thought of her cottage in the country. At least now she had a friend there who would understand. She didn't mean to burden Sam with her business but he wouldn't mind her running a few ideas past him, would he? He'd been really helpful about her father and mother, giving her a perspective on that relationship. If he was somewhere in the garden, maybe he'd listen to her sound off while he carried on working? She wouldn't even be taking up his time. He'd probably tell her it was only a job and that there were plenty more of those to be had if you made the effort. She needed someone to say the obvious things so she could believe in herself.

Parking outside her cottage, she didn't even go inside but walked up the drive to the keep. Sam could be anywhere, though she thought she remembered him mentioning planting some rushes by the moat to increase the habitat for wildlife. Her memory was correct because she could hear some voices down by the foot of the drawbridge and one of them was definitely the castle owner. Was Leo with Sam? She pushed through the thick glossy leaves of the rhododendron bushes to emerge on the slope running to the green moat. Sam was wearing waders and not much else, waist deep in the murky water. He was laughing and chatting with a young blonde woman who was passing him bulrush plants from the safety of the bank.

'This is what I'm talking about, Sam,' she was saying. 'Pictures of you on your website, shirt off. It worked for selling Poldark to the British public.'

'I'd look an idiot.'

'Trust me, you don't look an idiot.' She flicked some water at him.

'You're a menace, Cammy.' He splashed her back.

She squeaked. 'Not fair! You're getting my blouse wet!'

'You started it. You always were a menace. You've not grown out of that, I see.'

'You always said you like the fact that I was a rebel.'

Gemma stopped short. She was clearly breaking into a scene between two people who knew each other very well, yet Sam had never mentioned a Camille. Too late to retreat: Sam had spotted her.

'Hey, Gemma, you're home early.'

'Yes. Something came up at work.'

'Gemma, this is Camille, a friend from London.' He waded out of the moat. 'Come to help with the garden design.'

'Hi, Gemma.' Camille held out a hand, realised it was muddy, then wiped it on the grass. 'Sorry, you probably don't want to shake that just now.'

Or ever. 'I just came by to . . . it doesn't matter. Nice to meet you.' But it wasn't. Gemma had a sudden feeling that she didn't know Sam at all. Was this a girlfriend? Though they'd been to bed, they had never had the 'let's be exclusive' conversation. Sam had said dating meant no commitment – did it also meant freedom to pursue other relationships? If so, what had she been thinking?

'You're Leo's mum, right?'

'Yes.' That made her feel about a million years old.

'He's a great kid. Sam's told me so much about him.'

'Thank you. I'll . . . um . . . see you later. Better head back to the cottage.' She wrapped her arms around herself, confused and annoyed with herself. She knew better than to risk giving any part of herself to a man.

'Everything OK, Gemma?' asked Sam.

'Great. Never better. Bye, Camille.'

The visitor slicked a tendril of blonde hair behind her ear. Even her ears were pretty, slightly pointed like she had elf in her bloodline. 'Oh, I hope I'll see you again, Gemma. I'm staying a few days.'

'You are?' Sam seemed surprised at this announcement.

She turned to talk to him. 'It's a big project, Sam. If you want my input, it'll take that long. I'll make a start on that film we discussed.'

'Oh, OK. Thanks.' He didn't sound that keen but Camille gave a satisfied nod.

'It's fine. I don't have a job yet.' She faced Gemma. 'I've just graduated, you see, so I'm looking for work. Helping out here will be great for my CV.'

'That's . . . good. Have fun.' Before she did something unforgivable like burst into tears that the man she hoped would supply the comforting shoulder was occupied, Gemma reversed her steps and hurried back to her little castle of a cottage. Banging the front door closed, she wished she too had a drawbridge she could raise to ensure she could indulge in her mood uninterrupted.

She needn't have worried. No one came by. Leo texted to say he was having supper with Sam, Cammy and William. Did she want to come?

No, she didn't. She sent a polite refusal and went to bed without eating.

Chapter 18

Gemma found it very hard to go to work and act as if nothing had changed. It was impossible to face her colleagues without being hyper-aware that everyone knew her predicament, even though it was supposed to be confidential. All hope of keeping it a secret had gone when Gillian had spontaneously sent her home directly after a one-on-one in her office. They would've had to be very dense not to read between those lines. They were like a bunch of prisoners in the Conciergerie Prison during the French Revolution, knowing that her name had gone on the door for the guillotine the next day. It could've been any of them, still could be, but they were also relieved the blade had fallen elsewhere.

Gemma found she was getting a little reckless with her clients too, not biting her tongue when she normally would.

'So, you want to call little one Angel Simone?'

'Yes,' nodded the earnest mother looking down at her bundle of infant girl with a besotted smile.

'Lovely names. But your surname is Smith?'

'I know – dead boring, isn't it?' Mum rolled her eyes in a 'what can you do?' gesture.

'That's not what I meant. Have you considered what her initials spell?' Gemma looked to the dad hoping he was a little more awake than his wife. He had the massive arms of someone who worked out and several military tattoos. Hopefully, he'd be ready for action any time.

'Er . . . what?'

Evidently not. She would have to spell it out for them – literally. 'A S S.'

'Oh my gosh, she's right!' The mother hugged the baby to her chest. 'Joe, we were about to condemn her to years of teasing in the playground. I told you we shouldn't go with your mother's name!'

'Then what do you suggest?' he said grumpily. 'We've already promised her and she's been so kind – what with that loan for our house and everything. We've got to name the baby after her.'

Gemma decided to intervene before they came to blows – or tears – in her office. 'Why don't you switch the names round? Lots of people are called by their middle names, especially if there's another family member with the same one.'

'Switch them around?' said the man as if she had just suggested he tango naked in Bury St Edmund's town centre.

'Think about it,' she said mildly, uncapping her pen, waiting for the penny to drop.

'S A S – SAS!' crowed the mother. 'Our little girl is going to be so kick ass! Do you like it, babe?'

Dad's confusion cleared and he cracked his knuckles. 'That's cool! Yeah, I like it – so will the guys in my unit. We'll teach her to kick ass, not be one.'

Gemma worried as she filled out the forms that maybe she had moved the fate of the child in question from bullied to bully. Hopefully not. 'As long as you tell her that with great power comes great responsibility.' That was one of the man's tattoos, decorated with a little spider.

He chuckled and rubbed the soft head of his firstborn. 'Yeah, that too.' He bent closer. 'But kick ass first, OK, Angel?'

At lunchtime, Gemma hid in her office rather than join everyone in the staffroom for a gossip. She'd brought a sandwich from home so there was no need to emerge. She occupied herself by looking through the jobs section of the local newspaper. Did she really have to go through all that again? The CV? The dress-to-impress suit? The fake smiles and eager to please presentation? She felt exhausted just thinking about it.

There was a knock and Diana put her head around the door.

'You OK?'

'Great,' she replied insincerely.

'Good job with that couple just now. They sang your praises to Gillian.'

'She probably just thought I should've kept my mouth shut.'

'Maybe.' Diana smiled wryly. Registrars were supposed to be completely impartial. Offering advice was likely to backfire so they were told not to do it. 'There's someone here to see you – a friend, she says.'

'Oh, who?' Gemma couldn't think of anyone who would drop by at work like that.

'Young woman, blonde. Says her name's Camille.'

207

Oh God. Gemma dropped her head to the desk and bumped her forehead in despair.

Diana frowned. 'Like that is it? Do you want me to get rid of her?'

'No, it's OK.' She scrunched up the sandwich wrapper and lobbed it towards the bin. It missed. 'Send her in.'

'Yes, boss.' Diana shimmied out and Gemma could hear her voice outside. 'Ms Whitehall will see you now.'

Gemma played along by picking up her pen and trying to look busy. Camille entered in what Gemma uncharitably thought of as a burst of fragrant youth and unsullied potential. She imagined the flowers and jewels dropping from Camille's lips, compared to the dried-up leaves and beetles that tumbled from hers. She was definitely wrongly cast in this fairy tale to win the prince in his castle.

'Gemma, sorry to disturb you at work,' said Camille. 'I know we only met briefly yesterday but Sam's told me so much about you.'

'He has?' That sounded encouraging. Gemma put down her pen.

'Oh yes. He told me you'd been scouring the local records office for him. It's amazing you have the time, with a job and a son and everything.'

'History is a hobby of mine,' said Gemma defensively. Sam had made her sound like the fustiest old scholar.

'Well done you! So good to keep the brain working!'

Was Gemma the only one to hear the implied 'at your age'? 'It's nothing.'

'As I mentioned yesterday, I was hoping to polish up my

CV by helping Sam launch his garden properly at that September wedding.'

What September wedding? Gemma realised she and Sam really hadn't talked that much about their lives. 'Good for you.'

'I was thinking information boards and maybe even a video installation? The local press would probably cover it if we make enough of a story of the restoration and, let's face it, Sam is very photogenic.' She paused so Gemma felt obliged to respond.

'Yes, he is.'

Camille leaned forward. 'Between you and me, I've had a crush on him since the longest time. He was always my hero.'

'That's . . . nice.'

She clasped her hands in her lap. 'I know. I never saw him in uniform, I regret that.'

'Um . . .'

'But I'm so pleased to see him somewhere he can be really happy. I've always wanted that for him. He's a very special man.'

'Good.'

'So to help him, I wondered if you'd take me to the library and see if the records that you ordered are in? We don't have long until opening day so it will have to be a quick research job. I can't imagine you'll have the time, with everything.' She gestured to the office.

'I was going to make time.'

'No need now I'm here.' Camille smiled guilelessly. Was she really as innocent as she seemed or was she telling Gemma to back off her man? 'Sam said he was sure you'd be happy to pass the task on to me now I'm here to help. Old accounts, isn't it? I've had the academic training to understand what I'm reading, you see.' Implying Gemma was too thick to do so. 'It will just take you a moment.'

Never had she felt the lack of a completed university education more than she did right then. Gemma couldn't think of a polite way of refusing. The accounts were archived in public records so she could hardly claim they were hers to hoard, no matter how much she wanted to do so. She could imagine what story about her would be taken back home if she kicked up a fuss. *That Gemma is such a bitch – wouldn't let me even peek at the records. What is her problem, Sam?*

Her problem was that once again one small pleasure was being taken away from her. But she was bigger than that, wasn't she? 'OK, I'll take you to the library.'

'Thanks, Gemma. You are a gem!'

That wasn't exactly the first time she'd ever heard that compliment. 'No problem, Camille.'

'Call me Cammy.' Feeling something underfoot, Camille bent down, picked up the sandwich wrapper and lobbed it in the bin. 'Goal!' She raised her arms in a victory salute.

Sam was feeling miserable. Having Camille around the house was like playing host to a Disney princess, the sort that sang and birds twittered along while small woodland creatures crept out to worship at her feet. She was just so bloody upbeat. Everything about the garden exhilarated her from the matted hedgerows to the overgrown ponds. In desperation to have a break from her, he'd sent her into Bury by taxi to carry on the research Gemma had started. He was sure Gemma would understand once he explained. Not that his tenant really had the time to do the research he should be doing about his own garden. She would probably be grateful he'd relieved her of another task on her 'To Do' list. From the sounds of it, she was working herself into the ground, too tired to come over to supper the night before.

'How's your mum?' he asked Leo at lunch.

'OK,' said Leo in that non-committal way he answered most questions.

'Better?'

'Better? She's not been ill.'

'She was too tired to come to supper last night.'

'Oh yeah. Dunno. Didn't see her this morning. She'd gone before I got up. Do you want me to do some filming this afternoon, for the video?' Leo's interest was caught by the project. He'd been looking up free editing software online.

'Sure. If you think you can do it?'

'I can use your iPhone until you get a decent camera. It'll do.'

And so the afternoon was spent with Leo taking arty footage of Sam clearing the brambles from around a stone urn while his dad snoozed in a garden chair in the shade. It was actually quite fun; Sam had to admit he enjoyed the banter with Leo.

When Camille returned, full of her findings in the records office, Sam left her to brief his dad and Leo and cook supper together while he escaped. His dad was the only one who really understood what she was talking about and able to help out with some of the terms she hadn't found in the dictionary. His memory for the things of his youth was still razor sharp. They were happy in their team of three and Sam didn't like the idea of Gemma being on her own for another evening, not now Camille had extended an invitation – eagerly accepted by Leo – to eat with them. He could hardly protest without looking mean, but he was missing his quiet evenings, just him and his dad pottering around the kitchen together.

As Sam walked down the drive, he found his mood darkening. Camille might not look much like Jennifer, but she had the same voice, the same hyperactive way of behaving, organising everyone so that the world conformed to her wishes. Sometimes he just wanted to stuff her in a teapot like the dormouse in *Alice in Wonderland*.

'I suppose that makes me the Mad Hatter,' he murmured, stopping to unwind some bindweed from a gatepost.

Gemma's car was parked outside the cottage but there was no answer when he tapped on the door. Deciding she might be outside enjoying the evening sunshine, he went around the back. Now that was a sight for sore eyes. Gemma was indeed enjoying the sun, stretched out on a beach towel in her bikini, on her front with strings unknotted. Suddenly the world looked a whole lot brighter. She appeared to have fallen asleep so obviously it was his job to kiss her awake.

'Hey, beautiful.' He knelt down and dropped a kiss between her shoulder blades.

'Sam?' she murmured drowsily, beginning to turn over.

As much as he would welcome that, he decided to be a

gentleman. 'Stay right there.' He kicked off his sandals and took off his shirt. 'Didn't I mention the cottage comes with a free massage from the owner on special occasions?' He rubbed his hands together, dropped some sun cream on her lithe back and began gentle revolutions.

'Oh my word, that feels heavenly. I'd almost say you could double the rent for this, but then I'd really not be able to afford it.'

Her muscles, which had just been starting to relax, tensed again at the mention of money.

'Sssh. Just let it all go. I told you the massage was free. And only for very select tenants.' He worked on her back for a few silent moments, appreciating the long line of her spine and the nipped in waist. She had the strength and suppleness of a dancer. Sun cream absorbed, he leant forward and returned to kissing, stretching out beside her, weight supported by one arm.

'Sam?' This time his name held a question.

'Everyone's up at my house cooking supper. We won't be disturbed, I promise.'

'In that case.' Gemma rolled over and opened her arms to welcome him.

Gemma picked a long strand of grass and used it to tickle Sam's stomach. The man's torso was a work of art, muscled from labouring outside. A sculptor would be in raptures. Sadly, the shadows were lengthening across the garden and it was really a little too chilly to lay here with nothing on, not to mention the increasing risk that a search party might have been sent out to call them to supper. She could do without that mortification: caught by her teenage son stark naked with her landlord.

Sam brushed the stalk away. 'Pest.'

'We should get dressed.'

'I should. You look so perfect like that I declare you should always go around with no clothes on.'

She smiled. 'Bossy lord of the manor.' She pulled her T-shirt over her head.

'Rebellious wench.' With a groan he sat up and reached for his shorts. 'Gemma, thank you. I've been looking forward to seeing you all day.'

The itch of unease was back. What was she to him? Just a booty call at the castle gate? 'Sam, have you told Camille about us? That we're . . . you know?'

His face was hidden in the folds of his shirt as he replied. 'No. I don't talk about that kind of thing with her.'

'And if you did, what would you say I am?'

'You're my friend, my tenant. The rest is no one's business.'

'I see.' He wasn't making their relationship public, then. He'd warned her he only did no-strings-attached dating: she shouldn't be surprised. 'And Camille? What is she to you? She seems very possessive.'

He got up and hunted down his sandals. 'She's a friend from London.'

Like Gemma was 'a friend' at the bottom of the drive? 'She seems to know you very well.'

'Not really. Look, do we have to talk about this? I was feeling very mellow. These questions are spoiling the mood.'

Fine for him to say that but Gemma couldn't let it go so easily. 'So I'm a friend, she's a friend too, but does that mean that we are exclusive?' She gestured between the two of them.

He gave an angry growl. 'Why do you even ask? Have you got a date with another guy lined up? If so, feel free to give him a try, but, just so you know, I only date one woman at a time. You go out with someone else, then we're finished.'

'That's not what I was saying.'

He hopped into his sandals. 'Wasn't it? Have I ever given you any cause to think I wouldn't be faithful while we're together? There's nothing between me and Camille – never has been. The idea is . . . Christ, Gemma, I've lived like a monk for five years. You need to cut me some slack here – at least give me the benefit of the doubt. Just because I've a female friend visiting, doesn't mean I'm having sex with her.'

How had this become so ugly so quickly? She'd really found a nerve with her question about Camille. It sounded like he was protesting too much – like he had something to hide. 'This isn't about you, Sam, not really. I'm just feeling insecure and I don't know what you expect of me.'

He checked his phone then rammed it in his back pocket. 'I don't expect anything of you, Gemma. Supper is ready if you want to join us.' He stalked off, clearly offended by what Gemma thought had been fair questions to ask at the beginning of a relationship. She wasn't psychic; she couldn't see into his head or understand him unless he talked to her. But it appeared talking was off the menu.

'I think I'll pass on supper,' she murmured. He hadn't stayed to hear her response to the grudging invitation.

Gemma, Gemma, what are you doing? This wasn't healthy. He was making her feel like crap, like she was always in the wrong. She had enough going on without adding that to her pile. She had been hoping to confide in him about her money worries, her job prospects, how she might not be able to pay rent on the cottage past the end of the month, but he had gone right past the 'hello, how was your day?' straight to getting into the sack with her. Well, *on* the sack, she supposed she should call their recent encounter. Thank goodness for high hedges. She shook out the towel then went inside to stuff it in the washing machine. She needed her own motto tattooed on her arm: learn from your mistakes. Self-destructive relationships were best avoided. She was going to have to face the fact that Sam couldn't be what she needed and he didn't really want anything but sex from her. She should end it before she did something dumb like fall in love with him.

But she had, hadn't she? With no encouragement and many warnings not to, she had taken that toxic step into having feelings for someone who didn't want or need them. How could she have been so stupid?

The washing machine hummed, dowsing the evidence of their love-making in soapy water.

No relationship, no job, no income. Gemma felt sick. The conclusion was becoming clear. She had failed. After years of managing on her own, unless a miracle reprieve came along, it looked like she'd finally have to admit defeat and move temporarily back in with her parents while she hunted for a new job. Mum would say 'I told you so'; Dad would mutter his usual indirect words of comfort; Leo would be livid because it would mean a change of schools and much less independence under Granny's thumb.

But her mum would be right: Gemma had made a mess of everything. It was time she admitted it.

Sam stomped up the drive, driven by his anger. Why did women always have to spoil things by asking, probing, demanding? Couldn't they just accept a good thing when they had it? Gemma was funny, intelligent, beautiful; they enjoyed each other's company and had chemistry; why push?

Because she needs to know where she stands, said his more reasonable side. *Imagine it the other way round: a guy from the past moves into her cottage and takes over – you'd be asking questions too, right?*

But answers would involve telling her about Jennifer. The mention of Camille always coupled in his mind with that disaster; he couldn't tell Gemma about something that was so painful to him. It would be handing over a part of himself, not keeping things light as he'd intended.

Would that be so bad? If you want a real friendship with her, is there any harm her knowing? You're hurting her by giving her defensive answers and blaming her for asking in the first place.

He paused at the gate where he had stripped away the bindweed earlier. He muttered a swear word at the rooks. Dammit all, he owed her an apology. He'd overreacted. How was she to know that she was pressing on old bruises left over from Jennifer? Should he go back now and set the record straight?

His phone buzzed. It was Camille.

Supper on table. This was followed by a string of emoticons he didn't understand but guessed meant that he should hurry.

Give Gemma time to settle. He'd go round tomorrow and take her something. She liked the flowers Leo had brought her the other day. He'd take her a bouquet, a bottle of wine, and an apology. That should do it. He might even tell her the truth about Jennifer.

His phone buzzed again. Wasn't he Mr Popular? This time the message was from Gemma.

Just giving notice that I'm giving up the cottage as soon as this contract ends. Earlier would be appreciated if you can find someone else.

What! One little argument and she was flying off the handle. Thoughts of apologies vanished into the night.

Fine. I'll advertise. He pressed send.

Chapter 19

On the following Saturday, Gemma and Diana had a wedding in a tithe barn near the picturesque village of Lavenham, an ancient place of half-timbered buildings and well-tended gardens spilling over with summer blooms. That made it a perfect candidate for a setting for some grisly murder-mystery, thought Gemma sourly. They approached the barn with some misgivings as the couple had announced they were involving animals in the ceremony.

'Remember that pug who ran off with the rings at the golf course?' Diana asked as they turned off the A-road.

'God, yes. You found him humping a golfer's leg and had to wrestle it off him.'

'And the guy had the cheek to blame me! I don't get paid enough.'

'You'll get no argument from me. To be fair to the golfer, he did think it was yours.'

'The owner was wearing a huge white dress of puffy flounces like a cloud. I didn't fancy her chances in a foot race with a pug across the fairway. She'd've been blown to Ipswich.'

'You should've left it to the groom.'

'Yeah, like he was going to do anything. He was hysterical with laughter. Said he hated that dog. They almost broke up there and then. Someone had to do something.'

Cow parsley frosted the banks. It brushed against the car as the road narrowed.

'I hope we don't meet anything coming the other way,' said Diana. 'Not seen a passing place for ages.'

Gemma rounded a bend and met a tractor and trailer. 'Crap. Why did you have to say that?' With much swearing, she began reversing.

Diana studied her for a moment. 'Trouble in paradise, honey?'

'Paradise? I think you've got my address wrong. I live in "Whatever can go wrong, will go wrong ville".'

'I know about the job, obviously, but you're even more miserable this end of the week than when you first heard. I'm guessing all's not well with the love life?'

Gemma backed into an entrance to a field, hoping the dry weather would mean she'd be able to get out again. The way her luck was running, the rear wheels would sink in mud and she'd have to ring for a tow. 'What love life?'

'Like that, is it?'

'He's got that girl staying with him – the one who came to the office a few days ago. I asked him about her and he got all shirty with me, like I was accusing him of something.'

'And were you?' Diana arched a brow.

'I just asked if we were exclusive,' she said defensively.

'That kinda suggests you thought he might not be.'

'How else do I find out if I don't ask?'

'Gem, you do what most of us do: you watch how he was with her. Did he do anything suspicious?'

Had he? Gemma rested her forehead on the steering wheel. 'No. But they know each other really well. She admitted to having a crush on him. She's young, pretty, clever.'

'And you panicked?'

'Yes, I suppose I did. I just wanted to talk to him about all my crap, but then we got distracted . . .'

'Uh-oh.'

'That part was nice. Then he didn't want to talk.'

'Men usually don't. They often use physical stuff to communicate rather than words. What had that said to you?'

'That he was into me.'

'Well, that's good. It's his way of being close to you.'

The tractor rattled past and Gemma put the car in gear. Fortunately, the wheels didn't spin and they were able to pull out of the field entrance.

'He isn't into me now. I'm in Siberia as far as he is concerned. It doesn't matter. I suck at relationships and at life. I'm a complete failure.'

'Gem . . .'

'No, it's true, Di. I'm a complete disaster zone. August is a bad time to look for work. I'm going to be out a job as of September so it's looking like I'll have to move back in with my parents for a while.'

'Damn, girl, that's not good. What about Leo?'

'It's not like I want to do it! I've resisted for ten years. But I can't pay the rent with promises and I certainly won't do so with sex.'

221

'That does complicate things – you having a romance with the landlord. I can see what it feels like to you. Did you ask Social Security about Housing Benefit?'

Gemma had considered it, but felt too exhausted to go that route. And how could she bridge the gap between application and when they decided to give her the benefit? She'd heard horror stories of people getting badly in debt while waiting. 'Even if I get the benefit, I'll still have more bills than I can pay. Living in the countryside is expensive on fuel. I'm just . . . just tired of struggling. I need a break.'

'Now you're running home to Mum and Dad?'

'You say that like it is something bad.'

'Sorry. I'm just . . . surprised. You were always a fighter. Have you told Leo?'

'No. I'll tackle him later. He's not going to understand.'

'He might. Tell him like you would an adult. He might surprise you.'

From her vantage point at the registry table, Gemma felt melancholy watching the young couple get married in the tithe barn. It was a beautiful wedding, sunlight streaming through the high windows of the ancient barn, bathing everything in a golden glow. There were no lusty pugs to contend with as the animal turned out to be an owl. Just at the right moment, the groom held up his arm, which he'd covered with a gauntlet, and the owl flew from the back of the barn to land on his wrist, rings attached to its leg. It was truly an 'aah!' moment. The groom untied the rings and let the owl fly back to the handler waiting in the rear. As the bird flew past, a puff of wind from its wings stirred the bride's hair.

The groom then leant over and wiped away a tear that had fallen from her eye.

'Just for you, darling,' he said softly.

The bride bit her lip. 'You knew that was my ultimate fantasy!'

'I rather hoped that was me.'

This quip led to good-humoured chuckles from the guests.

Diana cleared her throat and carried on with the ceremony but everyone was aware that it was a special one, sprinkled with magic because the couple so obviously loved each other.

The bride's dream day didn't end there. There was a white horse waiting at the door when the couple processed out, mane and tail brushed to a shine and decked with flowers and ribbons. The groom mounted first then sat his bride in front of him, best romance novel mode.

'See you at the reception!' he called, urging the horse into action.

'Take your time, Jack!' called the best man. 'I'll cover for you.'

The guests laughed and threw confetti as the couple trotted away.

'Oh my,' said Diana, clutching her chest. 'Just sometimes . . .'

'Yes. Sometimes.' Gemma put the registry bag in the boot of the car.

It was tough to witness for those who had nothing like it in their lives, thought Gemma. People like her. Perhaps she was in the wrong job and redundancy was the way of making her wake up to the fact? It couldn't be good witnessing all these happy endings when her own life was a bleeding stump.

Getting home after dropping Diana, Gemma sat for a moment in the drive outside the cottage. Her thoughts went to the happy couple. They were probably now executing a perfect first dance, for once making the ridiculous wedding traditions meaningful. Good luck to them.

OK, life goes on.

Gemma got out and approached her front door. It was open so Leo had to be home from his duties at the castle. At least she had a wonderful, unique son to compensate for all the rest.

'Hello? Leo?'

'Mum, in here! Dad's come for a visit.'

With mounting dread, Gemma dropped her handbag, kicked it out of sight behind the wellingtons, and went into the sitting room. Ray was sitting on the sofa, a selection of snacks from her stores spread on the coffee table, a large tumbler of coke on the polished surface. He hadn't bothered with one of the coasters that were scattered for use. Gemma snatched the glass up but too late: a ring stain now marked the pristine tabletop.

'Leo!' No point complaining to Ray.

'Oh yeah. Sorry.' Leo went into the kitchen to grab a cloth. He swiped at the mark. 'It won't come out.'

'That's why we use coasters.' She couldn't cope with this, not now. 'Ray, I told you not to come here. Please, if you and Leo want to spend time together, catch the bus back to Bury. I'll fetch him later. Leo's not seen his gran and granddad for a few weeks. It will be nice for him to visit.'

Ray chuckled as if she had made a joke. 'Seriously? A bus?'

She was so desperate, she'd do anything to get rid of him. 'OK, I'll drive you in. Just let me change out of my work clothes.'

'Gemmy, we can't go to my parents.' Ray offered her one of her own crisps. She shook her head tightly. 'They threw me out.'

'What! No!'

'Leo said it was fine for me to crash here for a few days.'

Leo looked surprised at this statement. 'I said you'd have to ask Mum, Dad.'

'Yeah, well, so now I've asked. You wouldn't let Leo's dad sleep rough, would you? Because that's all that's left to me.'

'You are not staying here. I'm driving you back.' Gemma darted upstairs and slammed the door to her bedroom. She pulled her phone out and rang Miriam.

'Hello?'

'Miriam? It's Gemma. Ray's turned up here saying you've booted him out. Is that true?'

She heard Miriam sniff. Oh God, it was true. 'Yes, we did.'

'What did he do, Miriam?'

'He stole my Christmas fund. You know, the money I put aside each month in the old tea caddy? It's been a bit short a couple of times and I just thought . . . well, never mind. This time I caught him at it. That was the last straw. He's sponged off us long enough.'

'I'm sorry.'

'And to think I didn't take you seriously when you told me about the bike and the rest. I just thought you were being dramatic because Leo said he was OK with his dad selling them so he could get better ones.'

'Yeah, he and his dad had a little arrangement.'

'Don't let him stay with you, Gemma. Unless he wakes up and takes responsibility for his life, he's not going to amount to anything.'

Gemma thought that ship had probably sailed long ago. 'I'm trying, but it's hard with Leo being present.' She had an idea. 'Look, can I drop Leo with you for the night? It might get ugly over here.' She was imagining she might have to call the police to dislodge Ray and his son shouldn't see that. First priority was to protect her child.

'No problem. I'll make up the spare room for him.'

Plan formed, Gemma marched down the stairs. 'Right, into the car.'

'Not moving,' said Ray. He glanced round the room. 'Hey, where are the controllers?'

'You're not watching my TV, Ray. Are you getting in the car or not?'

He grinned at her, still treating this like a joke. 'Not.'

'OK then. Leo, your gran wants to see you. I'm taking you over now.'

'Mum, what's going on?' Leo looked between his parents, confused. Poor lamb.

'Nothing to worry about. She's missing you. Come on. Ray, I want you gone by the time I get back and don't touch anything.' Not that there was anything of value left.

Leaving Ray in occupation of the sofa, Gemma escorted Leo out to the car with his overnight bag.

'Mum, what are you going to do?'

'Ask your father to leave if he's still there when I get back.'

She started the engine. 'It'll be easier for him to back down when you're not there.'

'But he's got nowhere to go.'

'I'm afraid, Leo, that's a problem of his own making. If we step in, he won't learn the lesson that he has to provide for himself. He's thirty-three now, not thirteen. He's upset your gran badly. Be nice to her, OK?'

'But, Mum . . .'

'Your dad will be fine. It's high summer. He can sleep outside one night, or find a barn. Tomorrow he can sort out his life. But he is not staying under my roof. I . . . I don't feel safe with him there.'

Leo subsided. 'OK.'

On the way back to her cottage, Gemma wagered with herself the odds of Ray having voluntarily departed. He didn't really think she had the guts to push him into leaving. He always thought everyone would give him a pass. So she wasn't that surprised when she spotted him lounging on the sofa surrounded by the detritus of his raid on her cupboards. He was engaged in rolling a cigarette as she entered.

She snatched it and the tin of tobacco from him and threw them out of the front door. 'You will not smoke in my house. In fact, you will not even be in my house. Get out!'

'Bitch!' He lunged towards the door but then realised she would slam it on him if he went to retrieve his gear. 'Fuck!'

'If you don't leave, I'm calling the police.'

'You'd do that would you? See Leo's father banged up for coming to you for help?'

'You came to me for help. I said no. You leave. End of story – or it should be.'

'He's my son!'

'And this is my house.'

'Fuck you.' He collapsed back on the sofa. 'Not moving. Bring Leo back. I want to see my boy.'

God, Ray was like a toddler. Why were so many men just pure children? 'Just go. Please.'

'No. And I'll tell Leo how you ruined my chances of getting a job by dragging me into trouble with the police. That's what'll happen if you call them.'

'It's always someone else's fault with you, isn't it?' Gemma retreated upstairs with her phone, fingers hovering over the call button. Did she really want all that: blue flashing lights, ugly accusations, Ray hauled away screaming at her?

Then she remembered Sam's promise to her. She called him instead. Even though they'd fallen out, she knew she could count on his support. That was a revelation to think about once she'd got rid of Ray.

Sam saw his screen light up. A call from Gemma. He almost let it go to voicemail then realised it might be about Leo – they still had a mutual interest in him even if their relationship had hit the rocks.

'Yes, Gemma?'

Camille looked up from her draft of the information board for the keep.

'Sam? I'm sorry to disturb you but there's a problem at the cottage.'

'What kind of problem? Electrics?'

'I wish. No, um, it's my . . . Leo's dad. He's turned up uninvited and is refusing to leave.'

Domestic disturbances – always the worst call out for a policeman. 'Are you and Leo safe?'

'I took Leo to his gran's. I hoped Ray would be gone by the time I got back but he says he's not moving. He's been chucked out by his parents so he thinks he can bunk down with us. He's not welcome.'

'Have you called the police?' Whatever else had happened between them, however angry he was with her giving up so soon, Sam hated to think of her alone with the guy who slashed her tyres. He'd be down there like a shot if he knew he would be welcome.

Camille put down her pencil, eyes wide.

'No, but I thought of it. I just wondered, before it came to that, if you'd . . . you'd have a go?' Gemma gave a ragged sigh. 'Never mind. I shouldn't have asked.'

Thank God. The green light. And she was handling it right: getting the child clear, avoiding confronting the man herself. 'Of course you should ask. I'll come down right away and see what I can do. Stay away from him, all right? Best if he doesn't suspect I'm on the way.' Pocketing his phone, he stood up. 'Cammy, can you look after my father, please?'

'Of course. What's wrong?'

'Unwelcome guest at the cottage. I'm going to help Gemma get rid of him.' Sam grabbed his car keys. 'Hopefully, this won't take long.'

'That's fine, Sam. I'll look after everything at home while you're out.'

He wondered about Camille's 'at home' comment as he got into his SUV. It looked like a frank conversation with her was in his future – but not now. Gemma's trouble came first.

Pulling up at the cottage, he could see Gemma watching for him from an upstairs window. He gestured to her to stay there and showed that he had a key with him. Attack fast and get the guy out before he had time to react: that was the best strategy. He opened the front door and strode into the sitting room. The mess the man had made in what had to be just a few hours was appalling.

'Right you, you're coming with me.' He seized Ray by the back of his T-shirt and hauled him up.

'Fuck off! Don't touch me! You can't do this!'

'I fucking well can, mate. This is my house and I'm evicting you.' He dragged Ray to the car and shoved him in the passenger side. 'Shut up and get in.' He slammed the door and hurried to driver's side before Ray had a chance to gather his wits. 'I'm taking you into Bury and leaving you in the town centre. It's more than you deserve.' He started the engine and pulled away with a jerk that threw them back in their seats. 'What you do after that is your own business. If I ever see you back on my land, I'm not going to be so nice.' He drove away from the cottage, taking the corners faster than usual. 'Put a seatbelt on, you moron.'

Ray grappled for the strap. 'Leo's my son.'

Poor kid. 'What the fuck has that got to do with me?'

'She's stopping me seeing him – there are laws against that.'

'I don't blame her – and I think you've a weird idea of what the law says. I tell you one thing it does say, though: getting an underage girl pregnant is wrong, act of a first-class dickhead. Vandalism: that's another thing that's illegal.'

'Vandalism? I've not fucking done a thing. Leo let me in.'

Interesting. Ray hadn't linked the accusation to the tyre slashing but assumed Sam meant something connected with this evening. Sam tucked that piece of information away. He wasn't going to ask directly about the car as that would only give Ray ideas. 'The boy let you in but that doesn't mean you can refuse to leave when Gemma asks.'

'He wants me there.'

'Unlikely but also irrelevant. Gemma gets to say who stays, not Leo. She's the adult in the household.'

'It's not fair!'

Sam had had enough of this loser. He'd met too many like Ray in the cells at the police station to have any time for his sob story. 'Just shut the fuck up OK? I don't want to hear another word from you or I'm turfing you out right now.' They were miles from the main road on a particularly quiet stretch of country lane.

Ray subsided, having worked out that hitchhiking from here would not be easy. He wasn't the sort people would stop to help.

'Right, out you get,' said Sam as they'd pulled into the car park of the multiplex cinema.

'What am I supposed to do now?'

'Not my problem.'

'But I've nowhere to go!'

'Do I look like I give a shit?'

Ray reached for the door handle.

'And if I see you back on castle grounds, I'll lock you down in the dungeons and forget about you.'

'You . . . you don't have dungeons.'

'I do. Rat-infested. Complete with chains. Flood when we have too much rain.' Sam gave him his best death-ray stare, the one he used on Bolshie suspects. 'No one will hear you scream.' Too much?

Apparently not. 'You're fucking crazy.' Ray leapt out.

'That's right. Remember that.' Sam drove away with relief. He wasn't lying about the dungeons. He'd just hadn't got round to clearing them. At some point they'd make an impressive Halloween party venue but at the moment they were filled with packing cases. The image of chaining Ray down there was very appealing.

The cottage door was open when Sam returned. Gemma was taking out a black sack of rubbish.

'Your ex is a pig.' He got out of the car and lifted the lid of the wheelie bin for her.

'Tell me about it.' She dumped the sack inside. 'My kitchen looks like a plague of locusts has passed through. Everything that can be eaten without being cooked has gone.'

'Sure you don't want to prosecute?'

She threw her arms wide. 'And prolong the agony? I'd prefer just to get shot of him – but that's impossible as Leo does love him.'

'The jerk doesn't deserve it.'

'We never deserve the love our children feel for us. We just get lucky if they do. Want to come in for a moment?'

Sam jingled his keys. Did he? He'd put away the hope he'd had for a friendship with her. 'I'd better get back. I left Camille in charge and she's not used to Dad.'

'Right. OK.' She hugged her arms to herself. He quashed the instinct to give her a cuddle. They'd gone past that. 'Sam, before you do, I wanted to say I'm sorry.'

'Sorry?'

'For everything. Tonight . . .'

'That's not your fault.'

'Isn't it? You told me you didn't do involvement and I dumped all this on you. But I also meant I'm sorry for asking you about Camille. Di had some good advice. Told me I should've looked at what you did before leaping to conclusions. You did nothing wrong. I was just feeling insecure.'

It was big of her to make an apology. He did understand how it might've looked to someone who wasn't sure of her own attractiveness. To his eyes, she obviously had far more to offer than the child-adult that was Camille. 'I get that. And I'm sorry I didn't explain about her. Communication isn't my strong point.'

Gemma lifted her hand. 'You don't need to explain – if you don't want to. I'm also sorry I sent that text rather than tell you myself that I have to give up the cottage.'

That had hurt. 'You needn't leave just because our relationship hit the buffers.'

She laughed darkly. 'You thought that was why I messaged you? God, of course, you did!' She ran a hand through her dishevelled hair. 'That was horrible of me, not even thinking how it would look to you. It's nothing to do with us.'

A little shoot of hope poked above the surface. 'Then why?'

She swallowed against a sob. 'I . . . er . . . I've been made redundant, Sam. I'd only just heard that afternoon so was still reeling. I can't afford to live independently any longer. The slashed tyres and putting down a deposit here – those wiped out my savings. I'm going back to my parents to regroup and start again, probably find somewhere to live near them.'

Sam kicked himself for not having probed her reasons but just assuming the worst. He was at least as much at fault as her in their crash-and-burn argument. 'I think I probably should come in.'

He watched as she made some coffee, wondering what to say.

'Are you OK to drink it black? Ray drank all the milk,' she asked.

'Of course he did,' Sam muttered. 'Black is fine. Look, if you report him to the police, you can get a restraining order.'

'That involves courts, doesn't it? I'm not sure I can afford that. He won't dare bother us at my parents. He's terrified of my mum.'

Sam was beginning to understand what was making Gemma scuttle back there after the hard slog of fifteen years surviving as a single parent. 'You're scared of him, aren't you?'

'Anyone would be, in my position. I never thought of him as violent but after the car . . .'

'If it helps any, I'm not sure he did that. I mentioned vandalism to him on the way into Bury and he didn't click – thought I was talking about the mess he made here.'

'You think it was just bad luck in the council car park? Crap. Have I kicked a leprechaun or something to earn all this bad karma?'

'I don't think leprechaun's control karma.'

She managed a smile at that. 'You know what I mean.'

Sam cradled the coffee. Should he offer a rent-free holiday to her? That would break his rule about not getting involved and he really did need a paying tenant. His own bank balance was looking shaky. Still, this was Gemma.

'You know, if you need a month or two here to look for jobs . . .'

She covered his hand with hers. 'Thanks, Sam, but I can't accept help from you. If I'm going to move, I'd better make sure Leo gets in the right school for the whole year. I can't move him at Christmas. He already has enough social problems as it is.'

'Leo?'

'Yes. He doesn't get on well with other boys his age. They think he's a nerd.'

Sam was about to say he didn't believe it, that Leo was great with his father, but then he remembered his own school days. He'd been teased unmercifully for his gardening passion; only the fact that he was fairly sporty saved him. Leo was the kind of kid who got on better with grown-ups than boys of his own age. 'Sometimes people have to wait to leave school for them to truly flourish. It's like they're pot bound and need to be planted out.'

'Love the simile.'

'I try. After all, I'm talking to someone who uses the word "crepuscular". Do you want me to talk to Leo?'

'Let me break the news to him first. After that, please do what you can. I've run out of ideas how to help him.'

'Moving to your parents doesn't mean he can't come over here anymore, or see Dad. He likes it here.'

Gemma smiled. 'So, the Selfish Giant is ready to share his garden?'

'For some select few. Leo makes the cut.'

'Do I still, even though I spoiled it?' She was looking at him with an uncertain expression that suggested she expected a rejection. Her self-confidence was clearly at zero and he'd not helped with his crass comments.

He moved in and drew her into his arms, offering comfort, nothing more. 'You didn't spoil it, Gemma. I'm just not very good talking about things. I'll tell you about Camille another time. It's complicated and will take a while. I'd better get back.'

'Thank you – for everything.'

He kissed her forehead, then her lips. 'You're very welcome. And I'm sorry about your job.'

Driving back to the castle, Sam wondered where they now stood. They'd still ended it, hadn't they? That was a bit of a grey area. At least he had a clearer picture of what was going on in her life. He'd made light of her claim to have hit a seam of bad luck, but she was right: she did seem to attract hard knocks. No wonder she'd reached the point where she was finding it difficult to get back up again. Anyone would when life kept kicking them in the teeth.

He opened his front door to the sound of harsh sobs from his father. His heart dropped to his boots.

'Dad?'

'Oh, Sam! Thank God, you're back. Your dad burned himself.' Camille was trying to keep his father's hand under the running cold tap but he was resisting.

'Let me look.' His father's palm had a stark red mark in the centre. It looked bad. 'What happened?'

'He was in the kitchen. I think he must've forgotten that he'd put a pan on for pasta – there was no water in it but the hob was on. He went to pick it up and I heard him cry out.'

'Why was he in the kitchen on his own? I asked you to look after him!'

Camille's eyes filled with tears. 'I'm sorry. I didn't know he'd do that. He seemed so capable – he offered to make supper when he saw that I was working.'

'Dad's reached the stage where he fades in and out. He can never be left to do things like that on his own.'

'I know that now.'

Sam hugged his father to his shoulder. 'It's OK, Dad. We'll take you to hospital and get that looked at. I'm just going to wrap it up, OK? Camille, pass me the cling film.' He was furious with her, but it wasn't really her fault, was it? It was his for not finding a safe place for his dad.

'Cling film?' She rooted it out of a drawer.

'Best thing for burns.'

She did the wrapping while Sam helped his father hold his hand steady. 'I'm so sorry, Mr Ranworth.'

'Not your fault, Jennifer. I'm such a clumsy old fool. I don't know why I did that.'

'Come along, Dad.'

For the second time that night, Sam found himself driving

at high-speed to Bury. A&E was busy – it was a Saturday – but old folk were given priority so it wasn't too long before his dad was seen. The nurse on duty tutted when he saw the burn.

'I bet that hurts, William.' The nurse looked only a little older than Leo and yet called Sam's father by his first name. 'I'll just put some magic ointment on it and give it a proper bandage.' He turned to Sam. 'You'll need to keep it clean and dry until it's healed. Is he OK to take painkillers? Not on any other meds?'

'He's taking some for dementia. I'll have to ask his GP what they are exactly.'

'I'll send you home with paracetamol for now. If he is having trouble sleeping, ask your doctor to prescribe something a little stronger. All right, William?'

His father looked wearily at the nurse. 'Do I know you?'

Chapter 20

Gemma waited until the following morning before ringing her parents. She had to force herself. This was the moment when she really gave up, not just talked about it. How shaming was it to admit she couldn't cope? Wasn't she better than this? It appeared not. She kept her fingers crossed that her mother would still be out at church and she could talk first to her father.

'Aldeburgh 553467.' Her father always answered that way. It was a comforting habit, reminding her of the old days of telephone exchanges and switchboard girls plugging in wires to connect calls like you see in the films. Gemma felt a knot of tension loosen. Confession to him was a breeze compared to her mother.

'Hi, Dad.'

'Gemma. How are you?'

'Um, not so good actually.'

'Not that summer cold that's going round? Your mother's been a little under the weather.'

Bad daughter, thought Gemma, not checking up on her own parents. No doubt, her mother had marked this down against her in the long list of 'Disappointing Daughter traits'. 'Is she OK now?'

Her dad gave a rumbling laugh. 'Oh yes. Bounced back stronger than ever. You know your mother.'

'I absolutely do. I'm not ill, no cold. I just got some bad news.' Here it went. 'I've been made redundant, council cuts.' She braced herself for condemnation from a father who stuck at the same job from leaving college to retirement.

'Oh Gemma. Ah well. No one is safe these days. I'm sure it is no reflection on your ability.'

She metaphorically picked up her jaw, which was on the floor. 'Thank you.'

'Everyone going or just you?'

'Just me at the moment. My boss decided to go on the last in first out principle and there are some old fossils on the team who have been there for decades. Even though I've been there four years, I'm still the newest member. Anyway, this all means I'm looking for a new job. I'm on the council list of priority placements, but I'm not that hopeful I'll get anything as everyone is making cuts. I don't want to end up in debt.'

'Do you need money?'

'Actually, I was wondering if I could bring Leo and come home for a few weeks, find a job and look for a flat near you?'

'In Aldeburgh? But you always said you hate it here.'

'I don't hate it. I just wanted to prove I could manage on my own, but I've found I can't. Not right now anyway.'

Her father was silent for a moment. 'There's something else, isn't there? Something you're not telling me?'

'Isn't that enough?'

'I'm your father, Gemma. I know when my daughter is upset. Losing your job would trip you up, I'm sure, but it takes more than that to have the Gemma I know coming home.'

Had her dad always been so astute? 'There is something, yes. It's tricky. Ray's been bothering us.' And she'd fallen in love with someone who didn't want her. 'I don't know what to do to deter him and eventually Leo will suffer in the fallout.'

'Oh, Gemma, I wish I could do more for you about him.'

'I'm . . . I'm afraid of what Ray might do. He's been made homeless as his parents have finally chucked him out and I'm worried he'll exploit Leo's feelings for him . . .'

Her father tutted in exasperation. 'That man should grow up, act his age. He's had it coming for ages.'

'I couldn't agree more. So, would you mind if we came, just till I get myself back together financially?'

'Mind? Gemma, I would be delighted to help you – your mother too. You sound like you need people at your back with that pathetic little man circling.'

'He's Leo's dad.'

'We know that, Gemma, otherwise I'd handle this very differently, I promise you. He's had it coming for years. I only wish I could've given him the seeing to he deserved when you were fifteen.'

Since when had her dad started talking like a caped crusader? 'That's why it's so tricky. I've got to put Leo first.'

'And it's why we worry about you – all on your own.'

'Worry?'

'Managing with next-to-nothing – too proud to ask for help. Well, I'm pleased you have finally come to us.'

241

'You are?'

'I suppose Leo will need a new school? Can't bus into Bury each day from here – too far. Let me think . . . one of my golfing pals is the headmaster of a nice little private school here, near the Maltings. Shall I ask if they've room for Leo?'

'Dad, I can't afford school fees.'

'Of course you can't. But we can.' It was like being in the path of an avalanche. Her dad must have been saving all this up for years and finally she was giving him the chance to release his bounty. 'Ah, there's your mother now. Margaret, Gemma's coming home for a bit. That's good, isn't it?'

Gemma could hear the exclamations and questions from her mother but her father stood like a buffer between them, refusing to surrender the phone. 'No, it's nothing she's done. No, she's not got the sack. It's austerity, Margaret. Cut backs. I was thinking Leo might enjoy Jodlands School. Such a bright boy. Not bad at golf either and they do that there in Games. What do you think?'

Gemma said nothing and let him run interference. Had he always tried to do this and she just hadn't noticed? All those remarks off the subject – was that just his way of trying to divert her mother and her from an argument? He'd skilfully sent Margaret off on the matter of suitable schools, something about which she would have strong opinions – many of them. Managing went two ways in her parents' relationship and she'd only just woken up to this fact. 'Do you want to speak to your mother, Gemma?'

Could she avoid this for another day or two? 'I'm in a bit

of a rush. I've got to fetch Leo from his other grandparents.'
She waited to see if Dad would take the hint.

'I'll tell her you'll be in touch later then. Margaret, Gemma
has to dash. She'll ring later. When do you think we can
expect you?'

'Is next month OK with you? In time for the start of the
school year?'

'Of course. I'll clear out the box room for Leo. I'll let you
know about Jodlands.'

'Thanks, Dad. Love you.'

He gave a harrumph, which she now understood was his
'love you too'.

When she drew up in the car to collect Leo, Gemma was
worried that her son would be still stressed about the ugly
scene with Ray but she should've factored in the effect of his
other grandmother. Miriam's therapy for anything that upset
her was to go shopping. Her fascination with charity shops
was a necessary escape from her menfolk. On this trip, Leo
had taken his bank card, diverting Gran from the charity shop
route to visit the one remaining electrical store on the High
Street, and spent his earnings on the new laptop for which
he had been saving.

'It was in the summer sale, Mum, at PC World. I think
they're bringing out a new model in October so I got a really
good deal.' He showed her the box, which was still sealed.

'You had enough, already?' Gemma hugged her son.

'Gran helped me with the last fifty pounds. She said it was
an early Christmas present. Gran's epic, isn't she?'

Gemma knew that his grandmother would consider herself

well compensated just to hear such a lovely compliment. 'Thank you, Miriam.'

Leo's gran beamed proudly at him. 'I don't mind spending on someone who works hard for what he wants. You've done so well this summer, love.'

'Thanks, Gran.' Leo flushed beet red. 'It's been fun – not like real work.'

'Well, work can be fun. That's something your father has never learned. I'm glad you have more sense.'

From the stressed look in Miriam's eyes, Gemma wanted to ask if Ray had turned up there last night but she couldn't with Leo within earshot. 'Thanks for looking after him.'

'All sorted at home?' Miriam asked with a significant glance at Leo.

'Yes, back to normal. My landlord helped me.'

'Good. Let's keep it that way. For his own good.' Miriam didn't mean her grandson. The parental life support had been cut off, probably too late to make a difference, thought Gemma.

Heading out of Bury, Gemma let Leo chatter on about his laptop, its specs and better-than-decent graphics card. Was this a good moment to pull the rug from under him, when he had something else to look forward to? She decided there was never a good moment. She would just have to do it.

'Leo, I've got something to tell you.'

'Uh-oh, sounds serious.' He was trying to joke but his face paled, making the scruff, where he hadn't quite got the hang of shaving, stand out even more. 'Is it about Dad? He's not still at home, is he?'

'No, Sam persuaded him to leave. Are you OK with that?'

Leo shrugged. 'It wasn't cool of Dad to stay when you asked him to go.'

'No, it wasn't. But I'm afraid I've some different bad news.'

He swallowed. 'You're not ill, are you?'

'No! What made you think that?' She glanced sideways at him.

'Just that Katie in my class – her mum has breast cancer.'

'No, I'm not ill. Leo, look at me: I'm not ill.'

He met her eyes and nodded. 'Good, because you know I love you and stuff.'

'Oh, I love you too, darling.' Lost in the sweetness of the moment, Gemma missed the lights changing. Horns sounded.

'Mum!'

'Sorry. Yes.' She pulled away. 'My bad news is nothing like that. It's just that my job at the council is being axed and I'm being made redundant.'

'That sucks.' The mention of cancer had put the small matter of a lost job in perspective.

'It surely does. The thing is I don't think I can afford the cottage, or renting anywhere at the moment. I've asked Grandma and Granddad if we can move in with them for a few months, until I've found something else.'

'Sam wouldn't throw us out.'

'Sam is our friend. We mustn't abuse his friendship like that.'

'I suppose not.' Leo stroked the cellophane wrapped laptop. 'I like the cottage.'

'I know.'

'Who will look after Mr Ranworth if I'm not there?'

'Sam will have to make other arrangements. He would have to do so when school starts in any case.'

'And we really can't stay?'

'No, I'm afraid not.'

'OK.'

'OK what?'

'I understand.'

Gemma wondered for a moment if she would've preferred a teenage tantrum rather than this mature young man taking the news so well. That way she wouldn't have felt so guilty. Her son had changed over the summer. 'Thanks, Leo. I'm sorry I failed you.'

He shrugged. 'Not your fault, Mum. Besides Granddad has super-fast broadband.'

How to broach the subject with Camille that it was time for her to return to London? Sam hadn't realised how difficult it would be once someone had their feet under the kitchen table. Then again, he'd found it almost impossible to talk to Jennifer about the parting of the ways so was it any surprise that her little sister had the same gift of getting a firm hold on her place and refusing to take the hints that she would move on?

On Monday evening, Camille had pre-empted him in the kitchen again and served up a summer salad of cold chicken and home-grown vegetables and leaves. It seemed worse somehow that she was a much better cook than him, everything beautifully presented. Leo had ducked out of an invitation to stay, having the attraction of a new computer to lure him back home. That left the field clear for what Sam anticipated as an awkward conversation.

'I've given some thought to the display boards,' said Camille, serving William rather than let him choose his own food. Sam felt a little nugget of resentment lodge in his chest. 'If you are able to knock some basic signs together, I'll paint them for you. I thought a heraldic red – that's the old colour of the shield of the De Courcey family who owned the castle after the Norman Conquest.'

'Ah yes, the friendly neighbourhood oppressors.'

William began humming, his mind drifting to some moment in the past known only to him.

'I know you've worked really hard on the material, Cammy,' said Sam, 'but I won't have time to do the woodwork. It will be cheaper and, in the end, better presentation to order them in.' Sam cut into a tomato, relishing the scent that you only got from naturally ripened ones. He always thought of it as smelling of captured sunshine.

Her face registered her disappointment. 'But that means that they might not be ready for the wedding in September.'

'That's true, unfortunately, but there's really no hurry.'

'I thought you wanted to make a good impression?'

'I do – but I think that that a good job is better than a rushed one. The Tudor couple are going to be much more interested in the smooth running of their day than whether or not I've information boards up around the place.'

'You need them for the guests – and the press.'

'The press?'

She busied herself sprinkling dressing on her salad.

'Yes, I've rung a few papers to see if anyone wants to cover the opening.'

Sam's heart sank. 'Opening of what?'

'The official opening of the castle as a wedding venue.'

'Cammy, you cannot go around asking the press to someone's wedding. It's their day.' And it was on 9th September, the anniversary of Jennifer's death: had she not even noticed?

She waved that away. 'It's fine. I spoke to Jerry and Mary first.'

Sam blinked slowly. 'You rang my clients without asking me?'

'I told them I was your event organiser. They were totally cool about it. They liked the idea of being featured in the Daily Express.'

'You didn't?' He put down his knife and fork.

'Didn't what?' Camille was making a good show of innocently eating her chicken breast but Sam could tell from the shifty look in her eye that she knew full well she had overstepped.

'You took it upon yourself to invite the national press to the first wedding, before I'm even ready? The gardens won't be in any fit state to be scrutinised by the press.'

'Look, they won't be peering into the shrubbery to check on the weeds; they're after the big picture. They all love the story of the ex-copper turned castle owner. Anyway, what's the worst that can happen?'

'They'll make me sound an inept fool taking on too much. I've no staff in case you haven't noticed. This garden isn't a one-man job!'

'You've got me,' she said quietly.

'You are not staff. You are a visitor. And I think that visit has come to a natural end.' Was it too late to put her on a train tonight?

'Sam!'

'Just leave me with the details of the people you contacted and I'll try to undo the damage you've done.'

'But I've announced it – it's on Facebook and everything! I've invited some VIPs to see the arrangements and to attend an exclusive reception at noon before the wedding party arrives at three. I've got gardening journalists coming. Monty Don's agent said he might be free and I'm pretty certain I've got a firm "yes" from Bob Flowerdew.'

Oh God, she was the human equivalent of Japanese Knotweed. Pulling her up from the places she had spread in his life would result in blisters and burns. She'd only gone and asked all the most high-profile gardeners on radio and television.

'Camille, this is my castle. You didn't get my permission for any of this!'

'I did. I told you I was going to help make the launch for the first wedding go well.'

He threw down his knife and fork and wiped his mouth on the serviette she'd set out. 'No, you don't get to do that. You don't get to reinterpret what was discussed as photos and a video project as *carte blanche* to reorganise the whole day.'

'I think you're being ungrateful.'

'No, I'm being furious. You only get that level of media attention once, if at all and, frankly, I'm not ready for it yet.

You are risking my business here. I'm on a knife edge financially. If I fail at this, I'm washed up – ruined. Don't you get it? I was even thrown by the fact Gemma's giving up the cottage – I'm that short of cash!'

'I'll take the cottage,' she said quickly. 'I'm sure Mum and Dad will pay my rent when they know what a good thing I'm doing here for developing my career.' Real financial pressure had obviously not yet made itself felt in the life of a recent graduate and adored only surviving child.

'Hah!' said Dad.

Sam was angry, so much so his hands were shaking. 'You don't see what you've done, do you? You've completely fucked this up for me.'

'Sam!' she protested. 'I was only trying to help.'

He nearly said something unforgivable about how she was just like her toxic sister but restrained himself just in time. He had to get out before recriminations exploded from him. 'For Christ's sake, at least look after Dad properly this time. I'm going out before I say something I regret.'

He grabbed his phone and his wallet and strode out of the house. Knowing his land well he made his way to the overgrown paddock as far from any dwelling as he could go and released a shout of frustration. He then picked up a fallen branch and whacked it against a stone urn. It therapeutically resisted shattering until he'd got in at least four blows. He probably had splinters but that seemed a small price to pay.

Camille had let the genie out of the bottle. Could he stuff it back in? Not without damaging his reputation beyond repair. He supposed that in another year or so he would've been going down on bended knee to thank her for her initiative – the prospect of national press coverage and broadcast interest was impressive – but he knew that he just wasn't ready yet to show this diamond in the rough to an informed audience. Claremont was only just passable. They'd see how much more work had to be done, how it was nowhere near certain he could pull the site into financial viability. The insurance on the keep alone, as a venue, was enough to make him wake up in a cold sweat at three in the morning. Add to that, the real danger that he'd crack up on the day. Wouldn't that be great, to be reliving the worst day in his life in front of the world and his wife?

Finally exhausted from his ranting, he stretched out on his back on the cold grass and stared up at the stars. He couldn't do this alone so he was screwed because, as usual, he found himself on his own, up shit creek without a paddle.

Then his phone rang.

Chapter 21

With Leo happily ensconced in his bedroom, cursing the broadband speed but sufficiently online to satisfy him, Gemma cleared up from supper. They'd had the first of the lettuce alongside the quiche she'd managed to snag from the supermarket bargain shelf. Leo had been so proud to have provided part of the meal and Gemma had made sure she lavished praise on the little spray of green garnishing their plate. They both agreed it was far superior to anything you could get from a shop. Gemma reminded herself that this was a moment in his growing up to savour, a rite of passage. She should make a note of it in her much-neglected diary where she jotted down her special days.

It didn't take long to put the kitchen back in order so she took her post-meal cup of tea out into the garden. Shadows had eaten up the shrubbery. Moths flitted around the porch light and bats wheeled overhead, so fast the eye couldn't track their shape. A tall stalk of a plant with yellow flowers glowed luminescent from the border. As she watched, a new bud unfurled, a glorious trumpet to join the others. She googled it, discovering that her little garden was home to evening primrose. Funny, she had assumed that was a small plant like normal primroses, not that giant tower of a thing.

An angry shout went up in the distance, provoking the rooks to a cawing response. Calming her alarm, she rationalised that there was probably some football match on and the opposition had just scored. She'd heard that sound once when England bombed out of the World Cup – a collective protest from the pub near her old home that showed the satellite sports. Odd though: she didn't think anyone lived over in that direction.

No more shouts came but she did hear the crack of wood against wood. OK, not sport, maybe some campers? Perhaps Sam had decided to allow some as another income stream? Actually, that wasn't a totally bad idea if you didn't mind coming across urban strangers in Hunter wellies from time to time. Glamping was all the rage at the moment and his land was perfect for it. Maybe she should suggest it?

No, bad idea. He didn't want her to get involved. He had Camille for that.

But there was one thing she could help him with – and she thought he probably wouldn't mind. Besides, it wasn't him she was helping, but his dad.

Sam answered after four rings. 'Hi, Gemma.' He sounded hoarse.

'Sorry to disturb you. I hope you weren't still eating?'

'No, I'm out for a walk. Is there a problem?'

Of course, he assumed the only reason she would have to ring was because she needed help again, not because she had anything to offer him. 'It's nothing like that. I rang because, well, it's just that I registered a death today at work.'

'I guess you do that most days.' He sounded confused and deeply tired but too polite to cut her off.

'True, but this one was for an old lady who has – had – a room in the nicest home I know in Bury. Wild Thyme Lodge.'

His tone perked up. 'Wild Thyme Lodge? I tried them early on but they had no vacancies.'

'I know. That's why you have to move fast. They might have a waiting list, of course, but it struck me that your dad would like it there. It's an old house set in mature gardens but they've fenced the perimeter off well so that the residents don't get lost. They've a dementia specialist advising them.'

'And you know this because . . .?'

'People talk when they come to register a death and I did ask a few leading questions today. The lady had been living with her condition for eight years.'

'Right then: I'll ring them first thing in the morning.'

'I hope it works out.'

'So do I.' There was a silence. 'Gemma, thank you. I really mean that.'

'It's nothing.'

'No, it's not nothing. You thought of us. You didn't have to do that.'

'Of course I think of you.' She wanted to add, 'I'm in love with you, you idiot!' but held it back. That ship had sailed.

'Who knows: thanks to you, I might have one less crisis for me to handle?'

'And you have so many others?'

He gave a hollow laugh. 'Did you ever watch *Star Trek*?'

'Um, maybe once or twice.' Sci-Fi wasn't really her thing.

'So you didn't see the episode with the tribbles? It's pretty famous.'

Gemma smiled. 'Can't say that I did.'

'They're these cute fluffy creatures that someone brings on board a space station. Unfortunately, they breed worse than rabbits and soon take over, getting under the floors, into the machinery and even in the service ducts.'

She knew enough about *Star Trek* to know how much crawling through these weirdly large ventilation tubes went on. 'No, not the service ducts!'

'Yeah, serious stuff. Intergalactic travel grinds to a halt.'

'Disaster.'

'Yep.'

'Sam, do you have tribbles?' She wondered if this was a metaphor from some invasive species in the garden.

'Of a sort. Mine has blonde hair and access to a phone.'

'Camille?'

'Yep.'

'What tribble-like thing has she done?'

'She's only gone and made the first wedding in September into an all-singing-all-dancing launch with national press and broadcast media. I'm not ready, Gemma.'

He was right. Just as the cottage wasn't quite ready for her and Leo to move in, the garden was getting there but there was still a long way to go. 'Oh, Sam.'

'Yeah, she doesn't get what she's done. She said she was only trying to help.'

'She probably was.'

'She's just so damn young and inexperienced. It's like telling off Pollyanna for her optimism.'

Gemma felt an unworthy burst of pleasure to hear her rival dismissed. Not that they were rivals. She and Sam were over, weren't they?

'How can I help? Want to go for a drink?'

'That would be better than beating the crap out of another stone urn.'

'Ah. Where are you attacking innocent garden ornaments?'

'Far side of the grounds from you.'

Gemma had an inkling now what might have been the source of the earlier shout of frustration. 'Meet you at the pub?'

'Yeah, good idea. Save the stones from further abuse.'

Sam looked rumpled and stressed when he entered the pub. Gemma had decided to rescue him from the ordeal of talking to Tim at the bar and had taken a guess that he'd like a pint of the same brew he'd ordered last time. She waved at him from the seat at the rear she had picked, the one Tim had promised was out of his eye-line. Not that she was sure she believed the irrepressible landlord: he'd probably put in a mirror just to see what was going on behind his back.

'Here. This OK?' She pushed the drink over to him.

'Perfect.' He took a couple of gulps. 'That's much better already.'

Gemma couldn't tear her eyes from his hands cradling the bottom of the beer glass. It was hard to forget what they felt like on her skin now she'd experienced that. *You're here to help him get over this crisis,* she scolded herself, *not fantasise about the man.* 'So, do you want to talk about the situation with Camille?'

'I don't know.'

She plucked a strand of grass out of his hair. 'You don't have to. We can chat about anything you like to take your mind off things.'

'I'm not sure I can do that either.'

'Then we can just sit. Or I can talk so the silence isn't awkward.'

'I don't find silence with you awkward.'

That was a lovely compliment. 'Nor do I. OK. Let's just sit.' She let the sounds of the pub envelop them: the hum of conversation punctuated by Tim's raucous laugh, the clink of glasses and scrapping of chairs on the stone floor. The pub dog, a black Labrador, padded over and thrust its head into Sam's lap. Sam gave it an absentminded scratch.

'It's all about Jennifer really,' he said suddenly.

'Jennifer?'

'Camille's older sister. I lived with her for a few years in London. That's how we know each other, Cammy and I.'

Gemma held her breath. She knew that one wrong move would stop this confession. She sipped her drink, keeping her movements casual so he wouldn't feel pressured.

'Jennifer wasn't stable. Looking back, it is fairly clear she had an undiagnosed mental illness. What started out as a fun relationship soon degenerated into a burden I couldn't carry. She wanted me to . . . I don't know . . . to run her life for her.' He rubbed his face, ineffectually trying to smooth away the stress lines. 'She saw me as taking all responsibility for everything at home and even in her personal life. I was at fault if she wasn't happy, or if I didn't understand her mood. It was impossible, like living with a dictator who expects you to anticipate her every whim and threatens death if you get it wrong – though in her case it was her death that was waved around as a warning.' He subsided and spun the beer glass slowly, studying it from every angle.

'That wasn't fair on you.'

'No, it wasn't. But maybe I should've realised and got her more help?'

'Did you encourage her to go to her GP when you were worried about her state of mind?'

'Of course. I suggested counselling too – found some good people for her to see. And she went. I think she went – she told me she went.'

'Then you did what you should – what you could. She was an adult after all, not your child.'

He looked up at her, his eyes anguished. 'But I gave up chasing her to help herself, Gemma. I got so tired I stopped caring. I failed her.'

Gemma had enough self-blame herself to know that this was the real sorrow he carried. 'I'm not sure about that.'

He gave a dark laugh and took a swallow of beer. 'Oh, I did, believe me.'

'If you didn't care, then why are you still suffering?'

He shrugged.

'You mustn't confuse your exhaustion with not caring. You were struggling, out of resources, out of your depth. You're not Superman even though you might like to think you are. Sometimes you just have to hoist the white flag and say you give up. If the professionals didn't pick up on it and get it handled, then how could you?'

He was silent for a while, taking in what she had said. 'I guess you're right. Is that what you're doing now by going home? Raising the white flag?'

'I've decided it's a weakness not to ask for help when I'm drowning.'

He nodded, accepting that. 'And what if I told you that I felt relief when she died? She took an overdose and I wasn't there to stop her, but when I did find her, dead on the sofa, I couldn't be sad as I should've been – I felt numb. Dazed that it was finally over. How bad is that?'

'What makes you think I expect you to be good and pure all the time? Everyone has these ugly emotions from time to time; it's whether we act on them that matters. Did you dance round the room and celebrate?'

'No.'

'You were probably in shock. What did you do?'

'I called the ambulance, tried to give her CPR but I was far too late. It felt like it was happening to someone else.'

'There. Don't beat yourself up for being human. And I bet you did grieve, if not at first, then when you'd got over the shock.'

'I grieved for missed chances, for a wasted life, and I suppose for my old self that wasn't afraid of being with someone. He died too that night.' Sam reached out and took her hand. 'Thank you for listening. This is maudlin stuff. I don't usually do this.'

'Don't belittle what you went through. You're not being maudlin. And I'm just trying to be a friend by listening.'

'And you are – a much better friend than I am to you.' He let the pause stretch. 'What can I do to help you? We haven't really talked properly about what's happening in your life.'

'I'm fine. I'm a big girl. Yes, I'm running home for a while but I don't mean to stay there. I just want to Ray-proof my life and get a decent job. My dad will try to solve my problems with money. I'll let him spend on his grandson but not on me: that's my red line which I'm not going to cross. I feel OK about my decision as long as that's what I stick to.'

'You impress the hell out of me, Gemma Whitehall.'

'Why thank you, sir.' She gave him a wry smile.

His stroked her wrist, making her pulse leap. 'I don't think I've ever wanted anyone more than I want you right now. I've felt so alone since we argued. That was stupid of us. I miss you.'

With her body already waking up to the gorgeous man opposite her, Gemma wondered what harm it would do to act on that impulse? If he wanted her, she wanted him a million times more. 'We could do something about that, you know? Just as friends.'

'God, I'm so pleased you said that.' He drained his beer. 'Ever made love in an orangery?'

'Can't say I have.'

'Nor have I. I think we need to rectify that.' He got up and pulled her to her feet. 'Let's hurry.'

* * *

261

With Gemma's head resting on his chest, Sam knew he was never going to be able to come into his glasshouse without thinking of her. Relaxing after making love to her on the nest of seat cushions he'd built, he remembered how she'd laughed and called it her bower. She'd then teasingly removed her clothes and welcomed him into her arms. It had been the most sexy thing he'd ever seen.

'I should've made love to a friend more often,' he murmured.

He could feel her lips curling into a smile. 'I'm sure Neil would've been delighted.'

He winced. 'What I meant was I don't think my relationships before and after Jennifer have really been friendships. That's pretty lowering to admit.'

'So you were all "wham, bam, thank you, ma'am"?' She shifted to balance her chin on her crossed hands so she could look down at him. 'I don't think you're alone in that. Lots of us confuse ourselves, wondering why a relationship doesn't last when it's just built on attraction and nothing else. That fizzles without something deeper to power it.'

'That's your experience?'

She flopped back, which left him with a rather spectacular view of her breasts under the wash of golden light from the up-lighters hidden among the plants. She put the back of her hand to her forehead. 'My experience? That's so limited, I'm embarrassed to admit it. I suppose I'm going by what I've seen in others.'

He leaned over and dropped a kiss between her breasts. 'You are just the loveliest woman I've ever met.' His compliment didn't please her as he expected, instead she sat up and reached for her top.

'Thanks,' she said shortly.

'You OK?' What had he done?

She gave him a wobbly smile. 'Will be. The problem I have is that I can't quite stop at friendship with you. When you say such lovely things to me, my stupid heart wants the whole deal and I know that's not on offer.'

Wasn't it? Sam was no longer so sure. 'Gemma . . .'

She put a hand to his lips to prevent him speaking. 'You don't have to say anything. I totally get where you're coming from. You're still mending. You've only this evening got to the point where you can talk to me about your past. I can't expect a miraculously repaired heart and you can't hurry the process of healing. Just, you know, if you get to the stage when you are ready, promise you'll give me a call, OK?'

The door to the orangery squeaked open. 'Sam, are you in here?' It was Camille.

'Crap!' Sam reached for his boxers. Gemma pulled one of the seat cushions over her middle. 'Hang on, Cammy, stay where you are. Is it Dad?'

'No, he's in bed. I saw a light. I was worried about you. You didn't come back and you didn't eat anything. I'd made a dessert.' Camille had taken no notice of his warning and came round the stack of chairs. 'Oh.'

Gemma gave a huff of sound that might've been laughter or embarrassment, he wasn't sure.

'As you can see, I was busy.' Sam was sure his face was beet red.

She turned quickly round. 'Sorry. Um, awkward.'

'Hi, Camille,' said Gemma.

'I didn't realise . . .'

'Why don't you go back to the cottage? I'll be there in a moment,' said Sam.

'Yes, I'll do that.' Camille hurried away.

Once the door to the orangery closed, Gemma let go of the laugh she had been repressing.

'I'm glad you find it funny,' Sam said, irritated that she could see the funny side when all he could feel was humiliation being caught practically in the act.

She threw the cushion aside and buttoned her shirt. 'You don't get it: it feels kinda good to me.'

'How?'

'She's got a crush on you, Sam. You must've noticed?'

'Camille has *what* on me?'

Gemma sighed. 'Men: dumb as a pile of bricks. Yes, she idolises you and she's been sending me "keep off, you old bag" signals at every opportunity.'

'I didn't realise.'

'Yes, big boy, I'm getting that. So, to find us lounging naked in the glasshouse is a score for me. Does my ego no end of good.'

'You don't mind being seen like this?'

She shrugged. 'If it had been your dad or Leo, then, yes, I'd mind; but Miss Muffet? No.'

'Miss Muffet?' Sam's lips quirked in a smile.

'So, I suppose playtime is over?' She wriggled back into her jeans.

'I'm afraid it is.' It was a crying shame to see all the delectable flesh being covered up.

She went up on tiptoe to kiss him. 'Thank you for this moment – and for all the other moments. We probably shouldn't do it again though. I don't think my heart can take it.'

He pulled her gently to him, relishing the feel of her lithe body nestled against his. He couldn't speak, didn't want to risk committing. She was right that he needed time. The last person on earth he wanted to hurt was Gemma and he knew he was not good at relationships. He had stuff he needed to sort out before he promised her anything. He also reminded himself that Gemma was first and foremost a parent. Being with her meant taking on Leo too: he couldn't play at that and mess it up. He didn't rate his step-parenting skills highly enough.

'OK, back you go to make your apologies to Miss Muffet for shocking her like that.' Gemma caressed his cheek. 'It'll be OK, the opening. I have every faith that you'll work something out.'

Reminded of his duties again after his brief holiday, Sam sighed. 'Thanks. I'm going to give it my best shot. She hasn't left me any choice.'

Chapter 22

Leo was feeling the need for munchies. Battling the ridiculously slow broadband was frustrating and he decided he had earned a break. His new video of game footage was uploading so his channel would soon be back in business on YouTube with fresh content. He just had to hope he hadn't lost too many followers during his absence. But what to eat? He'd scouted the kitchen earlier and knew there wasn't much in stock but Mum made sure there was always cereal to fill him up.

Checking the time, he saw that it was midnight – way later than he thought. He crept downstairs, hoping not to disturb his mother.

'Leo?' She wasn't in bed as he had expected but was sitting curled up in an armchair, one of her books balanced open on the arm. 'Are you OK?'

'Hungry.'

'Ah. There's nothing very interesting to eat, I'm afraid.'

'Just getting a bowl of cereal.' He padded into the kitchen and filled his bowl to capacity. Mum looked different tonight. Sad maybe? He knew she was upset about losing her job so

Eve Edwards

he should try to cheer her up. He thought what she did was pretty cool, even though he'd never admit that to her. Not everyone would have the confidence to stand up and marry people every day. The very thought of speaking in public like that made him want to be sick.

He plonked himself down on the sofa and dug in with his spoon. 'You all right, Mum?'

She hugged her knees to herself. 'I'm fine, darling. I was just thinking.'

In the soft light of the table lamp, he was struck all of a sudden by how young she was. He didn't like thinking like that. Some of his classmates had sisters her age. She was what . . .? Just fifteen years older than him? He hadn't ever considered that before but she had been only a year more than he was now when she'd had him. What would he do with a baby if he got landed with one? Crunching on a big spoonful, he upgraded his mum from 'cool' to 'heroic'.

'What were you thinking?' His words didn't come out clearly through the mouthful of Cheerios but she made sense of them.

'Oh, I don't know.' She rested her head on the back of the armchair, eyes closed. 'Have you ever wanted something so much that it hurts?'

He nodded. He'd really wanted that laptop.

'But you know it's useless as you can't order the world to deliver it to you? It just doesn't work out that way?'

He wondered if he could save up for whatever 'it' was by taking more odd jobs when they moved in with his grandparents. 'What do you want, Mum?'

She laughed. 'It's nothing.'

'If it is important to you, it isn't nothing.'

'Aw, thanks, Leo.'

'So what do you want?' He hoped it wasn't too expensive because he only had a few months before Christmas.

'Only someone to fall in love me and share my life.'

'Oh.'

'See? It's not something that I can fix because it depends on other people.'

'I'm here, Mum.'

'I know, darling, but it's not too long before you leave for college and I'm thinking ahead. I'll be lonely. You're my wonderful son but I was thinking of a partner – another adult.'

He wondered if he should mention dating websites, but that would be weird with his own mother. 'Does it matter who the person is?' His mind then made the obvious connection. 'Is this about Sam? Do you like him?'

She pulled a face. 'Yes, I like Sam.'

'That's OK then because he likes you too.'

'I know he does. We're friends. But it's not going anywhere.'

'Why not?'

'It's complicated.'

He'd heard that line on TV before. 'They always say that.'

'Because it's true.'

'It shouldn't be: you're single, he is too. What's the problem?'

She got up and took his empty bowl from him, ruffling his hair in passing. 'Indeed. That's why it's complicated. Time for bed. We've both got work in the morning, remember?' She carried the bowl to the sink to wash up.

Leo went upstairs to clean his teeth. Turning the tap, the pipes sang and rattled from the trapped air. He didn't know why he hadn't seen it before now: Mum and Sam were perfect for each other. She liked old stuff and history; Sam had a castle. Sam hosted weddings; Mum conducted them. Sam wasn't bad looking for an older guy and Leo supposed Mum still looked good despite being almost thirty. If they got together, Mum and Sam would be happy, he wouldn't have to move or change schools, and he would have a place of his own, not a box room in his grandparents' house. Living in a castle would be epic, give him real bragging rights.

But the Wi-Fi would still suck.

Leo wriggled under the duvet, balancing his needs with his mum's. OK, the broadband would usually be a deal-breaker, but he would prefer Mum to be happy. Before he fell asleep, he vowed that he would do what he could to make it happen because the adults were too shortsighted to see a good thing dangling before their noses.

The following morning, Sam put down the phone with a thrill of pleasure. The manager of Wild Thyme, Mr Coralto, had been enthusiastic to meet his father, particularly after Sam mentioned William's background as a gardener at Kew. Mr Coralto took a particular interest in maintaining the grounds of the home and enjoyed the pleasure the residents took in their surroundings.

'My dad would probably do more than look,' Sam had warned. 'He'll try and help out.'

'Excellent. The more the merrier,' boomed Mr Coralto, who had a voice that needed no amplification.

They'd agreed to visit that afternoon.

Sam looked up to find Leo hovering. The boy had been behaving oddly all morning, talking non-stop about Gemma, mentioning what a good cook she was when she had the ingredients and how caring she was. He didn't need prompting to have a high opinion of her; he was already in her fan club. It was getting a little annoying.

'Need something, Leo?'

'I was just wondering if you wanted to come to dinner at ours tonight?'

'Did your mother ask you to ask me?'

Leo looked away. 'No, but I know she won't mind.'

'After a full day at work, she might.'

'I'll cook.'

'You can cook?'

'I can follow a recipe – and my lettuce is ready. We had some last night.'

Sam realised that he'd been dense: the boy had been angling to impress him with his first homegrown produce but been going the long way round to make it happen. 'That's great, Leo. It's a good feeling, isn't it? You must show Dad too.'

'Oh I will, but Cammy can give him dinner. I was thinking that it would be nice just to have you. On your own. I can make myself scarce.'

This was odd. 'If your mother would like company.'

'She will – I promise.'

Sam didn't have time to work out what the boy really

wanted. It passed through his mind that Leo might want to have a man about the place in case his father came calling, or maybe he was hoping Sam would let them stay on at the cottage? He couldn't explain that Gemma had already shut down that option. 'Fine. Ask her and let me know. I've got to take Dad into Bury. Will you keep Camille company? She needs help with her displays for the castle and the website.'

Leo grinned. 'Cool. See you later then.' He bounded off, letting the door bang behind him.

It was only when he'd gone that Sam realised he'd forgotten to have the conversation with Camille nailing down the time of her return to London. The trip into Bury would've been the perfect opportunity to drop her at the station but now he'd given her another day's grace by sending Leo to assist her. He had all the backbone of an earthworm. Feeling guilty about inadvertently exposing in a very literal sense his relationship with Gemma to Camille last night was part of the mix. He hadn't been able to face her this morning and she had avoided him.

His dad shuffled into the kitchen wearing one slipper but otherwise fully dressed.

'Dad, I've found another house with a nice garden that might suit you,' Sam said brightly. 'Would you like to visit?'

'What's wrong with this one, Sam?' his father grumbled. At least he was fully present for this discussion, not afloat on the seas of the past. Sam knew he had to press the matter while his dad could take an informed view.

'Nothing, but this is my house, isn't it? A bit cramped for us both. I was thinking of finding you somewhere of your own where you have friends around you.'

'You're getting rid of me? I thought we were rubbing along just fine. You certainly need a hand with your garden.'

'Dad, do you remember burning yourself?'

William looked down at his palm.

'I know you know that you aren't always on the top of things. You have moments where you forget what you're doing. I can't keep you safe here and that worries me. If you had a nice residential home somewhere nearby where there were people on hand to help, you can spend lots of time here, but still be somewhere where I don't have to worry about you.'

William sighed and sat down, his shoulders a little hunched as if defeated. Sam absolutely didn't wish for that. 'I don't want you to worry about me, Sam.'

'Then you'll come with me and see what it's like?'

'If it would make you happy.' William sounded very glum about the prospect. He was probably remembering the plastic plants at the last place they'd visited.

'I'm hoping it will make you happy, Dad. Let's just give it a chance. It's got to be right for both of us. Nothing will happen without you agreeing to it, I promise.'

When she got home from work, Gemma was astonished to find Leo prepping vegetables for the evening meal. She dumped the shopping bag on the table and gave him a hug from behind.

'Hey, what's all this, sunshine?'

He playfully flicked water at her. 'Sam's coming for dinner. Is that OK?'

'He is?'

'I want him try my lettuce.'

Gemma looked at the paltry few leaves left behind from yesterday's salad. 'OK then. But I think it might have to be a garnish.' She opened the bags to survey her picks in her last-minute dash after work around the supermarket. 'I wish you'd let me know earlier. I got us some fish but it's going to be a struggle to make it go round.'

He shrugged. 'I don't need to eat with you. I'll got up to the cottage once he's tried the lettuce and scrounge something off Camille. I told her I'd be over.'

Gemma knew her son well enough to know this uncharacteristic behaviour had a cause, not that she could fathom it. 'What's going on, Leo?' She recalled her unguarded words at midnight and her suspicion grew. 'Are you trying to set Sam and me up for a date?'

Leo flushed but continued peeling the potatoes with the ineptitude of someone doing it for the first time. 'No!'

She took the peeler from him. 'Here, like this.'

'Right. Got it.' He took it back and, with improved technique, tackled the last of the spuds.

'So are you going to explain why Sam's coming round for dinner?'

'I was talking to Camille this afternoon . . .'

Gemma turned away because it was her turn to blush. 'Yes?' she squeaked, unpacking the shopping.

'She says she's messed up. She went overboard with her plans to help Sam and really made him mad.'

'Sam told me.'

'I said we'd help her sort it out.'

274

'We will?'

'Yeah, of course. Sam's our friend. Helping her, helps him, and, anyway, Camille is cool.'

To a fourteen-year-old boy, Gemma could well see the attraction with the bright-eyed blonde. 'What do you think we can do?'

'The wedding is on 9th September. You won't be working by then.'

'Thanks for the reminder.'

'I thought we could stay around and help set things up – you know, a kind of last thank you to Sam for employing me and everything before we move?'

'He might not want our help.'

'You could offer, couldn't you?'

Gemma filled the kettle to buy herself time. She remembered the morning Mr Ranworth had nearly wandered into the road. It had been Leo that saved him. When had her son become a more selfless person than her? He had nothing to gain now he had his laptop. 'You're right. Sam's really worried about this opening. If we can stop it being a failure, then that's a really good thing for us to do. I should've seen it myself.' She hadn't offered to help last night because Sam had always seemed so adamant that his castle and his business were his to handle. She hadn't wanted to impose but she would get very old if she waited for him to ask for her help.

Leo nodded as if that was the only answer he expected. 'Great. I've been thinking about it and I thought that, as you know about weddings and stuff, you can do that side; Camille can finish the displays; I can do the website and help Sam if he needs it about the garden – that's in-between looking after Mr Ranworth, of course.'

'Of course,' she said faintly. If only his teachers could see this side of Leo, they wouldn't be complaining about his lack of social engagement at school. 'Wow, you've really given this some consideration.'

'We can all be there to help on the day as you won't be working at weekends any more.'

She was going to have to watch one of her colleagues conduct the wedding that she had originally been booked to perform: wasn't that a blow to her hopes of sliding away and never having to think about what she'd lost? 'OK, I'll ask Sam tonight.'

'Good.' Leo tipped the potatoes in the saucepan. 'Do I need to start cooking these yet?'

Gemma smiled. 'Not unless you want them to disintegrate into mush before we eat. You've done enough, Leo. I'll take it from here.'

Grinning with relief, Leo headed upstairs. 'I'm just going to take a shower before I see Cammy then.'

Shaking her head, Gemma filled the teapot. The relationships at Claremont were becoming convoluted. She and Sam were in a doomed affair. Camille had a crush on the castle owner. Leo had a crush on Camille.

Mind you, a shower was a good idea if they had a guest for dinner.

'Don't use all the hot water!' she called up the stairs.

* * *

Sam entered the cottage bearing a bottle of wine. 'Leo messaged me that it was fish so I guessed white, is that OK?'

'Perfect.' Conscious of her son hovering by the sink, she made her kiss brief and on the cheek. 'I'll pop it in the fridge.'

Sam rubbed his hands together. 'So, Leo, where are the fruits of your labour?'

Leo gestured to the windowsill. 'Over there. I've got to run. See you later, Mum. I'll go right upstairs when I get back. I won't come in here and disturb you, OK?' He dashed out of the cottage letting the door bang behind him, a typical Leo exit.

Sam arched a brow. 'What just happened? I thought he wanted me to see his lettuce?'

Gemma smiled. 'He did, but you forget that you have a pretty young woman at your house. Her attractions beat lettuce.'

'Leo's sweet on Cammy?'

'Sam, Sam,' said Gemma in a singsong voice, 'what am I to do with you? Don't you notice this stuff? He's fourteen: of course, he has a crush on her.'

'He knows she doesn't . . .?'

'He does know somewhere inside that girls her age do not consider boys of his age romantically but he's enjoying the idea of her. Don't worry: your father's there to act as chaperone.'

'And all that about not disturbing us?'

'Either he's worried he'll interrupt us like last night, though I hope Camille didn't mention anything . . .?'

'I don't think she would. We were both wracked with embarrassment over that so I can't see her blurting out the details to your son.'

'Phew. I did wonder. The second possibility is that he knows I want to talk to you and didn't want to break into a serious moment.'

Sam helped her lay the table. 'Talk to me? Sounds bad.'

'It's not, believe me, but dinner's ready so maybe we should eat?'

Gemma was pleased with the meal when she pulled the dish from the stove: not bad, considering how little notice she'd had. She'd made a parsley sauce for the fish and finished off the mashed potatoes in the oven with a cheese topping. The runner beans were a fortuitous gift from a work colleague who had a glut on his allotment and was feeling particularly sorry for her.

'This is wonderful,' said Sam as she put the plate down in front of him.

With a flourish, Gemma produced a lettuce leaf and placed it on top of the fish. 'The finishing touch.'

'Ah, yes. No meal is complete without something you've grown yourself.'

'Then you'll be pleased by the blackberry and apple crumble for dessert.

'You're really spoiling me, Gemma. Thanks.'

'You're lucky I had enough food in. Leo only broke the news you were coming when I got home.'

'He didn't?' Sam groaned. 'I'm sorry. I told him to ask you at lunchtime.'

'He's my son – you don't need to apologise. Anyway, it's worked out fine. We all got what we wanted.'

Sam unscrewed the cap on the white wine and poured her a glass. He then raised his in a toast. 'To Leo and his schemes.'

'I can drink to that.' She took a sip. 'Ah. That hits the spot. On the subject of schemes, he's been having a heart-to-heart with Camille. He wants to help with the opening – and so do I. In fact, he's demanded I do. It's quite shaming to realise my son is more noble than I am.'

Sam opened his mouth to speak.

'Let me get this out, Sam. I realise you don't ordinarily ask for help but these are extraordinary circumstances. Your business is on the line. As you know, I'll be out of a job at the end of next week as I'm taking the redundancy. They're giving me a couple of months pay so I have a little cushion while I look for work. I'd like to offer to organise the wedding and the reception for the VIPs that Camille invited. In other words, I'll volunteer here for a couple of weeks before we move.'

He cleared his throat. 'You don't have to do that.'

'I know I don't, but you're my friend and I care about Claremont.'

'It's not your responsibility, Gemma.'

'I know that too but, if you have to sell up, I can't see anyone else stepping forward to look after it. They didn't in the last hundred years so I'm doubting there's anyone waiting in the wings to take over.' And Gemma had become absurdly attached to the old place, in particular, the way it had struggled to survive over the centuries despite so many attempts to raze it to the ground.

'No, there's not,' he conceded. 'There was a developer interested in the land but with a mind to building houses near the village. No one else is mad enough to revive the garden.'

Time for some straight talking. 'To be frank, Sam, I think

you're going to need a lot more money eventually to invest in this place. You can't run it on a staff of one.'

'I know, but I was hoping I had more time.'

'I've had a few ideas if you want to hear them, about how you can diversify your income stream.'

He winced and took a gulp of wine.

'Oh dear, I sound like Camille, don't I?'

'A little. But the difference is you aren't fresh out of college with stars in your eyes.'

'Yes, I bypassed the whole college thing, sadly. What she's suggesting is good – it's just the speed at which she wants things to happen that's at fault.'

'You think I was too hard on her?'

'No, of course not. She's dumped you in a pile of trouble. She needs to know that or she'll not learn anything from this experience. And that's what I have to offer: plenty of experience of visiting wedding venues and I know what makes a successful one that gets repeat business.'

He gave her a wondering look. 'I suppose you do. I hadn't really thought of that.'

'You thought I just filled out forms?'

'Is there an answer to that which doesn't get me into trouble?'

'Probably not.' She laughed. 'Look, Sam, you've got potential here but it needs developing. You can't rely on weddings to keep you afloat.'

'So, what do other places do?'

'Have you heard of glamping?'

He nodded.

'Get some yurts and develop the far paddock as a posh camping site. There's one the other side of Ipswich you can visit to see how it's done. City people really like that kind of thing. They've got used to it from the festival scene.'

'Anything else?'

'Stop me if I become a bore. I made a list.'

'Hit me with it.'

She unfolded her notes made while she waited for the crumble to cook. 'Festivals are another possibility. Start by running a medieval one with jousting, birds of prey displays and local food. Some of the stately homes do it around the area so I can't see why your castle can't join in the fun. It's much more appropriate in this setting and it will bring in the families and publicise that you're here.'

'OK. Jousts.'

Was she going on too much? 'Another idea: organise seasonal experiences.'

'I was already thinking of Halloween at the castle. Spend a night in the dungeon.'

'Not my idea of entertainment but someone will dig that. Weddings dry up over the winter so you need to offer something else. Christmas at the Castle. My Lord's Valentine's Day Dinner. Medieval Murder Mystery nights. There are companies that will come in and run the murder evenings for you, bringing the actors to take the various parts.'

Sam gave her one of his heart-stopping smiles. 'I'm not sure as a former Metropolitan police officer I should allow that kind of thing in my castle.'

'No, that makes it even better! Brilliant idea: you could be the detective! That would the the USP. I think I'm getting carried away. I could go on but our food is getting cold. I'm going to shut up.'

Sam polished off his meal and pushed the empty plate away. 'You've given me a lot to think about. I'm not sure I can do all this and my immediate problem is the opening.'

'That's why you need to give in gracefully and accept our help – me and Leo. I think Di and her husband would also come onboard if I ask them. They've sons around Leo's age – they could help do some gardening if you give them pocket money for it.' She kept quiet about their tendency to kick a football at anything recently planted. 'Then there's the village people.'

Sam chuckled. 'Not YMCA?'

She rolled her eyes. 'No, I mean Tim and the others. Ask if any of them have time to help. If you're getting national press interested and VIPs, I bet you'll get volunteers. What helps you, helps the village.'

'Cammy did mention Monty Don and Bob Flowerdew were possibles.'

'There you are: that's sorted. The ladies of a gardening persuasion will be up here with their secateurs before you can say "Gardener's World".'

Sam frowned, but she was relieved to see that it was in thought rather than from stress. He was taking this better than anticipated. 'Phil and Neil – they'd want in too. In fact, they'd never forgive me if I left them out.'

'That's my point: you don't have to do this alone.'

He reached out and squeezed her hand. 'When did you get to be so wise?'

'At about a quarter to six when my teenage son put me right about the duties of friendship.'

'Come here. You're too far away.' He pulled her to sit beside him. 'Is this OK?'

Gemma nodded. Neither of them seemed able to stick to their resolution that things were over between them. As soon as they were close enough, they kept coming back together like the north and south poles of two magnets. They were hopeless.

He looked into her eyes, deep emotion shining in the depths of his gaze. He was such a hidden well of strong feelings, like the castle well he'd just found in one of the lost gardens. There was so much work to do to clear both. 'Thank you, Gemma. For this – and for the tip about the home. Dad liked it and is coming round to the idea – at least, he is if he remembers that tomorrow. The manager loved Dad and said he could move in if we get our skates on. It looks like it might be the perfect solution.'

'Oh Sam, I'm so pleased.'

Sam sat back and tapped her nose. 'OK, I agree.'

'Agree to what?'

'Do your worst, Gemma Whitehall. Call in the cavalry – write me a business development plan. I promise I'll pay you for that once I've chased the wolf from the door.'

'No need. It's an offering of . . .' She wanted to say love but that was unfair at this moment when he'd finally unbent enough to accept help, '. . . friendship.'

'And I'm grateful.'

'So, the peasant at your gate isn't such a bad thing then? You'll let me help?'

'Peasant? I'd say you and Leo were more like an invading army of Templar Knights, but I surrender.'

Chapter 23

Surrendering led to unexpectedly rapid consequences. Sam had imagined Gemma would wait until she gave up work, not that she would start phoning everyone on her list of potential volunteers the very next day. She left him to contact Neil, which he did with some reluctance as he anticipated his friend was going to tease him unmercifully. After Sam had explained his request for all hands on deck, Neil immediately agreed that he and Phil would come up the next weekend and for the big day itself.

'What I can't get over though, is that you, Mr I-am-an-Island, is actually asking for help,' said Neil, wonderingly.

Sam had been hearing strange noises in the background of the call and a particular loud grunt couldn't go unremarked. 'Neil, where on earth are you?'

'I'm in the gym near work.'

The noise now made sense as that of running machines, but Neil's presence there did not. 'You are at a gym – in your lunch hour?'

'Is that so strange?' Neil's tone was a little spiky.

'Frankly, yes.'

'It's all right for you, with your body like a Greek god and regular exercise. Now I'm married, I need to work harder to keep Phil's interest. He said the other day we were both getting a little out of shape and he's taken up running. He goes out at seven each morning.'

The ink was barely dry on his marriage certificate and already Neil was fretting. His friend was never going to have a quiet life. 'That doesn't mean that he's going off you.'

'I didn't say that, but I can't imagine standing next to him when he's all ripped and no longer my comfortable old Phil, not without trying to tone up to match. People will wonder what he sees in me. *I'll* wonder what he sees in me. So, here I am, drinking a protein shake and summoning up the courage to join in.'

'Probably should've done it the other way round.'

'What?'

'Exercise then shake.' His friend's worries reminded Sam again that relationships were on ongoing work in progress, not completed by wedding bells no matter what the fairy tales suggested. 'You need to talk to him about this, Neil. That man loves you as you are. It's fine to get fit but not if you're doing it because you're scared.'

'Me talk to him, like you talk to the women in your life?'

'You would've been proud of me: I did in fact, talk to Gemma about Jennifer.'

'Oh my word, you must be serious about her.'

'It's not like that. We've moved on to being friends.'

Neil snorted. 'How on earth did you get her to accept that steaming pile of manure?'

'She knows about my commitment issues.'

'You mean how you're plain petrified it will go wrong again?'

'That was the gist of the conversation.'

'And this is the woman who is helping to save your business from being flushed down the toilet? My man, when are you going to wise up to the good thing within your grasp? You'd be an idiot to let that one go because you are afraid to come out of your castle.'

'How about you talk to Phil about your body issues before you read me a lecture about my fear?'

'Good point. I will. The question is: will you?'

When Sam ended the call, he was deeply uncomfortable that he and Neil had been talking relationships. He didn't normally do that and imagined few men of his age did. Neil had always been an exception, right out there with his emotions. He'd talked and Sam had listened: that had worked for them both for years. Gemma's entrance into his life was having a transformative effect and he wasn't sure he enjoyed the changes. Part of him did want to creep back in the castle as Neil suggested and draw up the bridge.

Deciding that he really had to take a leaf out of his own book of well-meaning advice, he tracked Camille down to the keep where she was measuring up the spaces she wanted to use for her historical displays.

'Cammy?'

'Sam!' The way her face lit up when he sought her out told Sam he'd been a complete idiot. Gemma was right. How had he missed this? The girl did have feelings for him. Just because he'd never considered a romance with someone almost two decades younger than him, *and* Jennifer's sister, didn't mean that she hadn't developed her own hopes.

'I really appreciate all you've been doing to turn things around so we'll be ready.'

'Thanks. I'm enjoying myself. What do you think about a display about the building of the keep in here?'

'That's great, but not where the weddings take place. We need to keep the walls clear. How about in the entrance, over there?'

'Perfect.' She relocated with her measuring tape.

'Cammy?'

'Gemma's offered to project manage the wedding and I've accepted her offer.'

The smile didn't quite reach Camille's eyes. 'Oh wow, that's good.'

'Yeah, she is the expert on how to run the ceremonies. And I'm bringing in more help – we'll need to team up to pull this off. We'll all have to work together, OK?'

'Absolutely. It's definitely not a one man – or one woman – job. You need us all, Sam.'

'I realise that now, but Cammy, you do know, don't you, that I'm . . .' what was he? '. . . single at the moment, and if I was going to change that, well, Gemma and I, we have talked about dating – eventually. I'm not looking for anyone else. I've got lots of unresolved issues to work through from what happened with Jennifer. You're doing a better job dealing with her loss than I am.'

'Oh, Sam. I completely understand.' She hugged the tape

measure to her chest like a bride her bouquet. 'You just need time.'

'That's right. Time.'

Hoping he'd said enough, Sam went off to hack at the brambles strangling the castle well. It was dangerous left like that – someone could stumble in – Leo or his dad, God forbid. Better to see the danger clearly and fence it off.

Having put in a good few hours at the well, Sam returned to the cottage only to head right into another crisis. Leo was valiantly trying to stop his father walking out of the front door with a suitcase.

'Mr Ranworth, please!' Leo begged. Leo looked close to tears. 'Let me get Sam.'

'He doesn't want me here so I'm going back to Kew.' His father's face was set in adamant lines. 'I don't stay where I'm not wanted.'

'I'm here, Leo. Let me handle this. Dad, what's going on?' Sam wrestled the suitcase from William. It was so light he realised his father hadn't remembered to pack any clothes. That made it all even more poignant. His father sat down on a kitchen chair. At least he was back from the edge and no longer threatening to walk out. Sam didn't like the idea of physically restraining him – he wasn't sure he could.

'He was talking to your sister on the phone,' said Leo in a low voice. 'Everything was fine but then I think she said something about how glad she was you'd found him a nice home to go to.'

Sam silently cursed his sister. He'd mentioned he'd found a

strong contender, not that Dad had agreed. 'I think she rather jumped the gun.' He knelt beside his father. 'Dad, I promised you I wouldn't send you away unless you wanted to go.'

'I don't want to go to that place with plastic plants.' His poor dad had woken up confused. Dementia had a way of wiping out progress. 'The doors were locked!'

'Don't you remember where we went yesterday? The place with the big garden? You liked it when you were there. You and Mr Coralto hit it off. It wasn't the place with the fake pot plants.'

William's gaze skittered around the room, resting anywhere but on Sam's face. 'Hah. Hah-hah! Hah. Hah-Hah!'

Sam got up and put a hand on Leo's shoulder. 'Don't get scared, Leo. Dad does that when he's not feeling so good.'

Fortunately, Leo was taking it in his stride. 'I know. When he gets like that I try to distract him. What about giving him some flowers to plant out?'

'Good idea. There's some on the potting bench in the back garden. Best if you ask him. At the moment, in his mind, I'm the guy trying to lock him away.'

'Mr Ranworth? I need some help with some cuttings,' said Leo, taking the old man's hand.

'What? Who are you?'

'Your junior gardener. I'm pretty clueless about this stuff as you know.'

'Everyone has to learn. No one is born knowing how to be a gardener,' said William, focusing on the teenager.

Sam breathed a sigh of relief. If his dad was back to quoting his favourite gardening lore then they were coming out of the crisis. 'I'll bring you some tea.'

William's spine straightened as he assumed the dignity of his status as head gardener. 'You do that, dear boy. White and one sugar, remember?'

'Yes, I remember.'

That boy was really worth his weight in gold, thought Sam, watching Leo steer his father towards the potting bench. He felt a pricking in the corner of his eyes as Leo put a sunhat gently on William's head and guided him to stand in the shade. He couldn't be prouder if Leo had been his own son.

Camille bounced into the kitchen from her bedroom upstairs, the energy back in her step now she had a team of volunteers to help her with her plans. Sam had seen some boys from the village turn up to assist her that afternoon – the landlord's sons among them – but he'd kept clear. She seemed to have everything under control, sending them fetching and carrying for her. Team work was about delegation and he had that down from his time in the Met.

'Everything OK? I heard voices,' asked Camille.

If she'd been in and heard the row, why she hadn't rushed down to help? 'Fine. Dad was having a bad moment.'

'I thought it was probably something like that. Sam, the displays are arriving tomorrow afternoon. They put on a rush on the order when I explained about the opening. Will you be around to take delivery?'

'Yes, but where will you be?' She wasn't finally going home, was she, just when he decided he could put up with her presence for another fortnight so she could see her plans through to the conclusion?

'I was going to go into Bury to ask about flowers for the

arrangements in the keep. There won't be enough in the garden to make a big enough display – you need everything you have in the borders. I've got a number for a wholesaler and they said they can see me tomorrow.'

At least she wasn't planning to denude his grounds of all colour. 'Camille, the wedding displays in the keep are Gemma's responsibility as wedding organiser. That's what we agreed.'

'But she doesn't have time . . .'

'How do you know? Have you asked her?'

'Well, no . . .'

He pulled out his phone and texted even though Gemma was at work. *Quick question. Do you need help with flower arrangements?*

The reply was instantaneous. *No. Got it covered.*

He turned the phone round to show Camille. 'See.'

'Oh. OK. I suppose I'd better cancel?' She was still testing the boundaries.

He had his suspicions about her true motives. 'What would've happened if I'd let you go ahead without asking Gemma? Give me an honest answer. Put yourself in her shoes.'

'I suppose it would've upset her?'

'Exactly. Did you mean that to happen?'

She twisted her hands together before shoving them in the pockets of her jeans. 'No.'

'Maybe it's not fair of me to put you on the spot, Cammy, but we agreed that we are doing this as a team. If you are trying to score points off Gemma, it's going to mess that up.'

'I wasn't trying to score points.'

'Weren't you? Look, can we just agree that we all have to respect everyone on the team and not let personal agendas get in the way?'

'I don't have an agenda.'

Her denials were so flimsy he didn't think he need challenge them. He'd told her he wasn't looking at anyone other than Gemma. She'd get the message eventually that he saw through her little games. 'Great. Then thank you for all your help and let's all stick to what we agreed, OK? That way we'll all end up friends.'

'Got it. Friends.' She said it in such a way that he could almost hear the 'not likely'.

'So, you'll be here to take delivery of the displays?'

'Yes. Now I will be, I suppose. I'll phone and cancel my meeting.' Her tone was a little scratchy. It was a good sign if he was annoying her as that would be a fast cure for any unwanted feelings for him.

'And you can show the locals where to erect them?'

'Locals?'

'The landlord from the pub, Tim, and his oldest son are coming over. He claims they're good at that kind of thing.'

'Really?'

He smiled at her sceptical tone. 'When people volunteer, I'm hardly in a position to ask them to prove their abilities. Just roll with it, Cammy. You'll like Tim.' That's if she didn't hate him after an hour in his company. Tim had worked hard to earn his reputation as the Marmite of pub landlords.

* * *

On her last Friday at work, Gemma packed up her few personal belongings from her desk. She'd refused a leaving party on the grounds that it would be extremely awkward for everyone. It was like they were survivors of a shipwreck adrift in an open boat pulling straws to see whom to sacrifice. OK, that was an exaggeration. No one was threatening to eat her. Yet she certainly didn't feel like celebrating her four years that had been so suddenly discarded. She opened the card they'd all signed. The messages were muted: variations on 'good luck' and 'hope it all works out'. They must have felt *schadenfreude* signing that. The whip round was welcome though. Under Di's influence they'd not bought her a bunch of flowers that would fade in a week, but a token for M&S. At least she could splash out on new undies or a decent bottle of wine. Come to think of it, Leo needed new shoes for school. He'd hate buying them there but the menswear department gave good value, better than the stuff he liked that fell apart in a month.

She tucked the card in her handbag, lamenting the fact that the dream of new briefs had been, well, so brief. A thong of a dream.

Di tapped on the door. 'You OK, Gem?'

'Fine. Just clearing out.'

'Here's an idea.' Di marched over and thrust a magazine in her hand.

'A makeover?'

'No, read the article.'

Gemma skimmed the piece on the woman they were giving a new look. 'A celebrant?'

'Uh-huh. With all these requests for unique, non-religious weddings and funerals, there's a growing demand for an experienced celebrant to take the ceremony. I don't know anyone locally doing this. I checked online and the nearest is the other side of Ipswich and I think he's a Druid, so that's not everyone's cup of tea.'

'I guess not.'

'You could set yourself up as freelance. Four years' experience in the council service. You're attractive and well spoken. I can see you being very popular if you market yourself properly.'

Gemma brushed her fingers over the image of the sixty-something lady from Islington who ended the piece channelling a Helen Mirren vibe, sharp silver haircut and equally sharp expression. 'You really think I could do that?'

'I'd say it's something worth thinking about. You've shown you've a head for business with the advice you've given Sam. I mean I knew you were a smart cookie but even I didn't know you had all these ideas brewing. Why not turn some of that business acumen on yourself?'

'This doesn't totally suck as an idea.'

Di laughed. 'High praise indeed. And when I get given the boot on the next round of cuts, I might just come and work for you.'

Gemma grinned. 'My door will always be open.'

'Phone the Druid. Ask him how it all works, how you register and the rest.'

'OK, I'll add that to my check list. Organise VIP reception. Arrange wedding flowers. Phone Druid.'

Di checked the reception. 'Great. My appointment's a no-show. Tell me about the floral displays.'

Gemma leant back against the filing cabinet. 'I'm using the language of flowers for each arrangement. The Tudors were really into that kind of thing.'

Diana looked blank.

'You must know that scene in *Hamlet* where Ophelia hands out flowers to everyone, each containing a meaning?'

'Gem, I hate to admit it but I didn't get through the play when it was on TV, even with David Tennant. So they used flowers like a kind of Tudor Hallmark card?'

'I suppose you could say that. Anyway, I've been researching it. I'm going to put little explanatory cards next to the arrangements and the garland over the dais where they'll be married.' She showed Diana her file of research. 'It's all in here. Do we know yet who's doing the wedding?'

Di winced. 'It's me, hon. And Gillian. We're short staffed so she's taking more weekend duties.'

'Of course you are. Do more with less: the new council motto.'

'Are you OK with us being there?'

'I'd rather it was you than anyone else.' Gemma remembered the conversation they had months ago when this wedding first appeared on the list. 'Are you dressing up?'

'Me? I can't imagine they had many black people in Tudor England.'

'That's where you're wrong. They were there, not in huge numbers, but as servants and diplomats, entertainers and sailors.'

Diana impulsively hugged her. 'Gem, what am I going to do without you?'

'Be miserable?' she suggested hopefully.

'That's a certainty. OK, I'll dress up. Are you?'

'Sam realised that if he were going to do these Tudor or Medieval themed events, then he'd need a few costumes for staff. He's got himself and Leo a doublet and hose and ordered a dress for me.'

'It almost sounds like you've got a happy family there.'

She tucked the file deep in her tote. 'Don't, Di. That's not what's going on.' It hurt too much to be teased.

'Isn't it? That guy is dumber than he looks if he doesn't do something about it soon.'

'We've reached a truce. He'll run in the opposite direction if you try to herd him towards me right now.'

'I shouldn't come dressed as a shepherdess then?'

Gemma had a brief flash of what Diana would look like in the peasant-style blouse of that costume with all her assets on display. 'I think your girls would upstage the bride.'

Diana adjusted her bust. 'Understood. I'll come up with something modest and I promise I won't let you down.'

Gemma loaded her belongings onto the passenger seat of her car. There wasn't even enough to warrant opening the boot. Looking around the car park, she said a final goodbye. It had been fun while it lasted and at least she was taking Diana's friendship home with her. Pulling out of the exit, she waited for a gap in the traffic before joining the cars heading out of Bury.

That was when the ambulance rammed her.

Chapter 24

Sam was up a ladder when he heard Leo calling him, panic evident in the boy's voice. Not his dad again?

'Over here, Leo! By the stone lion.' He climbed down quickly, dumping his hedge trimmer.

Leo raced into view, his face ashen.

Sam held out his arms to field the running boy. 'Hey there, slow down. Is it Dad?'

Leo grabbed Sam's forearms, breath sawing in his chest. 'No . . . it's Mum.'

Sam went cold. 'Gemma?'

'Diana, Mum's friend, she called, wanting to speak to you. Mum's in hospital. She's called my grandparents already and they're on their way but I've got to get there. Can you take me?'

Heart pounding, Sam pulled the boy into a one-armed hug. He had to keep calm for the boy's sake. 'OK, OK, tell me what she said. We'll go as soon as I know where we need to be.'

'She said Mum got hit by an old ambulance outside the council offices. It was her last day and everything.' Leo hiccupped.

'Was she on foot?' He sickened at the image that presented.

'No, in the car.'

That was a little more hopeful. There can't have been high speeds involved outside her office. 'Injuries?'

'Diana didn't know. She told me not to worry, just to come, but a real ambulance was called and took Mum to A&E. That sounds bad, doesn't it? Can we go now?'

'I'll just grab my keys.' Sending Leo to the car, Sam jogged towards the house, dialling Camille as he did so. She didn't reply. He tried Tim.

'Hey, Sam, you should see this display. It's looking good.'

'Tim, Gemma's been in a car accident. I'm taking Leo to the hospital right now.'

Tim's jovial tone turned serious. 'How bad?'

'I don't know. I need a favour.'

'Just ask.'

'Can you keep an eye on Dad? He's not had a good couple of days.'

'No problemo. Send Gemma our best. Let us know how she is.'

'Will do. Is Camille with you?'

'Yes.'

'Can you mention her phone's switched off? I need to be able to get in contact in case there's news.'

'Consider it done.'

'Thanks.'

'No thanks required. Get going.'

Sam grabbed his keys and checked on his dad. 'Tim's coming to see you, Dad,' he called into the front room where his dad was watching the racing.

'Tim who?'

'A friend. You'll see. Make him feel at home. He's got lots of hanging baskets at his pub. Ask him about those.'

Hoping that would distract his father from any more forays outside with his bags packed, Sam dashed to the car. Leo was already there, trying the doors even though they were locked – a habit left over from living in the city. Sam clicked them open.

'Right, let's go.' They scrambled in and Sam floored the accelerator. The car headed down the drive, flying over the speed bumps, but it wasn't fast enough for either of them. 'Can you call Diana back and ask her for an update?'

'I've been trying but her phone's not picking up.'

'She might be in the hospital. Your mum's going to be all right, I promise.' That was a stupid thing to say, but he couldn't bear to see Leo suffering.

'Should I phone Granny and Granddad, see how close they are?'

The boy was more on the ball than he was. 'Good idea.'

Sam listened in as Leo bravely updated his grandparents with the little he knew and that he had a lift to the hospital so they didn't need to divert to collect him. Leo ended the call and cleared his throat. 'They're already on the road, coming as fast as they can but it'll be an hour before they reach the hospital.'

'We'll be there in ten minutes.' Sam was breaking all road laws that he could without being a dangerous driver. Fortunately, his police training had taught him how to handle a high-speed chase. 'Do you want to tell your other gran? Gemma likes her, doesn't she, and she's closer?' If Gemma's condition was serious, then Ray's parents might be in a better place to support Leo than Gemma's parents – or him.

Gripped by such a feeling of devastation at the idea of losing her, Sam had to face the fact that he already loved her. He'd only just understood what had been growing inside him since she first stood up for her gnome and now, maybe, it was too late? No, he refused to be too late again. Gemma was not Jennifer. She'd be OK – he'd make sure of that if there was anything anyone could do with time and resources. He'd sell the damn castle if he had to.

'Phone Gran? Yeah, I'll do that.' This time Leo broke down on that call, beginning to sob as his gran offered him the telephonic equivalent of a cuddle. She promised to meet him at the hospital too.

As the miles passed, neither of them made any reference to the tears. Sam took a breath, trying to be the better man. This was about Leo, not what he thought of the individual in question. Gemma had made it plain Leo loved the guy. 'Do you . . . do you want to tell your dad?'

Leo looked up at him, expression bleak. 'I don't think that would be a good idea. Not until we know.'

Thank heavens for that. 'Yeah, good decision. That can wait.' The tosser would probably use it as an excuse to move in to 'look after' his son. 'You can stay with us, you know? That's if your mum has to be in overnight.' Or longer, but he wasn't going to raise that possibility.

Leo gave him a shaky smile. 'Thanks, Sam. You're the best.'

Sam pulled into the hospital car park. Best what, he wondered? He didn't have time to answer the question as they were in the A&E reception and Diana was beetling towards them.

'Leo!' She folded him to her breast even though he was many inches taller than her. 'Your mum's in surgery now but they said they would have a clearer picture of her injuries soon and would let me know. They also said not to worry – she's not in danger – but trust the doctors. She's got a good team seeing to her.'

Wanting the real update and not the reassuring one tailored for the son, Sam needed to talk to Diana without alarming Leo. 'Hey, Leo, would you get me something from the vending machine – and something for yourself? This might be a long wait.'

Leo looked relieved to have a task. 'What do you want?'

Sam passed him a handful of coins. 'Black coffee.' Leo went off to search for the machine. 'How serious?' Sam asked Diana.

'I don't know. They're not saying much.' Diana looked distraught, her usually neat bob of hair rumpled. 'It all happened so fast. Gemma didn't have a chance: her little car against a heavy old ambulance. A secondhand one. Some kind of conversion job into a campervan.'

'Did the other driver stop?'

'What do you think? It had no number plates. We're not dealing with an upstanding member of the community.'

'You saw the accident?'

She nodded. 'I was just leaving work. It was so strange: it looked like the ambulance was waiting for her. But ambulance, right? You quite often see those parked in strange places. It takes a moment to clock that it's not a real one – probably why the owner likes it. Anyway, it accelerated out of a side street and went straight into her Fiesta like driving was a game of dodgems. Normally, the collision should've just shunted her into the empty bus lane but a taxi was coming down at speed and rear-ended her. Her car span and hit a concrete bollard.'

'You think it was a deliberate shunt?'

'Looked that way.'

Sam then remembered the slashed tyres. Gemma had put that down to vandalism after he suggested Ray hadn't known about it but had they been wrong? Ray didn't drive or have access to an old ambulance, did he? He toyed with that possibility for a moment. Something told Sam that this was the wrong track. It seemed extreme for that loser, far more actively aggressive than his usual mode of waiting for the world to deliver. 'I know this seems an odd question, but does Gemma have any enemies?'

'Gemma? Of course not!'

'Did you see the driver?'

'Only a glimpse. He was a big guy. Bald.'

'Have you seen him hanging around at all?'

Diana bit her lip. 'I suppose he looked a bit like the man who was involved with the wedding scam we busted a month ago, but I couldn't swear to it.' The connection was made. 'Oh my God, do you think he's taking revenge on Gemma? If he was, I feel so guilty! It was me who blew the whistle on that fake wedding. Gemma was just the one conducting the ceremony.'

But Gemma had been the one standing up in public view. The scammers weren't to know and probably didn't care about the backstairs workings of the office. They might've been trying to intimidate the registrars into not daring to object next time they turned up. Perhaps they'd been intending just to give Gemma a shunt but that plan had got out of hand by the bad timing. 'You're going to have to tell the police – tell them this is more than a hit and run.'

'But this is Bury St Edmunds! I can't believe this would happen here.'

'You get low-lifes everywhere, Diana.'

She thumped her forehead. 'I know that. Of course, I know that. I'll call them.'

Leo returned with the drinks. It was punishment to sip the black coffee but that suited Sam's mood. He should've paid more attention. He had enough experience in the police to suspect that slashing four tyres was more than a random attack by a vandal. If it had been some kids on a spree, he would expect more than one car to be damaged, and possibly some other stuff done, like setting fire to the wheelie bins, keying car doors or tagging. To go right for a Fiesta at the far end of a car park, walking past other nicer vehicles that would make a more satisfying target, and then going to the effort of ensuring all the tyres were ruined: that showed deliberate malice.

Before he'd finished his coffee, Miriam arrived accompanied by her husband in his motorised scooter.

'Gran, Granddad!' Leo fell into his grandmother's arms.

'Oh Leo. It'll be all right, I promise,' crooned Miriam.

Waiting for the flurry of their arrival to pass, Sam introduced himself to the elderly couple.

Leo's grandad offered his hand. 'I'm Gordon. Pleased to

meet you, Sam, but not under these circumstances, obviously. What's the news about our girl?'

'She's in surgery. They said not to worry but, of course, we are,' said Diana.

'I'll go see if I can get anything more out of them. They know me here.' Gordon directed his scooter over to the admissions desk.

Miriam patted Diana on the shoulder. 'Don't fret, love. Gordon knows his way around this place. He used to be a hospital porter until his back got to him.'

Gordon returned after an earnest discussion with the lady on duty. 'It's as I thought. They're backed up at the desk and forgot to tell you she's already out of theatre and in recovery.'

'Why didn't they say anything?' protested Diana.

'You have to understand these places, Diana. You can sit here for hours waiting for information if you don't keep asking. They're fire-fighting bed crises over there and don't always have time. The good news is that they say the operation went well but they'll have to see how she is when she wakes before they can say anymore. She'll definitely be staying a while though.'

'Do we know the extent of her injuries?' asked Sam. He was only just now letting himself feel a little relief. He could begin to function again.

'They were operating on her ankle. It was a bad break and required pins. What they're most worried about is concussion and possible whiplash injuries. Those are what they need to assess. They thought at first she might've fractured her skull but the scan ruled that out.'

'Will I be able to see her?' asked Leo.

Gordon took his grandson's hand and gave it a squeeze. 'I know you want to but let's wait and see what the doctors say. The main thing is that she's not too badly hurt. It could've been much worse. Your mum is going to be just fine.'

Not long after, Margaret and James Whitehall arrived, prompting another round of explanations, with James declaring gruffly that he'd phone a friend who was an orthopaedic surgeon if he wasn't satisfied with the care she was receiving. Feeling excess to requirements, Sam left Leo in the care of both sets of grandparents. He had to do something or he'd go crazy. He couldn't pull strings like James, or wheedle infor-mation like Gordon, but he did have his own skills. Sam drove to the site of the crash. Gemma's car was still there, stranded in the bus lane, waiting a tow. It looked like a crushed tin can. It was a miracle she escaped with just a broken ankle. He studied the junction. The minor road opposite was an alleyway between shops. He walked down it, looking for security cameras. He found one on the backdoor of an antiques shop. Would the alignment catch a vehicle parked on the street? Only one way to find out.

He went back to the front of the shop and peered inside. The grills were down but he thought he saw someone moving about in the back. He reached through the shutter and knocked on the door. A man came out from a backroom, wiping his hands.

'We're closed,' he mouthed. Of course they were: it was eight in the evening. He was lucky the man lived above his shop.

Habit had Sam reaching for his warrant card but he came away with his wallet. Flipping that open, Sam held up his

National Trust membership card, hoping it would fool the guy that this was an official visit of some sort – enough to open the door.

The shopkeeper gestured to him to go round the back. He met Sam by the unloading bay.

'Who are you with? Electricity? Gas?'

Sam grimaced. 'Sorry, that was just to get you to open the door.' He showed the man the wallet.

'The National Trust are doing house to house calls now are they? I let my membership lapse a while ago.'

The man thought he was touting for new business for the charity. 'I'm not here representing anyone.'

'Then what do you want?'

Sam gestured to the street. 'My friend was caught in an accident a couple of hours ago.'

'Oh yes, I was here. Terrible business. Is she OK?'

'I think so but I've not seen her yet. She's in recovery.'

'If you want more information, I'm afraid I didn't see anything – not the accident itself, only the aftermath. I was busy cashing up for the day.'

'Actually, I was wondering about your CCTV on the back-door. Have the police asked for it?'

'They called in briefly to ask if I had witnessed the crash but I said that I'd not seen it happen so they left. That camera only shows the side alley, not the front.'

Sam knew from his own time juggling budgets that the police didn't as a rule put a lot of resources into traffic accidents and they didn't yet know this was deliberate. 'Is the camera switched on?'

'Yes. I've always thought that door is the most vulnerable point in the shop so I make sure it's on. I probably shouldn't have told you that.' The shopkeeper now looked worried.

'Don't worry. I'm not planning a heist.'

The shopkeeper smiled. 'No, you don't look the sort. But then, what do burglars look like?'

'May I see what it shows just before the accident?'

'Why?'

'My friend's work colleague says the other vehicle involved was parked in this alleyway. They were driving without licence plates so we're hoping you might've caught the driver on camera.'

The man gave him an untrusting look. 'Who are you again?'

Time for full disclosure or he had a feeling the door was going to be shut in his face. 'My name's Sam Ranworth. I own Claremont Castle. The woman in the accident is my girlfriend.' It felt odd saying that, but easier than a convoluted explanation about their on-off relationship.

Suspicion vanished as the man had a place to pigeonhole Sam. 'I think I've heard of you.'

'You have?'

'I occasionally drink at the Castle Inn in Claremont Magna. Tim's got a book running on how long you'll last. You're the London man who's trying to restore the garden.'

Thanks for your vote of confidence, Tim. 'Yes, and I did not know about the bet, but I'm not surprised. I think Tim believes we're all put in his village to amuse him.'

The man smiled in recognition of that fact. 'That's Tim down to a T. I'm Fred Burnet. If Tim knows you then you must be OK. I'll show you the recording.' He invited Sam inside. 'I don't keep them more than twenty-four hours as they use up so much space on the computer so it's good you came round tonight. What time was the accident?' He accessed the security feed on his desktop.

'You'd have a better idea than me. Around five?'

'That sounds about right.' Fred re-wound to the right time. 'Go back a little bit further.'

They both watched an ambulance back into the narrow lane at four forty-six right outside the rear door of the shop. That was a bit of luck.

'He's blocking my fire exit, bloody fool. And you're right: no plates. Can't quite see the driver though. The reflection on the windscreen spoils that.'

'Can you take it frame by frame from the moment he moves? We might get lucky.'

Fred clicked through the footage.

'Stop! There!'

'Yes, I see it. Blurred but not bad. Angle's a bit distorting. You can see the basic body type. He's not going to win any beauty prizes, is he?'

Sam tapped the screen. 'It's better than that. Look at his hands on the steering wheel.'

'Oh my word. What does that say?'

'O V E and I'm guessing the one out of sight is R. Over.'

'Weird.'

'I'd put good money on the left hand saying "Game". It's one of the tats favoured by one of the gangs in London. If you see my knuckles coming towards you then it's . . .'

Fred grimaced. 'Game over. Infantile but I understand.

310

There can't be many people in Bury St Edmunds with that on their knuckles.'

'I hope not. Would you contact the police, tell them what we found?'

'What's your name again?' Fred got out a piece of scrap paper.

'Sam Ranworth. If they're worried that we've been doing our own investigation, you can tell them that I was until recently a Met police officer. Detective Inspector.'

'That explains it, having that information about the gangs and so on. I'll give them a call.'

'And please, whatever you do, don't delete the file.'

'I'll email it to you if you like, just to be sure. I'd hate to mess this up by losing it. Knowing my computer skills, that is a possibility.'

'Thanks. Appreciate it.'

'The least I can do for our local castle owner.'

Sam looked around the shop, noticing now the fine collection of antique swords and helmets. 'I don't suppose you'd like to come to our opening?'

Fred smiled in delight. 'I would enjoy that. It always seemed a crying shame to see that place go to rack and ruin.'

'I'll add you to the list.' He told Fred the date and time.

'Send my best to your lady,' called Fred.

Sam paused at the back door. His lady. That felt strangely appropriate. 'Yes, I will.'

Chapter 25

Gemma regained consciousness for a second time. The first had been just enough to suck some water through a straw and assure the nurse that she knew who she was. This time she took note of her circumstances. Panic flared. She was immobilised: her head in some kind of brace and her left leg tethered.

'There you are.' It was her mother. *Her mother?* A cool cloth wiped her forehead. 'I imagine you must be feeling terrible but it isn't bad, really it's not. They've put you in a neck brace just in case but there's no spinal injury. Your ankle has been operated on and they've inserted some pins and a frame to keep it aligned. Leo says to tell you that you look like a cyborg and that apparently is "cool".' She rolled her eyes, making Gemma smile despite everything: her old-fashioned mum saying 'cyborg' was hilarious if only she didn't feel too beaten to laugh.

'Leo? Is he OK?' croaked Gemma.

'He's fine. He's with his granddads having something to eat in the café. Miriam's just left to get you an overnight bag. She won't be long. I persuaded Diana to go home – she was here from the moment you were admitted and stayed to see that you were all right.'

Gemma wondered at all these people rallying around her, but the person she most wanted to be among them appeared absent. 'Sam?'

Her mother pursed her lips. 'Yes, he was here too. He brought Leo but disappeared when we arrived.'

'It's his father. He has to care for him.' Though she couldn't but feel a little disappointed he had gone. He had chosen not to count himself into her inner circle.

'Ah, I see. But I hoped . . .' So had Gemma. Her mother shook herself. 'Would you like some water?'

'Please. Tell me what happened.'

Her mother retold the account Diana had given them. 'It is awful to think how close it was, Gemma. Your father is, of course, furious. He never liked that Fiesta of yours. He's going to insist you take my little Volvo. We don't need a second car. Your safety is more important and maybe now you'll listen to us.'

Gemma ignored the lecture. Driving didn't seem like something that she'd be able to do for quite some time. 'Did they say how long I'd have to stay here?'

'No. I think that's something they want to discuss with you. The surgeon who checked on you before end of her shift did mutter a few things about making sure you had an accessible bathroom at home so I'm hoping it won't be more than a few days. We'll put a bed downstairs and there's the cloakroom by the front door. Or if you'd prefer to be upstairs, then I'm sure we can manage to get you up there somehow. It'll be nicer to be in an upstairs bedroom, I would've thought. We can move a television in there to keep you entertained. I've a spare one in the kitchen.'

'You're talking about taking me to your home?' Gemma had been thinking about her narrow cottage stairs but the mention of the spare TV clued her in to the picture in her mother's mind.

'Of course. This just brings coming to us forward a few weeks. Unfortunate, I know, but I can't see another solution, can you?'

Gemma realised something she should've cottoned on to when she first asked to retreat to her parents: she really didn't want to go. The impulse had been pure running away. What she really wanted was her fairytale cottage with its battlements and impenetrable hedge of blackberries, its gnome guard and wilderness back garden. 'Mum—'

Her mum patted her hand. 'Don't worry about all that now. One step at a time, all right?'

'But I promised Sam I'd help with the official opening of the castle – and Leo's minding his dad for him.'

Her mother waved that away as if it were no more than a cobweb. 'Pish, no one expects you to do that. Sam's a grown man; he'll manage. You have to concentrate on getting yourself better.'

Sam and Tim surveyed the sitting room of Gemma's cottage.

'What do you think? A bed down here? We can rig some curtains across to give her privacy. There's a loo out the back – a bit basic but it works,' suggested Sam.

Tim nodded. 'She has a double upstairs, yes?'

Sam nodded.

'There's not enough room for that but we've a spare bed in our B&B accommodation. I'll bring that over and set it up for her.' He checked the downstairs toilet. 'Not thinking much of your landlord standards here, Sam.'

Another thing for him to feel guilty about. 'It was on the list for refurbishment. The one upstairs is better.' But not by much.

'You'd better bump it up to the top. It might be all right for a guy taking a quick whiz standing but that's nowhere near suitable for a lady.'

Sam hadn't realised Tim was so sensitive to female sensibilities. 'Agreed.'

'If we move fast, we could get the plumber to put in a shower in a couple of days. That will be easier than a bath. Is the landlord paying?'

Sam thought of his vanishing savings. He had taken the decision on the drive back from Fred's shop that he would spend everything he had if necessary just to give him a chance to prove to Gemma that he was not a complete commitment-phobe and that their relationship still had a future, if she would give him another chance. He would do everything he could to stop her retreating to her parents. Almost losing her had the effect of clarifying what he really felt and he'd fallen in love with her some time ago. It had just taken his brain a few weeks to catch up with his heart. 'Yes, of course. The plumber will come round so quickly? He always seems to dodge my calls.'

Tim rubbed at a circular stain on the coffee table but it didn't come off. 'He will when I tell him to. No one in Claremont Magna wants me as their enemy.'

Sam grinned. 'Tim, you're a scary man.'

'Too right I am. And you really found footage of the fucker who did this?'

'Already sent to the police.'

'And he had knuckle tats?'

'Yes.'

Tim nodded. 'Then he shouldn't be too hard to find if he's stayed in the local area. An old ambulance and those tattoos: someone's going to know him. Send me a still from the video. I'll ask the wife to put the word out to other pub owners on our WhatsApp group. If he raises a glass in Suffolk, we'll know.'

'Thanks, Tim.'

When Sam arrived back at his own cottage, he found his father sitting at the kitchen table flicking through Gemma's research on the garden. He wondered which Dad he would get: the one in the past or present. He couldn't deal with another meltdown now. Neutral topics only were on his agenda.

'Dad, have you eaten?'

'My boy, I'm so sorry about Jennifer,' his dad said, tears in his eyes.

'It's not Jennifer, Dad, it's Gemma.'

'I know Leo's mother had an accident. No, I meant that I'm sorry Jennifer died. Camille told me.'

Damn her. He'd explained that his father forgot. 'It happened a long time ago now.'

'It's just that I get so confused.'

'I know that too.'

'I always thought she was a fragile flower.'

'Jennifer?'

William wiped a tear with his cuff. 'Not well equipped to survive out of the hothouse.'

Sam broke off a piece of kitchen towel and handed it to him. 'No, she wasn't. I failed her.'

'You didn't fail her, Sam. No one could keep her alive for long. Some people just won't take to the outside world.'

'I'm sorry you had to remember this now. You might not remember but you were at the funeral and a great support to me at the time.'

'I was?'

'You took me on a garden tour of Italy. Do you remember?' He opened a bottle of red, needing the comfort of a good vintage to soothe him after a hellish day.

'Oh my goodness, yes!' William's expression brightened. 'That was with you? Of course it was. My memory is so patchy these days. Those magnificent cypress trees on Lake Como!'

'That's right. I'll show you the photos later. I've got them on my laptop.' He offered his dad a glass.

'Not for me. I preferred the old days when we had albums.'

'Me too, if I'm honest. I don't get time to arrange them.'

His dad sat up straighter. 'That nice young man, Tim, has been talking to me too.'

'Young?'

'Everyone seems young to me.'

'Did you like him?'

'A bit of a character, isn't he?'

'You can say that again.'

'Reminds me of a chap I knew in the war.'

Setting his wine aside, Sam ran some water into a saucepan. From the evidence of the dishes in the sink, it looked like Camille or Tim had given his dad a meal. For his own dinner, it would have to be quick-cook pasta. 'Forget about any of us castle owners; he rules the village, I'd say.'

'He asked about the home you took me to and I remembered that there was a nice one with that man who had planted those stunning magnolias, wasn't there?'

'It's called Wild Thyme Lodge and it's in Bury so only a short drive away.'

'He said I should give the home a go because if you've got a new lady in your life your old dad will cramp your style.'

'That's not the reason for moving you.' Sam sliced open the top of the plastic packet and tipped half into the water. Once the pasta soaked some of that in, they bobbed to the top like survivors of a disaster in yellow lifejackets. 'I really think you'll like the company.'

'I enjoy being here. I like Leo.'

'But he goes back to school in a week or so. The cottage will be empty all day.'

'Tim said that too. He said I should go for a visit to see if I like it. In his opinion, a fine-looking man like me should be chatting up the ladies of my generation – what a nerve that man has!' His dad chuckled.

'I think the village has let him get away with being outrageous for too long. He can't help himself.'

319

'Would that be possible? Go for a visit, I mean?'

Bless you, Tim. 'Of course! That's what the owner suggested. Do you want me to give him a ring?'

'If it's not too much trouble. I know you have a lot on your plate.'

Sam grinned and showed him the serving of pasta he had just tipped out of the sieve, which was indeed full to the rim. 'Dad, nothing is more important than finding you the right place to live.'

Gemma watched the door for her Saturday afternoon visitors but there was no Sam. She knew he was busy with all the volunteers arriving for the weekend but she'd imagined he might squeeze in a quick visit, just to see how she was. She didn't mind if he had to bring his dad with him as she liked William. Leo came, of course; though after a hug and a few words, he retreated to his phone. She felt reassured by the evidence that he was back to normal and didn't feel the need to hover like he had last night. Her parents and Leo's grandparents all came, taking it in shifts so they didn't exceed the maximum number allowed on the ward. Even Diana came with her husband, Henry. They were heading over to help out at the castle and had arranged to take Leo.

Leo looked up from his phone. 'Sam's put me in charge of the under gardeners,' he announced.

'Under gardeners?'

'Leo means the other teens – my boys and the lads from the village who have signed up,' explained Diana.

'You're OK with that?' marvelled Gemma.

320

He shrugged. 'Sam said I know the place best so I was his main man for the job. Oh yeah, Mum, I told Gran I'd stay overnight at home. Beach Granny and Granddad are going to be with me. Is that OK?'

Gemma wondered what state she'd left the kitchen in on Friday morning. Probably horrendous. 'Of course.'

'There's so much to do for the opening,' Leo said, sounding like he was about forty, not fourteen.

'Yes, there is.' That reminded her. 'Leo, can you get my bag out of the locker?'

He rooted through the cupboard. 'This one?'

'That's it. It's got the details of the flowers I've ordered and how I planned to arrange them. Give them to Sam, will you, so he can find someone to take over?' She'd really looked forward to seeing that through to completion but there was no way that was going to happen in her parents' house. 'I think all the other details for the reception are in-hand but the information is in there if he has a question.' She crossed her fingers, hoping the jobs wouldn't be hoovered up by Camille – silly, but she would prefer anyone else to take over.

'OK. Will do.' Leo tucked his phone away and stood up. 'I think we'd better go.'

Diana leant over and kissed her. 'We'll spring you from this prison soon enough, partner.'

Gemma hated to be left behind. 'I'm counting on it, Di. The food's crap.'

'Concentrate on getting better, OK?'

'Will do.'

Henry gave her a smile and put an arm round Leo. 'Let's

go round up our hooligans from the café. You make them work hard, OK?'

Leo looked so proud at that moment. 'That's the plan.'

'Good luck!' called Gemma.

Left alone, Gemma flicked through the magazines they'd left her. She came across the article on the celebrant Diana had pointed out. Could she? Why not? It wouldn't stop her looking for other work but she had at least six weeks of recovery to fill. Planning a new business venture would be a sensible use of time. Surely the overheads for setting something like that up were minimal, maybe some insurance and a website? She searched up the Druid and sent him a message, a little disappointed he could be contacted by regular email rather than demanding carrier pigeons or messages in runes.

The doctor in charge of her case reached her at five.

'Sorry it's so late, Gemma,' she said, picking up the notes at the bottom of the bed. 'We're running a skeleton service this weekend.'

'Pretty appropriate considering it's an orthopaedic ward.'

The doctor smiled. 'Glad you can see the funny side. That bodes well for your recovery. Now, looking at this, it seems everything is going to plan. The ankle is the worst with the joint disputed – that's why there's the frame holding it in place. I know it looks frightening but it really is doing a good job of mending.'

'I'm coping by not looking at it. My son tells me I'm part cyborg.'

'Not for long, you'll be pleased to hear. We'll take the frame off your leg once we're sure the break is stabilised and the pins inside are doing their job, but I don't think that should stop you going home if you have suitable accommodation. How's the pain?'

Gemma winced. 'Not too bad as long as I keep distracting myself. Visitors help.'

'I see.' She flicked through the chart. 'Hmm, I'm sorry I can't give you anything stronger. I've got you just on paracetamol because of your condition, of course.'

'What?'

The doctor looked up from the notes. 'Sorry?'

'What condition?'

'Oh dear. I really shouldn't have said that but I wanted to explain about the meds.' The doctor turned the chart round. 'Did no one tell you your blood results? I thought someone would've discussed them with you by now. The nurse said she would.'

'No! Tell me what's wrong!'

'Gemma, you're pregnant. Must be early days, I guess, if you didn't know?'

'Oh my . . . no . . . what?'

'I see that's come as a bit of a shock. I just assumed . . .'

Assumed that a grown-up woman would be on top of her own reproductive health. She hadn't even noticed in the turmoil of the summer that her period was late. How stupid could she be?

'Look, I'm sorry to spring this upon you but it's important we get the dosage right so you have all options open. Any doctor will advise you to make an appointment with your GP as soon as you can.'

'But there's been no harm done – to the . . .?'

'To the foetus? Not from paracetamol.'

The doctor left Gemma reeling. How had this happened? Of course, Gemma knew *how*, what she meant was through what oversight? To be six weeks along, it had to have occurred right at the beginning of her relationship with Sam about four or five weeks ago as pregnancy was calculated from the date of the last period, not conception. But they were responsible adults. They'd used protection when they'd started sleeping together. True, she wasn't on the pill as she was on an oral contraceptive holiday on the advice of her GP after some cramping issues. She had been intending to go back on the pill but the first available appointment had been a couple of weeks away. Sam had been taking care of that side of things. Too late now. Had she learned nothing since she was a teenager? Was her body some super-fertile zone that mocked any futile attempts by condoms to stop her falling pregnant? Not that Ray had even used that much to protect her. Sam had though: he'd always come prepared.

Gemma then remembered her first time with Sam. They'd made love several times during the night, including one very sleepy one near dawn. Had they forgotten? Oh God, they completely could've done; it was all too hazy.

She thumped her forehead. 'You idiot!'

The older woman in the bed opposite cleared her throat. 'Are you all right, love?'

Was she? *Perspective, Gemma. It's a pregnancy, not a terminal cancer.* Leo was the joy of her life. There was nothing stopping another child adding to that. 'I will be.'

'That's the spirit.' The lady turned back to her knitting. 'I'll make you some little cardigans.'

Oh no, she'd heard. Looking around the four-bed ward, Gemma realised everyone knew and all were sending her sympathetic looks. Her face had to be scarlet.

This is not an embarrassment, it's a blessing, she scolded herself fiercely.

She had to tell Sam.

Gemma picked up her phone but put it down again. It was not something she could confess over a text. If he didn't care enough to visit her, then he didn't deserve to be the first to know.

Oh God, she was getting weepy. She really must be pregnant with all sorts of hormones washing around inside her. She couldn't talk to Sam in this emotional state.

Gemma knew she was really being a coward, putting this off. How would he react? It wouldn't be pretty, that she could predict. He'd been clear he wasn't ready for responsibilities. But it was his little swimmers that had got her into this mess so he would just have to buck up and . . . and what? She'd been around this track at fifteen, telling a man that she was carrying a child he didn't want any part in raising. Sam wasn't Ray and would probably be more supportive, but that didn't stop the sinking feeling that he just wouldn't want this complication in his life.

Despair filled her. She'd promised herself never to have another child on her own. It looked like she'd just broken her cardinal rule. History was on repeat.

Chapter 26

Sam ran into the hospital, aware that he only had half an hour left of evening visiting time. He'd had a frantic day, what with meeting the plumber about the refurbishment of Gemma's shower room, taking his dad on his visit to Wild Thyme Lodge, and organising the work at Claremont for the opening. Neil and Phil had arrived in the morning and they were helping hold the fort, dishing out the list of tasks and making sure people stuck to the programme, but this had been the first moment Sam had where he could escape his other duties. Sam had told Leo to let Gemma know when the boy visited in the afternoon that Sam would come in the evening, but over supper Leo admitted he'd forgotten to mention it.

'Mum won't mind,' he said blithely. 'She had more visitors than she was allowed anyway. She won't've noticed.'

That made Sam feel a little better, though he kicked himself for forgetting what poor message carriers fourteen-year-old boys could be.

'I'm here to see Gemma Whitehall. Do you know where she is?' Sam asked the nurse on reception.

'Along there. You only have twenty-five minutes of visiting time left.'

'Yes, I know.' He'd spent five of them buying Gemma some sorry-looking freesias from the hospital shop. He should've brought her a bunch from home. 'Thanks.'

Gemma appeared to be asleep when he turned into the small side ward. His arrival garnered surprisingly hostile looks from the three ladies in the other beds. He'd seen piercing looks like that from crows waiting for him to plant out his seedlings. Perhaps they were worried about him disturbing Gemma's rest but it would be worse to go home without her knowing he'd called in. He gave them a bland smile and went over to Gemma's bedside. Bending over, he touched her wrist.

'Sorry I'm so late.'

'Sam?' Gemma's eyes fluttered open. Her head looked very strange, perched on top of a neck brace. He thought, completely inappropriately, of coconuts at a shy. 'I'd given up on you.'

A lady knitting in the bed opposite snorted in disdain as she threaded her needles with fine white wool.

Sam shot the stranger a quelling look and pulled the visitor's chair as close as possible so they could talk with lowered voices. 'Leo was supposed to tell you I was coming but he forgot.'

Gemma smiled sleepily at the mention of her son. 'How's he got on with his under gardeners?'

'He's been a star. He's such a wonderful boy, have I told you that?'

'I don't think you have.'

Knowing she'd lap up every detail about her son and the castle, he recounted the afternoon's achievements and how the opening no longer seemed so impossible with so many people turning up to help. 'I noticed that Leo and Tim's youngest appear to have hit it off.'

She blinked in surprise. 'Tim's youngest? I can't imagine that.'

'You might if I tell you that he is the opposite of his father. I've not met Connor before. Tim says he's shy and spends most of his time up in his bedroom playing computer games.'

'Ah, now I see how Leo and Connor might've bonded.'

'I heard Leo telling him something about that Magisnark thing.'

'Magikarp.'

'They agreed it wasn't cool to hunt Pokémon anymore but they still liked the game. I let them up into the keep so Connor could catch it.'

Gemma smoothed the sheet over her stomach. 'Oh Sam, thank you.'

'For what?'

'I've been so worried about Leo not having any friends.'

'Are you joking? In the last month, he's made friends with me, my dad, Cammy, and now half the village. The only boys he doesn't hit it off with on the gardening team are Diana's two but that's because they're just different types. Leo's your dependable sort whereas they're more immature, not used to thinking of others.'

'I suppose they are.' She smiled but her eyes glimmered with tears. He hoped they were happy ones.

'They kicked their football into the moat and spent most of their time trying to get it back when they should've been working. Their dad told me I should dock their pay.'

Gemma closed her eyes and smiled. 'Henry's great, isn't he?'

'He's been a big help. He's down at your cottage giving the plumber a hand with the new shower room.'

Her eyes opened. 'The what?'

'I'm doing up the downstairs toilet, putting in a shower so you can come home.' Sam knew he'd been beating around the bush but he only had fifteen minutes left. 'Gemma, I've been a fool not making it clearer earlier. I want you to stay at the cottage. I don't care how long it takes you to find work or pay the rent. You like the cottage, don't you? I know Leo does.'

'Sam . . .'

'Let me finish so you can make a decision. I've thought it all through. We've only known each other a couple of months so it's probably too early to talk about the long term. But I want you to know that I like the person I am with you.' He wished he wasn't saying this with three eavesdroppers not even pretending they were not listening in. 'You are fun, intelligent, gorgeous, everything I want in a partner. But I don't want to rush you. I'm having the cottage kitted out so you can recover there – that'll give you time to work out if you want to stay and if we have a chance together. I'll arrange for extra help from the village if necessary.'

'But how?'

'Tim will know someone. That's not a problem.'

'I can't drive.'

'I can. I'll take you where you need to go.'

'But haven't you got enough to do, what with your dad and everything else?'

'There's good news on that front. He had a lucid moment last night and agreed to visit Wild Thyme Lodge – that's where we went this afternoon so he could stay a few days and see if he likes it. I had to strike while the iron was hot, so to speak. Fingers crossed he'll like it enough to stay on there.' Sam cleared his throat, emotion clogging his voice. He'd almost lost this incredible woman. 'You did that – you found that for me.'

'I just gave you the tip.'

'But you helped me without hesitation, not worrying about getting involved.' He laced his fingers with hers. 'When I was driving Leo to the hospital yesterday, breaking every rule of the highway code I could get away with to be here as quickly as possible, I realised that I had worried so much about taking responsibility for people after failing Jennifer that I'd been blind to the fact I'd been making other people responsible for me. My self-sufficiency was an illusion. I need you, Gemma. Thinking I might've lost you completely blew up all my idiotic ideas that somehow I'd insulated myself against loss. Please stay at the cottage and see if you can need me too. We'll make it work, I promise.'

The nurse appeared at the entrance to the ward. 'It's eight o'clock. Visiting time is over. I'm afraid, sir, you'll have to leave.'

Of all the stupid timings: he'd not got through even a fraction of the things he wanted to say, hardly begun to make his case how he could become someone worthy of her. 'Please at least think about it. And if you're worried about Ray, I'll stand guard, evict him if he turns up, but I don't think he will. And as for the other business, that guy will soon be arrested.'

She looked startled. 'What other business?'

'Didn't Diana tell you?'

The nurse tutted.

'Tell me what?' Gemma increased her grip on his hand.

'The tyre slashing – the collision – one of the wedding scammers was behind it. I found footage to prove it on the CCTV on Fred Burnet's antique shop. One of them was waiting in that alleyway to shunt you. There's enough on there to identify him.'

'It wasn't an accident?'

'No. He was trying to scare you off but got rather more than he bargained for when the taxi appeared out of nowhere. His little shunt became a serious accident. He has to be wondering if it's going to catch up with him.'

'So not Ray?'

'No, none of it was anything to do with him.'

'I'm so relieved. It would've been awful for Leo.'

'Sir, I'm sorry but you really have to go,' said the nurse. 'We have rules for a reason.'

He rolled his eyes so Gemma could see his exasperation. Leaning over to kiss her, he whispered:

'Think about it. I'll come back tomorrow.'

'Sam . . .' She tried to keep hold of his hand.

'If I don't go, they won't let me back in tomorrow.'

'OK, but can you come alone? We really need to talk.'

That didn't sound good. 'If that's what you want.' He brushed a kiss near her ear. 'Take care.'

On the way back to the castle, Sam wanted to howl. He'd messed it up, spilled it all before her without the careful preparation he'd imagined. Not surprising that she hadn't reacted well to his offer. His money was on her finding a way to let him down gently tomorrow, all that about needing to talk was code for a breakup conversation usually.

He pulled into the parking bay in front of his cottage. Through the lit windows he could see Neil leafing through Gemma's file on flowers while Phil tapped away on the laptop. Camille was nowhere to be seen but then, Tim had mentioned something about his older, display-erecting son, Finn, inviting her out with the young people of the village. Stealing himself for the third degree, he entered the house.

'How's Gemma?' asked Phil.

'Sleepy.' Sam hung the car key up on its hook.

'And?' Neil didn't need to elaborate. They knew he had been intending to ask her to stay.

'Not good. She wants to talk tomorrow.'

'That might not be bad,' suggested Phil.

'No, Phil, it's always bad,' said Neil. 'I'm with Sam on this. How about a glass of something to soften the blow?'

Neil was letting him off gently, with no interrogation. 'Yeah, why not. I cocked up. I was late.'

'Did you give her flowers?'

Had he? 'I think I left them on the bed.'

'Sam, you are not a smooth operator.'

Phil raided the drinks cabinet and came up with a bottle of port. 'This do?'

Sam waved him on. 'Fine. Just like being back at college again.' He and Neil often had late night drinking sessions to take the edge off a rough day.

'One thing I know, Sam,' said Neil staunchly, 'is that, even though you are a fine man, faint heart never won fair lady. You go back tomorrow and do better.'

'I don't think she's that into me, Neil. I told her once that I didn't do commitment.'

'Rubbish. Tell her you were wrong. You may be a bit grizzled around the edges, but you are an attractive man, Sam. Take it from someone who knows. You just need to prove you are worth the long haul.'

Phil put a small glass of port in front of Sam. '*Courage, mon brave.*'

Sam waited for them all to have their serving and raised his glass. 'To her ignoring the fact I'm a complete idiot and liking me anyway.'

'I'm not drinking to that' declared Neil. 'To Gemma, may she recover quickly and grab for herself the most eligible castle owner in England!'

It wasn't Sam who returned in the afternoon but Diana.

'Gem, you really need to leave this place: you are missing out on all the best gossip stuck in here.'

Gemma smiled but inside she was twisted up with the knowledge that she had the juiciest bit of gossip herself. 'Oh? What do you mean?'

'Guess who turned up to help this morning at the castle?'

'Di, I'm not at my best for guessing. Help me out here.'

'Gillian – and her new man!'

'Gillian has a boyfriend? I'm so pleased for her.' Gillian had always seemed a little lonely, spending Christmas at her married sister's and taking holidays solo.

'But the best thing of all is the identity of the man.' Diana hugged herself in delight.

'Go on.'

'Gregor Niyazov!' She announced it as if that should mean something to Gemma.

'Gregor Niyazov? Niyazov? What? You don't mean that sweet little guy from the sham wedding? The one who wanted to buy a wife in exchange for hard work?'

'That's the one. I don't know how it happened exactly, perhaps Gillian chased him down after work, but they've been dating all summer apparently with no money being exchanged. And boy, does that man know how to work! He's become Sam's righthand man, up ladders, in the moat, under the bridge: you name it, he's there with his cheery smile and his ability to turn his hand to anything. I think I'm a little in love with him myself.'

'But isn't he a bit young for Gillian?'

'That doesn't bother him and if it worries her, it doesn't show. She's got a new hairstyle and looks ten years younger.' Diana leaned forward. 'I imagine he takes the same earnest enthusiasm to bed with him.'

'Lucky Gillian.'

They both giggled like schoolgirls, which was terrible of them.

'What are we like?' Diana dabbed the corner of her eyes with a tissue. 'So, when are you coming home?'

'Actually, I'm being discharged later. I texted Leo and my parents to let them know.'

'And where are you going back to?'

'That's the thing. I want to go to my cottage.'

Diana nodded. 'Henry's been helping. There's a new loo and a shower now, but I don't think the tiles are finished.'

'I'd manage but I don't know if I'm really welcome there. Sam says I am but he doesn't know everything yet.' Then again, neither did her parents. They might not be so eager to see her in Aldeburgh if she was doing the single mother thing again. But surely twenty-nine was different to fifteen, not so shaming?

Diana helped herself to one of the chocolates she had brought Gemma. 'What do you mean everything?'

'I don't think he knows yet quite how much trouble we'll be.'

'Honey, that man needs some trouble in his life. He's also too lonely if you ask me.'

'So I'm his Gregor Niyazov?'

'But much better looking and probably not so hard-working.'

Chapter 27

Paperwork complete, Gemma wondered when her family were going to arrive to rescue her. Leo had texted that he'd sorted out a lift and that it had been agreed she would go back to the cottage *to start with*. That sounded like her mother speaking, rather than Leo. Gemma braced herself for a few days of nursing from her parents – small price to pay if she was in the surroundings that felt like her territory rather than theirs. She had sent Sam a text explaining that he shouldn't come to the hospital but find her at home for the talk they needed to have but hadn't received a response. She tried to forgive him for that, knowing he was busy and didn't know it was urgent, but it was irritating nonetheless. She felt like she was carrying a grenade with the pin removed; everything might blow up in her face at any moment.

At seven, Sam himself appeared in the ward entrance.

'Hi, Gemma.' He kissed her briefly. 'Ladies.' He nodded to their spectators in the others beds.

'Didn't you get my message?' asked Gemma.

'Yes, I did. Didn't you get mine from Leo that I'd offered to give you a lift?'

'Not as such. He didn't mention it was you.'

Sam looked worried. 'Are you disappointed? Did you want your father to fetch you instead?'

'No, it's great! I can't wait to get out of here.'

'OK then. I'll just grab a wheelchair. They've supplied you with crutches?'

She gestured to the pair the she'd been given the day before. 'And I've got a soft neck collar to wear when I'm at home.'

'I think we can manage all this in one trip if you can put your bags on your lap.' Sam efficiently loaded her into the chair. 'Got the prescriptions?'

She displayed her little white bag from the dispensary.

He grimaced. 'Paracetamol? I'd be demanding something a bit stronger than that if I were you.'

Gemma cleared her throat and tried not to look at the lady opposite. A little white cardigan was now buried at the bottom of her handbag. 'Goodbye, everyone!' she called as Sam wheeled her out.

'Good luck! With everything!' replied the knitter.

'They seemed a friendly bunch – to you at least. Did I do something to upset them?' Sam asked as they made their way to the lift.

'No,' lied Gemma. 'They were probably just not keen to be seen in their nightdresses and no make-up by a handsome stranger. Women have their pride.'

'I wasn't looking at them.' Sam pushed her out into the car park. 'I'm going to have to lift you into the car: are you OK with that?'

'Don't do your back in!' warned Gemma.

He grinned and tossed her crutches and bags into the boot. 'No danger of that.' After opening the passenger door, he reached for her. Lifting her to his chest, he paused. 'Alone at last without the beady eyes of your audience. God, I've missed you! Gemma, don't ever do that to me again.' He kissed her forehead fervently.

'Get caught up in an accident caused by a wedding scammer? I'll try not to.'

He placed her on the seat. 'Who, by the way, was picked up by the police in Ipswich last night.'

'He was?'

'He made the mistake of going out for a drink and one of Tim's spies spotted him. The idiot was still in his old ambulance – I think he lives in it – and that has damage to the front of the vehicle. The police will be round to take your statement next week but I'd say the evidence is pretty strong even without your testimony.'

'So I don't have to worry about him again?'

'No: he's unlikely to be driving anywhere for a while.'

Gemma hadn't realised that this had been at the back of her mind as another thing to be concerned about. She felt almost weightless with relief.

Sam buckled her in and went to his side of the car. 'Ready to go home?'

'Oh yes.'

He drove carefully, treating her like precious cargo that wouldn't cope with a bump or a jostle. He chatted about the preparations, which were going well apparently, outlining what he thought she could do over the next week from her housebound state. Gemma realised after a while that this unusually chatty Sam was attempting to stop her embarking on the talk she had requested. Should she just spring it on him? But he was driving: that would be unfair and possibly dangerous. She had to trust he'd give her five minutes when they arrived.

But he drove past the cottage and up the main approach to the keep.

'Sam, where are we going?' she asked, seeing the lights were on in her cottage, so someone was home.

'I want to show you something.'

'Can't it wait until the morning?'

'It's a surprise.'

That didn't really answer her question. 'Will it take long?'

'That depends on you.' He looked quite nervous so Gemma didn't press. If he thought she'd disapprove of his arrangements for the opening, then he was wrong. She didn't think it her place to impose her ideas, just help him realise his.

He drew up right by the drawbridge to the keep and not by his cottage. Gemma was increasingly mystified.

'I think I might have to carry you,' he said apologetically. 'I didn't really think this whole "on crutches" scenario through.'

'That's OK with me. As long as you . . .'

'Don't do my back in. I know.' He scooped her out of her seat and strode across the wooden planks.

'Are you going to tell me yet where we are going?'

'Nope.' He let her balance on one foot briefly while he opened the door to the keep.

'Am I going to like the surprise?'

'I really don't know.'

'As long as you've not redecorated the keep like an eighties wine bar.'

'Oh damn, I knew I should've stopped Cammy ordering in the brushed steel counters and cocktail shakers.'

They entered the guardroom. Gemma gasped. It looked magical. Candles were burning on every ledge and in the new wrought iron chandelier hanging in the centre.

'Where did you get that?' she asked, pointing.

'The antiques man, Fred Burnet.'

'Is he responsible for the suits of armour?'

'Yes. If you look closely, they have a price tag. He's hoping I'll sell a few for him. They're replica, not real.'

'They're amazing.'

In the centre, there was a pile of cushions covered with a red velvet cloth.

'Your bower, my lady.' He lowered her onto them, checking her ankle was well supported. Sam flicked a remote and a hidden stereo started playing lute music.

Gemma stretched out luxuriously like a cat in patch of sunshine. 'What do I say now? Bring on the food and wine?'

'If you like.' He produced a bottle of champagne from behind a suit of armour. 'This is to toast your return and to cry confusion on your enemy, currently sitting in Bury police station.'

Oh Lord, this was awkward. Gemma winced as he popped the cork. She put her hand over the top of the flute glass he passed her. 'I can't. I'm really sorry, but I can't drink that.'

He replaced the champagne in the cooler, head slumped. The music cut off. 'I'm sorry too. I should've taken the message last night but Neil said I just had to try harder.'

'You *are* trying hard. You're doing brilliantly.'

But he wasn't listening. 'I asked Leo what you liked and he said "old stuff". That's why I brought you here. I wanted to offer you a lot of old stuff, including me.'

She smiled at that. 'Thirty-nine isn't old. Sam, please, just listen a moment . . .'

'It's fine. I get that you don't want to risk your happiness, Leo's happiness, by throwing in your lot with me. I'm a bad bargain.'

'Would you just listen!' She threw a cushion at him. 'Sam, I'm trying to tell you something. I'm pregnant. Six weeks along.'

He sat back on his heels, gaze dropping to her flat stomach. 'How?'

'That was my first thought too when the doctor sprang it on me. I think it was that time you stayed overnight. Didn't we forget just the once . . .?'

He surprised her by burying his head in the cushions next to her. 'God, I'm so sorry.'

'Sam, don't be. It takes two to tango so I'm not blaming you. And, whatever happens, I love it already. I just want to know how you feel about having a child with me.'

'I do everything wrong, don't I?' Her big strong Sam was cracking up but perhaps he needed to so he knew she would catch the pieces and put them back together again? 'I try to offer you a new life here and I mess it up by getting you pregnant. I wasn't trying to trap you, Gemma.'

'I know you weren't and I don't see it like that. I've had a kid on my own before, remember, and it works out OK in the end – hard work but OK. I was just wondering if you'd be up to doing this one together?'

'You'd want to have a family with me, even though you know I'm bad at this stuff, kids and so on?' He still looked braced for rejection.

'Bad? Where did you get that impression? You've taken Leo under your wing, haven't you?'

'But I'm not his dad.'

'Thank God for that. You're a hell of a lot better than that. I think you'll be a great father – and I'm a pretty good mother – there: I've finally said it – so it's going to work out.'

He looked close to tears but shoved them back wherever guys managed to lock up their emotions. She had never loved him so much as this moment as he finally got his words right. 'Gemma Whitehall, it would be my honour to have a family with you. I want you, I want Leo, and I want that poor kid in there too.' He placed his hand on her stomach. 'So no champagne for you? Do you mind if I have a swig? I need it for the shock.'

'Go ahead, but not too much. You've got to carry us back down the stairs, remember?'

That pushed his protective button. He'd got as far as one mouthful. 'You're right. I'm going to be a dad. I can't start by dropping my child's mother down a spiral staircase. Are you warm enough? Do you need anything?'

'Sam, you impossible man, I don't need anything but you! Come and lie beside your lady.'

Taking the greatest care possible, he crawled up the cushions and reclined beside her, letting her head rest on his chest.

The music switched on again. They lay looking at the candles together and listening to the sweet serenade of the lute.

'I love you, Gemma.' It came out of nowhere, but he'd clearly been thinking it for a while as they lay there.

'I love you too, Milord Sam, Castle Owner and soon to be father.'

He played with her hair a moment. 'If it's a girl, at least I'll be able to lock up any annoying boyfriends in the dungeon.'

'Girl? I assumed it would be a boy, but I'd like that. As long as we don't call her Cersei.'

'Why would we want to inflict a name like that on her?'

'Exactly.' She turned to smile up at him. 'The lady in the bed opposite knitted a cardigan for her.'

'What? You mean they all knew and I didn't?'

'That's why they were all giving you hard stares. They knew I was desperate for you to visit and you didn't come until late.'

'I couldn't help that, Gem . . .'

'I know. But I needed you.'

'I'm here now. And do you know something? I need you too.'

She nodded. 'That's how it should be.'

Chapter 28

G emma's father took hold of the handles of the wheelchair. 'Where next, young lady?'

Gemma adjusted her ruff. It was far less comfortable than her neck support left behind at the cottage. However did Tudor people put up with them? This had to be one of the worst ever fashion choices. 'I'd like to check on the keep a final time.'

'There's no need, and you know it. It's perfect. Your mother has arranged the flowers exactly to your plan and everything is set up.'

Gemma bit her lip, consulting the list on her lap. He was right: her mother's years of flowering arranging for her local church had come into their own. She'd done a fine job on the display, bringing a design sense to Gemma's language of flowers instructions. 'Then what about the reception for VIPs in the marquee?'

'Tim and Gaynor have that in hand.' The pub had offered to provide the catering for that event to keep it separate and cleared up before the wedding reception began later.

'Car parking?'

'Gregor is on top of that.'

'Showing the guests to the right venue?'

'Leo and his under gardeners are standing by. Camille is in charge of the list to make sure the VIPs and the guests for the wedding service don't get mixed up.'

As Camille had created this potential confusion it seemed only just to put her on that tricky job of separating the sheep from the goats. Mind you, it shouldn't be too taxing as the journalists were unlikely to be wearing codpieces and ruffs. 'Wedding caterers?'

'Doing their own thing in the orangery and they will not want anyone else getting in the way.'

'Diana and Gillian?'

'You know they're here already. Gillian is setting up her table and Dr Faustus is presiding.' Diana had stunned them all by turning up in an alchemist's outfit like a teacher from Hogwarts. She was in danger of stealing the show.

Gemma checked her watch. The first guests were expected imminently. No Monty Don after all, but Bob Flowerdew was coming with cameras. 'Dad, do you think this is going to work?'

Her father came to the front of the chair and crouched down. 'Gemma, look at me.'

She met his patient gaze. 'Yes?'

'You have your mother's tenacity and a creative ability all of your own. This is going to be a triumph.'

'Thanks, Dad.'

'I'm proud of you.'

She was really going to weep now. At least she could blame it on the baby – not that she'd broken that choice bit of news yet. 'Thanks.'

'Not because you're marrying a castle owner at Christmas, though your mother is quite chuffed about that . . .'

She smiled through her tears.

'We both are proud of you – I am proud of you – because you are you.'

'Is that you telling me you love me, Dad?'

'I thought I'd said that?'

'You did. Give me a hug.'

Her father gently and a little awkwardly pressed her to his chest, then let her go. 'Ah, here are two people with an even better claim on you. She's all yours,' he called to Sam and Leo. 'I'd better see what her mother is getting up to. I've promised to keep her away from Bob Flowerdew.'

'Why? What's she likely to do?' asked Sam. 'Badger him for an autograph?'

'Much worse. She's always going on about his hair when she sees him on television. I wouldn't put it past her to go up behind him with her flower arranging scissors and claim it is an accident when his plait is snipped off.'

Sam blanched. 'You'd better hurry then.'

When Gemma wiped her eyes, she saw that Sam and Leo were dressed in their doublet and hose.

'Reporting for inspection, Mum,' said Leo with a grin. 'What do you think?'

Hose did not do much for the long limbs of a teenager but she wasn't going to breathe a word. 'You gentleman look wonderful.'

'Great. I'd better check on my team.' Leo sprinted off, short cloak flying from his shoulders like a sixteenth century superhero.

Gemma turned to admire Sam. He'd wisely gone for breeches rather than the short doublet of Elizabethan portraiture. He'd started growing a beard so he was looking very piratical. Gemma put her hand to her heart. '*O brave new world, that has such people in't.*'

He bowed. 'Thank you, my lady.'

'Are you really OK, Sam?' She search his face, knowing that this day was an important anniversary for him.

'Yes, I really am. Cammy and I placed some flowers in Jen's garden earlier.' Gemma had suggested the castle well area be turned into a little herb garden in remembrance of Jennifer. 'We both think this is a healthy affirmation of life, having the castle officially open on this day. It's time to make good memories.'

'I'm glad.'

'And Cammy told me she's leaving.'

'She is?' Gemma hadn't known quite how she was going to make that happen.

'And guess what? She's moving in with Tim and Gaynor. She has her sights set on their son.'

'Oh God, I think Tim's finally got competition. The power struggle at the pub is going to be epic.'

Sam laughed and grabbed the handles of the wheelchair. 'It's going to keep the village in gossip, that's for sure. I calculate we have five minutes.' He started pushing her away from the car park.

'Sam, we can't!'

'We absolutely can.'

'But the opening!'

'This is more important than the opening.'

That shut her up. He bumped her over the edge of a lawn and pushed her past his father who was admiring the borders with his sister.

'Where are you going with Gemma, Sam?' called Helen.

'Never you mind, nosy little sister!' he replied.

'Bossy big brother!'

'Now, now children, stop it!' ordered Sam's mother, coming out of the cottage with drinks on a tray for her grandchildren.

'We'll be back soon!' Gemma promised. She'd only just met Sam's female relations that morning so didn't want to make a bad impression. 'We can't abandon them!'

'Yes, we can. I'm the king of the castle, after all. My minions will fill in for me.'

Sam pulled her round a corner and into the area they had decided last week must be the Knight's Grotto when Sam pulled a stone statue of a chess piece from the overgrown yew hedge. He wheeled her into the centre of his wild beauty of a garden, then knelt before her. In his hand was a ring box.

'Gemma Whitehall, I have prepared something to say to you.' He looked adorably embarrassed now.

'Go on,' she prompted.

He cleared his throat histrionically. 'Here goes. *I wonder by my troth what thou and I did till we loved?*'

She laughed in delight as he began on her favourite John Donne poem. 'I've already agreed to marry you, you know that, don't you?'

'Ah yes, but we haven't got engaged yet.'

'We're doing it backwards, are we?'

'Well, we did start on the family first, so I'd say yes. We're not being traditional. Shall I continue?'

Oh, how she loved this man! 'Pray, do go on, sir.'

'I'm going to cut the next bit as it goes on about snorting.'

'OK, get to the good part.'

'*And now, good morrow to our waking souls.*' He opened the box to display a simple large diamond, surrounded by two small ones. 'Gemma, thank you for waking me up. You stormed my castle and conquered my heart. Will you do me the honour of accepting this ring – and me – and my castle?'

'Sam, I do.'

He slipped the ring on her finger. 'Did you like the bit about conquering the heart? Neil wrote that bit.'

'Tell him he got it spot on. He's going to make the most amazing best man ever.'

Sam groaned and put his head on her shoulder. 'I'm having sleepless nights already.'

'Not to worry: I'm there for you now.'

'Yes, you are. Ready to go back to our opening?'

'I am.'

'Do you care to explain why you invited a Druid to the reception?' He pushed her across the long grass.

She turned to look up at him. 'I will, but later. Isn't it wonderful we now have so much "later" with each other?'

Sam caressed her cheek. 'A new chapter in the history of Claremont Castle, and we get to write it together.'

The End

350

If you enjoyed this book by Eve Edwards, then read on for a little surprise, Eve has something she wants to share with you . . .

Are you a single genre book reader? Or do you watch only one kind of film? I imagine that you seek out the right book or film to suit your mood or to challenge yourself. You will then be able to understand why I, as a writer, like to be able to tell different kinds of stories: those suited to the thrill seekers, the romantics, and the armchair detectives among you. As I believe you might well be all three kinds of readers on different occasions - like I am - I thought I'd share some news with you. While wearing my Eve Edwards' hat, I happily explore the trials and tribulations of an ordinary life, the light and the dark moments; but I also enjoy a knotty mystery that needs unpicking strand by strand. This is why I'm delighted to announce that I'm turning to Crime! (I'd better quickly add 'Fiction' before you call the police.)

The new series is called the Jess Bridges Mysteries and is appearing under my pen name Joss Stirling. Jess is like no other detective you've met before. Chaotic, risk-taking, hilarious, vulnerable, she finds herself in at the deep end with her first mystery, *Black River*, when a body washes up at her book club. Oh, and did I mention she was skinny dipping at the time? As she often says, 'you had to be there'. Fortunately, she soon comes across a more traditional detective in the Thames Valley Police, DI Leo George, who is also on the case. Leo is enigmatic where Jess is an open book, but together they have something the other needs to solve the crime. If you are intrigued to find out how the Thames Valley's newest detective duo solve the mystery, then try the chapter that follows.

Eve

Chapter One

Jess

I don't know what your book club is like, but mine is the sort that ends up with me stranded naked in the river with a dead man and a murderer on the loose.

Or maybe that is just me?

How did this happen? I suppose you could say it started when Cory told me it would be a great idea for me to join her group.

'Just a few of us mums – our night away from the husband slash partner and the kids. Bring-and-share supper. Lots to drink. Lots of gossip. A bit of discussion about the book – eventually.'

'And if I don't qualify as a mum?' I watched Cory push her three-year-old in the swing in the back garden of her Summertown house in north Oxford. It was a minute patch of lawn edged with lots of planters that Cory confessed to restocking each year as she suffered from an incurable case of black finger. Nothing survived in her care over winter. My hopes weren't high for her scented geraniums. We were both sipping our evening glass of white, a congratulations for getting through another shitty day.

'God, Jessica, you don't need kids to come along! In fact, you'd be our exotic alternative, the one living the life innocent of NCT classes or PTA politics. I bet you don't even know what a traybake is – or pelvic floor exercises?'

That was when I realised that reproducing brought with it almost as many acronyms and codewords as the army. Then again, from what I'd seen, maybe parenthood was a bit like entering enemy territory and you needed some discipline to get through?

I still wasn't sure I wanted to enter this contested area that appeared to belong to professional mothers. What did I have in common with them? I didn't have kids, a husband (or ex-husband), a house or career prospects. On the other hand, almost all the women I knew were in this life stage, what choice did I have if I didn't want to embarrass myself angling for friendships with those years younger than me? 'But you do talk about the books you read?'

'Oh yes. Most of us went to uni. Except for Jasmine. She opted for modelling and has ended up earning more than the rest of us put together.'

I wasn't sure I was destined to like Jasmine and told Cory so.

Cory drained her glass and handed it to me to hold so she could launch Leah more vigorously. 'We all agreed to hate the bitch naturally, but she's so sweet we couldn't keep it up. She'll win you round too.' Leah squealed as the swing hit the point where it made the frame judder; Cory slacked off a little. 'The point is, Jess, we all have dormant brain cells that need stimulating at a minimum once a month. Stave off Alzheimer's. You can never start too soon.'

'Well, that's an optimistic outlook, Cory.'

She ignored my dry tone. 'Believe me, you can only get so far on Disney Princesses and the Marvel Universe.' Cory had Leah and Benji, a boy of five who currently wanted to be Spider-Man when he grew up, so considered herself the expert in both topics. 'I really think you'll like it. Adult conversation and culture.'

Standing by the swing set with the munchkin trying to launch herself into space, I discovered that I'd do anything to please Cory. Even risk an evening of book talk with fecund thirty-somethings. And as real friends do, I agreed to join the book club to keep Cory company. That was why I was now hiding in the bushes without a stitch on trying to work out how I could get home without anyone seeing.

Conclusion? It was not possible and I had the horrible creeping feeling that things were going to get much worse.

Cory said she'd come back once she'd caught up with the dog that had run off with my rolled-up clothes. I'd hoped at least for knickers and bra, but the bundle had kept together surprisingly well in the big jaws of a flat-coated Retriever. I suppose the name was a bit of a clue, though I was not sure what the owner was going to do with his mutt's offering of a Primark polka dot sundress and scanty panties.

She still hadn't returned. I shivered. My head was swimming with too much white wine – and my body from the real dip it had just taken. Our summer book club meeting – *a picnic by the swimming spot called Parson's Pleasure, in University*

Parks, it'll be fun! Our chosen good read, *Wild Swim*, a trendy book by the improbably named Jago Jackson. This travelogue-come-social-commentary featured him leaping up each day from his lodgings in an Oxford college to discover another hidden treasure in the upper reaches of the Thames, ranging from Port Meadow to Cheese Wharf. Even the swimming places around Oxford sounded like something served in the Senior Common Room. Parson's Pleasure was the oldest spot, famous for its male nude bathing and featured in Oxford folklore, until it was officially shut in 1991. Closure was just a challenge to people like me. Parson's Pleasure lay on a bend in the Cherwell where the water dithered for a while under the overhanging willows and washed against the punt rollers that allowed the flat bottomed boats to progress upstream. By day, it felt a place for *Brideshead Revisited* student picnics with college scarves, champagne and teddy bears. At night, the black waters enticed you to join the desperate and the drunken who had ended their days here.

Jago had now adopted it as his own place for a daily dip. Cory's ex, Brendan, made the documentary that accompanied the book – another reason for us all to come down hard on it. Jago only stopped in his praise of swimming to make acerbic comments about the various new tribes now living in his city, of which Yummy Mummies were, of course, one. His pen did not spare the people who dared to enjoy the same places as him and introduced such abominations as kale smoothies and oat-milk cappuccinos to staid Oxford cafés. My book club friends howled at his caricature of them, calling out his thinly veiled disdain for their life choices.

'Hey, Jago!' Cory had roared at the picnic, waving a celery stick like a machete, 'I may drive an Audi, job-share and have an *au pair*, but I also have a degree in international development, get paid a pittance at DfID to go on project assessment visits to Syrian refugee camps, and you still dismiss me?' Cory was a civil servant working part-time for the Department for International Development in London.

'I don't think he means you,' said Jasmine. She absolutely was the epitome of the term 'yummy': coffee-coloured hair, big dark eyes, svelte figure. Where her little boy Reuben came from, I'd no idea, but I was voting 'stork' because there was no way that midriff ever housed a baby.

'You mean I'm not young, attractive and still sexy?' asked Cory, ready to rumble even though her wine intake had been modest as befits our designated driver.

To be honest, Cory wasn't really the poster girl for the Yummy Mummies, more the Over-Stretch-Marked Mums.

'No! What I mean is that Jago hasn't bothered to talk to a real woman,' said Jasmine, deftly avoiding a fight. 'All the fellow wild swimmers he interviews about the life are either hoary old men or eccentric lady artist types. The sort who have long grey hair, an allotment and make pots.'

'Or smoke pot,' added Frances, our one-liner expert. An acerbic forty-something with family back in Hong Kong, she now ran the HR department in a law firm – another part-time job-share mum burning the scented candle at both ends.

'And we wouldn't know anything about that,' I said archly.

Their faces were blank.

'You mean, you don't?'

'Not since college,' said Frances.

'Not even then,' said Cory.

Jasmine kept silent.

Right. OK.

'So Jago doesn't like empowered women,' I said, hoping to deflect the conversation from drug taking.

'Exactly!' said Cory.

'Then I say we should claim the riverbank here as our own. We can't let media darlings like him steal our identity as women.' I'd had my fill of media darlings when living with my ex, Michael, TV's favourite psychologist. 'We have a right to the same water Jago swims in. Parson's Pleasure is not just for naked dons!'

'Actually, there's a traditional spot on the river for women, called Dame's Delight,' said Jasmine helpfully, pointing upstream.

'I want to be a Parson not a Dame.' Maybe there's something wrong with that statement? 'Whatever: I'm going in!'

'But you can't!' protested Jasmine. 'The park's about to close. Even if you swim out, your stuff will be stuck on inside the railings.'

'Just watch me.'

'Oh God, I don't want anything to do with this. Jess is going to do one of her crazy things.' Frances was already gathering up her blanket and picnic bag. This was my third book club and she already had my number. 'I've got to get back to pay the babysitter. No time to be arrested for public indecency.'

The others decamped with her, leaving just Cory and me.

'Jess, this isn't a good idea,' said Cory plaintively.

None of my ideas are good. 'I'm committed now. I'm like Eddie the Eagle having left the top of the High Jump at the whatever Olympics.' I rolled up my underwear in my polka dot dress and put in at the bottom of a tree. If I'd thought about that a little more, I would've realised that wasn't a good place because, you know who else liked tree-trunks . . .? I pushed my way through the undergrowth – not so funny, naked – and kicked off my sandals before entering the icy water.

Ah, Jago, now I understood why you bother to get up for this. It felt sensual and might've been the closest I'd come to orgasm for a while now. I waded in past my lady bits and squeaked when the water reached my waist.

'You go, girl!' crowed Cory, clearly having decided that, as no policemen rushed up to arrest me, it was safe to be supportive.

'Join me! The water's lovely!' I did breaststroke out into the middle of the Cherwell and lay on my back, bosoms saying a perky hello to the unscandalised sky as the current drifted south towards the punt rollers and the next bend in the river. This is the life. I might have messed everything else up but at least I still had the ability to live free and easy under the apple boughs. A wild child wild swimming.

Barking and a scream from the bank broke into my reverie.

'Nooo! Give that back!' wailed Cory, running off after the aforementioned Retriever retrieving my clothes. 'I'll get them for you, Jess!' That was the last I saw of her. When I scrambled out, I saw that she hadn't even thought to leave me the picnic blanket. From skinny-dipping to starkers in the shrubbery.

Welcome to my life.